JOSEPH NASSISE

Riverwatch

POCKET BOOKS
New York London Toronto Sydney Singapore

POCKET BOOKS, a division of Simon & Schuster, Inc.
1230 Avenue of the Americas, New York, NY 10020

Copyright © 2000, 2001 by Joseph M. Nassise

Published by arrangement with Barclay Books, LLC

All rights reserved, including the right to reproduce
this book or portions thereof in any form whatsoever.
For information address Barclay Books, LLC, 6161
51st Street South, St. Petersburg, FL 33715

ISBN: 0-7434-7096-6

First Pocket Books printing October 2003

10 9 8 7 6 5 4 3 2 1

POCKET and colophon are registered trademarks of
Simon & Schuster, Inc.

Front cover illustration by Anna Dorfman
Photo: David Sacks/Getty Images

Manufactured in the United States of America

For information regarding special discounts for bulk purchases,
please contact Simon & Schuster Special Sales at 1-800-456-6798
or business@simonandschuster.com

This book is dedicated to my parents:

*For my father, who by his example
taught me how to be a husband and a father.*

*For my mother, who by her constant encouragement
gave me the courage to chase my dreams.*

Thank you both for always believing.

ACKNOWLEDGMENTS

I'd foremost like to thank my wife, Dawn, who found the original handwritten manuscript of this novel in a shoe box in the closet and insisted that I submit it. Without her, this book wouldn't exist.

In addition, my thanks also go out to my agent, Bob Diforio, for taking a chance on an unknown writer; my editor, Amy Pierpont, for working closely with me to bring this book into your hands; the many members of the Horror Writers Association whose votes placed this book on the Bram Stoker Award ballot in its original small press version; the judges of the International Horror Guild Awards who likewise saw fit to nominate it in their best first novel category; and to my friends Jon and Drew, for offering encouragement and critique of not only this work but my writing in general.

1

AN UNEXPECTED DISCOVERY

It's a tombstone.

The notion came out of nowhere; seeping into his consciousness the way fog sweeps off the sea on a cool summer evening, insidiously sliding into the center of his thoughts. Once there, it stuck hard and fast. The stone did, indeed, resemble a gravestone. The outer edges had been beveled at a slight angle, giving it a simple yet unmistakable sense of dignity. It had also been sealed to the dirt floor with mortar.

If it was a tombstone, then whose was it?

Why put it here, hidden beneath a river?

It just didn't make sense. Staring at it, Jake decided it had been a difficult afternoon. This latest addition to his troubles had started fifteen minutes ago, with Rick's arrival in his trailer.

"We need you in the cellar, boss."

"What the hell for, Rick?" Jake Caruso replied without turning. "You know Blake wants these estimates finished before two o'clock. I don't have time to look at every little thing that goes wrong. That's why I appointed you foreman, remember?" Jake was tired; the work had been going well, but Blake was on his back about even the tiniest details. It was starting to get to him. *Why can't the man just back off and let me do my job?* Jake wondered, not for the first time.

Rick's reply surprised him. "I know, boss, but I think you'd better come on down. It's important."

His solemn tone was what caught Jake's attention. Turning away from the work before him, Jake looked at Rick and started in surprise. His friend's lips were pressed tightly together. The tension in his jaw was easy to see despite the man's effort to hide it. His usually ruddy face had gone sickly gray, and the cheerful light in his eyes had dulled to a lusterless sheen.

Jake's aggravation with the interruption vanished. Rick was the perpetual optimist. For him to look this bad could only mean that something major had gone wrong. Images of bloodied flesh raced through Jake's mind, with visions of men crushed by powerful tools.

"What happened? Somebody hurt? Should I call an ambulance?" Jake asked, reaching for the phone.

Rick held up his hands in a placating gesture. "No need for that. Nobody's been hurt. The crew in the basement found something I think you should look at, that's all."

That was it. When pressed for more details, Rick refused to say anything more.

Tossing his pen aside and running a hand through his already disheveled hair, Jake agreed to go look.

The two men left the trailer and crossed the lawn to the wide veranda that encircled the house. Climbing the steps, they entered through the front door. Moving along the foyer, they passed through the dining room, the butler's pantry, then down the flight of servants' stairs that led into the basement, where Jake's crew had been working for several days.

The home's original owner had made use of the land's natural features, routing a nearby stream directly through the cellar. The stream's steady flow turned a large waterwheel, which in turn generated electricity for the estate. Ultimately, the owner's eccentricity had caused more harm than good, for over the years the stream had backed up and pooled in the building's basement. Now it was nothing more than a deep stagnant pool.

Blake, the present owner, had decided that the cellar was to become a wine-storing area. Jake's men had dammed what was left of the stream out on the east side of the property earlier in the week and spent the last two days pumping the last of the water out of the cellar. The streambed would be filled with concrete and a foundation laid for the hardwood floors, as Blake had requested.

As they descended the flight of rickety old steps, the smell of mildew and rot wafted up toward them. It reminded Jake of childhood days spent hunting crayfish in swampy creek beds. The stench was the same. At the base of the stairs he paused and surveyed the job his men had done. Bright lights had been erected to illuminate the area, and in their harsh glare Jake judged the height the water had risen over the years by the dark stain left on the wall. Beneath this mark, layers of green slime and algae still hung, shimmering in the light. The air was heavy with dampness, making Jake feel as if he were walking through a vertical curtain of dew. He could see the wide trench that extended from one side of the house to the other, neatly bisecting it before disappearing out the opposite side. Rick led him over to the edge and pointed down.

°   °   °

Now, staring at the stone, Jake realized that Rick was speaking.

". . . the last few inches of water about an hour ago, and I sent a few of the men into the trench to start widening it out. I was hoping we'd be able to start laying the pipe for the drainage system this afternoon, then we uncovered this thing."

Jake's gaze had not left the stone. He guessed it to be about six feet long and three feet wide. One corner had been chipped away, exposing an open space beneath and revealing that the stone was at least several inches thick.

"I had one of my men break it open just to make sure it wasn't an old storeroom or well shaft. When I saw what it really was, I didn't want to touch anything else until you'd had a chance to take a look," Rick said, handing a flashlight to Jake.

Jake took the flashlight and jumped down into the trench, moving closer to the stone. The muck at the bottom of the trench sucked at the soles of his shoes and coated them with a foul-smelling mud. He didn't care; his interest was on the slab of stone before him. Bending down beside it, he ran his hand along the surface where the men had cleaned off the layers of mud that had collected over the years. He was surprised to find it extremely smooth.

"Don't bother," Rick said from his position above. "There isn't any writing on it. I already checked. But take a peek into the hole beneath it."

Jake flipped on the flashlight and shined its beam down into the darkness beneath the slab. The light pierced the gloom lurking there, giving him a clear view of what lay beyond.

He realized what it was that had upset his foreman.

Stone stairs lay just beneath the stone.

Leading down.

Deeper into the earth.

"What the . . . ?" Jake mumbled to himself. He reached into the opening with one hand and ran a finger lightly over the top step. It was coated with a thick layer of dust that stirred slightly with the movement. There was no sign that any of the water that had lain overhead so long had seeped through. On a hunch, Jake reached sideways and felt the inner surface of the nearby wall.

That, too, was bone dry.

It also was solid stone.

Jake sat back on his haunches and looked up at Rick. "We can't do any more work until we check this out. Send a couple of men out to my truck. There should be some crowbars in the back."

Ten minutes later, Jake and Rick were heaving at the edges of the slab with the help of several others. It was hard work. The stone had lain there long and was heavy. They wedged several of the bars between the slab and the stone walls, using the first step as leverage. In that manner they managed to get enough torque to snap the stone from its seal. They slid the stone far enough to the side to leave an opening wide enough to admit a man. The stairs below were clearly revealed. They could see that the steps descended about twenty feet, then stopped at the opening of another tunnel.

Jake was preparing to go down to investigate when Rick caught his arm. "Should we be going down there?" he asked.

"Sure. How the hell else are we going to find out what

it is?" Jake's eyes gleamed. Visions of dark caverns and secret chambers danced in the back of his mind.

That frightened look was back on Rick's face. "I don't know if that's such a good idea, Jake. We don't know how safe the tunnel is or what it might have been constructed for. For all you know it might be the gravesite of one of Blake's ancestors. I don't think the old man would appreciate you poking around in the family crypt."

Jake remembered his initial reaction to the stone, and a chill raced through him. *What if it is a crypt? Does that make any difference? If I am going to finish the job, I'll have to discover what lies below and relay that information to Blake. I can't very well go to him and say we stopped working in the cellar because we found a hole in the floor. Blake would be furious. He'll at least need a valid reason for the delay.* He explained as much to Rick, who shrugged and reluctantly agreed, but the troubled look never left his foreman's face. Jake knew Rick was just going along because Jake was the boss. *Well, so be it then,* he thought. *That's the way it is.* Jake turned back toward the steps before him and forgot what Rick was feeling, caught up as he was in the excitement of exploring the unknown. Jake gingerly rested one foot on the top step, checking that it would support his weight. Then he stepped down with trepidation, worried about booby traps and the entire structure's stability. When nothing happened, he repeated the process, moving down onto the next step, then the next. Behind him, Rick picked up one of the crowbars and followed. After the first few steps Jake grew more confident and quickly descended to the bottom, where he waited for Rick to join him.

Together they shined their lights into the darkness of the tunnel ahead.

The passage extended directly ahead, farther than the beams of their flashlights would reach. Jake felt his excitement rise as he stared down the tunnel.

The air was dry but cold, and Jake was thankful for the sweatshirt he'd donned before heading out the door. He set off down the tunnel, with Rick close behind. The tunnel continued for several hundred yards. About halfway down its length, it began to rise gradually toward the surface.

Eventually, their lights revealed a ninety-degree turn. When they reached it, Jake hesitated a moment, wondering what he might find around that corner. A strange feeling of unease suddenly crept over him, and the walls seemed to be closing in. He was struck by the urge to turn around and get out of the tunnel as fast as he could. He was about to tell Rick they were turning back when his good sense reasserted itself. *Go back now?* a voice whispered in his mind derisively. *Just because of a little claustrophobia? I've come this far. I might as well see what's on the other side.*

No sooner had Jake convinced himself to keep going than Rick spoke up in a slightly quavering voice, "Jake? Don't you think we should wait until . . ."

Jake wasn't listening.

Intent on what lay ahead, he stepped around the corner.

The tunnel ended some three feet ahead in a perfectly laid wall of brick.

"What the hell?" Jake stepped forward and slapped the wall with his hand. A flat sound reached his ears in response.

When Rick caught up, Jake said, "Give me that crowbar, will you?"

Rick handed Jake the crowbar and watched as Jake took a step back and swung the bar at the wall. It rebounded off the surface and nearly struck Jake in the face, but he seemed not to notice. He stepped up and put his ear against the wall, listening.

A frown crossed his face.

He stepped back and swung again.

"Hear that?" he asked.

Rick shook his head.

"There's an echo," Jake told him. He struck the wall again, harder. This time, Rick also heard the echo.

"I think there's a room on the other side of this wall."

By then Rick was also getting caught up in the excitement of discovery. "Want me to have the jackhammer brought down?" he asked.

Jake absently handed the crowbar back to Rick as he considered his next move. More than anything, he wanted to do what his foreman had suggested. He knew that he shouldn't, however. There could be a good reason the area had been sealed off. He didn't want to put anyone in danger.

He decided it would be best if he checked with Blake first.

Jake let Rick know of his decision, and the two men returned the way they had come.

Leaving Rick to dismiss the men for the day, Jake headed back to his trailer. Excitement or not, he still had a deskful of paperwork that needed to be finished before he could call it a day.

Much to his dismay, he found he couldn't concentrate

on the work before him. His thoughts kept returning to the stone, and the tunnel it had concealed. Again and again, he found himself asking the same question.

What is behind that wall?

In the darkness, he stirred.

At first, there was just a vague feeling of confusion. Confusion a child might feel when waking in a strange room in the middle of the night; yet what was waking here was anything but a child. Against the disorientation, he fought to hold on to his dreams. Though dreams were but a poor substitute for reality, they were all he had. His only companions. To anyone else, they would have been nightmares; dark visions of death, gloriously colored with the rich crimson flash of freshly spilled blood. They were his link to life, his last toehold on the edge of sanity. Without dreams he would long ago have succumbed to the fate that his enemy had planned. But then, like now, his desire for life had been too strong. Long ago, when he'd first felt the crushing bonds of his prison, when he'd first recognized the true nature of his imprisonment, he'd retreated into the cold embrace of the darkness that surrounded him. He surrendered himself to his dreams, finding in them the sanctuary he needed to survive. Over time, he'd forgotten what was real and what was not, the line between illusion and reality blurring. He'd come to see his dreams not as a mere reflection of reality but the very image itself.

Then, as the first faint tugs of reality prodded his consciousness, he fought against them, not yet ready to relinquish that which had kept him safe from the hateful silence and despair that had surrounded him for so long.

Then, like the slow trickle of a muddy stream, he began to remember.

Sights and sounds and images from days that had long since fallen into dust came to him, fragments of a time forever frozen in the depths of his mind.

Memory returned.

He awoke.

He moved to leave his prison, only to find that his sentence had not ended, but had merely been exchanged for another.

He screamed then, a long, howling cry that would have been awful to hear had there been a throat from which it could have issued forth, a cry filled with such rage and frustration that it would have turned the listener's blood to ice and bones to stone, had it been possible to hear.

In the midst of that cry, another memory surfaced.

The image of a face formed in the darkness of his mind. The face of one he had known long ago, the face of the one who had imprisoned him in the darkness of eternity, the one who had brought him such misery and pain.

The face of his enemy.

Cold, reptilian reason took over then, strangling his silent cry, shoving aside his emotions. A calculated cunning immediately set to pondering his current situation.

Summoning his strength from somewhere deep inside, he sent out his newly regained senses and discovered something more.

Men were near.

He could sense them, could hear the clank of their tools and the sounds of their voices. He could feel the minute vibrations that descended through the earth each time they moved above him.

For the first time in countless ages, he began to hope that he might soon be free. Once he was, nothing would stop him from having revenge on the one who had imprisoned him.

Exerting himself, he cast his consciousness out farther, past the walls of his prison, across the fields just beyond, among the living. Searching, seeking, briefly touching the minds of all he encountered before moving on, jumping from one to the next . . . until, at last, strength deserting him, his consciousness rushed back like the snap of an overstretched rubber band.

But in that last instant, he'd found him.

His enemy was old now, old and frail, no longer the awesome force that had once defeated him in battle. His foe's powers had waned; the man's body had grown feeble with age.

Having expended what little strength he'd had, the beast slipped back into the restless edge of sleep.

Yet this time, he remained aware.

And in the depths of his inhuman mind, a plan began to form.

2

LEGENDS

Fingers flying across the keyboard, Samuel Travers watched the words appear in neat lines of glowing green script on the screen in front of him with a deep sense of satisfaction.

He'd been writing since nine o'clock that morning, a steady five hours of work. At first it had been difficult, every sentence leaving him unsatisfied. Nothing seemed to fit, nothing had sounded quite right. The first half hour had been completely wasted, with nothing to show for it but half a pack of cigarette butts in the ashtray beside him. In desperation he'd tried an old writing exercise, copying names out of a phone book to stimulate creativity, and suddenly the words he'd been trying to summon together with such difficulty moments before had flashed into his mind as clearly as if they'd been etched in stone. He'd given a whoop of delight, swept the phone book onto the floor with a swing of one arm, and plunged into his tale with reckless abandon.

For the last four hours, his mind racing, his fingers trying desperately to keep pace with his thoughts, he'd been too absorbed in the crystal story line that was flowing out of his head to pay attention to anything else.

The creative stream was finally starting to wind down. The flood had become a weak trickle, and he knew it wouldn't be much longer before even that went dry.

It was just about time to call it quits for the day.

What he had written that day was good. *Damn good,* he thought. *Now if I can only keep it up until it's finished.* Taking a long drag off his cigarette, he cast a silent prayer to the Nine Muses to let him do just that.

Tipping the scales somewhere around 170, Sam stood just under six feet, with short curly hair the color of used motor oil that was slowly receding across his brow and eyes. Sam had taken the less traveled road after college, going to work as a writer for a company that produced fantasy role-playing games. Having been in love with the strange and fantastic for as long as he could remember, the job allowed him to stay in a world where demons, ghosts, and things that go bump in the night were a reality, at least on paper. While enjoyable, the job didn't pay that well, so Sam was forced to supplement his income with a second job at a nursing home in Glendale.

As he sat staring at the pages of the fantasy tale he was in the midst of writing, his thoughts turned to the latest session of Swords and Sorcerers that he had scheduled for Jake and Katelynn later that night. It had been a week since his friends had ventured into that underground maze beneath Zolthane Mountain that Sam, the adventure's writer, had created and named the Crystal Caverns. Katelynn and Jake often acted as an unofficial test group, working through his latest creations for their strengths and weaknesses before Sam sent them off to his editor for production. As usual, Sam was anxious to return to that fantasy world of imagination. Last week had seen Chelmar the Wizard and Alganea the Warrior-Maiden trapped in a dead-end cavern by a pack of flesh-hungry ghouls. Despite the week they'd had to ponder the problem, Sam still couldn't see how Jake and Katelynn were going to get their characters out of their deadly predicament.

Looks like you might've made this one just a hair too difficult, he thought to himself. *If they can't find their way out of the maze, you're going to have a lot of rewriting to do.*

A quick glance at his watch told him it was just after two. He was working a rare day shift that provided the perfect opportunity to take Katelynn to work with him that afternoon so that she could interview Gabriel Armadorian, one of the nursing home's patients and Sam's friend, for her thesis. Knowing he had to be there by three-thirty, Sam decided he had just enough time to grab a quick shower and a bite to eat before going to pick up Katelynn. He saved the fresh text he'd written on his computer, then wandered into the kitchen, trying to hunt up the fixings for a sandwich or two, his thoughts wandering through the details of that night's adventure.

He didn't know it then, but before the night was through, Sam would find himself wrapped up a situation beyond his control, one that would make those he faced in the twilight realm of his imagination seem positively dull in comparison.

Across town, Katelynn Riley was anxiously awaiting her friend's arrival. As was her habit when nervous, she checked through her book bag once more, assuring herself that she had everything she needed.

Notebook? Check.

Pencils and pens? Check.

Tape recorder? Check.

Tapes and extra batteries, just in case? Check.

That's everything, she thought with satisfaction, and relaxed back into the chair by the front window, where she sat watching for Sam's car. He had promised to take her to St. Boniface's today when he went in for his shift, to introduce her to Gabriel Armadorian, the nursing home's oldest patient. He had assured her that the old man was still lucid and in complete possession of his mental faculties.

From the comments that Sam had made, Katelynn was fairly certain that Gabriel was privy to a good deal of information that she was unable to find elsewhere on Sebastian Blake, the man who was the subject of her thesis. She was eager to sit down with Gabriel to discuss the issue at length. What a coup it would be for her to uncover and support information that not even Dr. Hemington, her mentor, had previously seen.

A horn sounded from outside, snatching her from her musings. Seeing Sam's car in the drive, she quickly slipped into her coat, snatched up her pack, and hustled out the door.

"All set?" Sam asked, as she settled into the passenger seat.

"Sure am. Thanks a lot for this, Sam." She leaned over and gave him a quick kiss on the cheek.

He smiled at her in return. The two had known each other for several years, having enrolled at Benton University at the same time. A chance introduction had blossomed into a deep friendship that had lasted well past college. At times Sam found himself wondering just why it was that they'd never been more than just friends. *Wasn't friendship one of the most important pillars in the foundation of a relationship?* It wasn't that he didn't find her attractive; he certainly did. She kept herself in shape with daily workouts of swimming and aerobics, toning her body without losing its soft feminine curves. Her hair was the color of chestnuts and curled at the shoulders. Katelynn had a wonderful laugh, a beautiful smile, and a pert little nose that reminded him of an elf. Sam knew from past experience that she was kind, caring, and generous. *So why hadn't they fallen in love?* Sam figured it was just one of the great mysteries in life and left it at that. Sometimes it didn't pay to look too closely at such things. They were friends, and that was what was important. At least that was what he told himself.

Suddenly, Katelynn interrupted his thoughts. "Tell me about Gabriel, Sam."

He thought about it for a moment, then said with a laugh, "I'm not sure I can."

Despite all the time they'd spent together, Gabriel was still pretty much an enigma to him. He had the feeling that the old man would remain that way no matter how well they got to know each other.

Sam remembered the day they had admitted Gabriel to the nursing home. The stretcher attendants were wheeling him in, his stroke too recent for him to be mobile, and as they'd passed the nursing desk were Sam was stationed for the night, the old man had opened his eyes, looked at him, and said, "Come pay me a visit sometime, Sammy. I think we've got a lot to talk about." It had taken Sam a minute or two to get over his shock, and by then the group had passed through the double doors and down the hall to the guest rooms. He'd wondered how the old man had known his name, then decided he'd simply read it off his name tag. But when he'd been changing in the locker room after his shift, he'd discovered he'd forgotten to put his tag on that night. There it was, sitting right where he'd left it the night before, on the top shelf of his locker, the white letters of his name staring him in the face. Once the shivers had gone away, he'd convinced himself that one of the attendants must have been playing a joke on him. Knowing his interest in the supernatural, they'd convinced the patient to go along and try to give Sam a scare. He'd had to admit it had worked beautifully, and left it at that. But he hadn't forgotten the incident all weekend, and when he went back to work the following week he did just what the man had asked, paid him a visit.

From that night on, the two of them had been friends.

Knowing Katelynn was patiently waiting for some kind of answer, he struggled to describe how he felt whenever he was in Gabriel's presence.

"You ever notice how they portray grandfathers on television? Nice old guys who always have the right answer, who can always give the kid who's the star of the show the right piece of advice?"

Katelynn nodded. She knew exactly what Sam was talking about; her own grandfather had been just like that. He'd always known when something was bothering her and managed to cheer her up with just a few words. When he died a few years ago, she thought she'd never be able to stop crying.

"Well, that's Gabriel. He makes me feel like a kid all over again, awed and amazed at everything he says. He can take an everyday object and turn it into something miraculous, just by having you look at it in a different way." He grinned sheepishly. "Sounds pretty corny, doesn't it?"

"Not at all. Keep going."

"He seems ancient to me. Totally at one with nature and the world around him, peaceful, serene, as if nothing could ever faze him. And he's an incredible storyteller. Sometimes, when I'm working the late shift and he can't sleep, I'll sit in his room and he'll tell me old legends, tales filled with wonder and magic, good and evil, tragedy and happiness."

They left the town limits and headed west on Route 3, heading down the side of a mountain to where Glendale lay at the base, fifteen minutes away. They crossed the covered bridge that spanned the Quinnepeg River, and a few moments later drove into the town of Glendale. It was bigger and more industrial than Harrington Falls, less quaint and more seedy. St. Boniface's, the nursing home where Sam was employed, was on the far side of town, and it took them another fifteen minutes of fighting the afternoon traffic before they arrived.

Once inside, Sam had Katelynn wait in the lobby while he ran downstairs to the locker room, changed into his uniform, and clocked in his time card. When he returned he led her upstairs to the third floor. Mr. Armadorian was in Room 310, at the end of a long L-shaped corridor.

Outside the door, Sam said, "I told him you were coming, but just in case he's asleep, why don't you wait here a sec and let me go in alone."

Katelynn nodded and stepped back to comply, but a voice called out to them from inside the room. "Are you two going to stand out there all day, or are you coming in to keep an old man company?"

Sam grinned, shrugged his shoulders, and led Katelynn inside.

The first thing Katelynn noticed were his eyes. A clear robin's-egg shade of blue, they seemed to gaze out at her with the open wonder of a child. They were eyes she'd often read about but never actually encountered— mesmerizing eyes, eyes that seemed to see right through a person. If not for the obvious kindness that poured out of them in waves, their impact would have been quite frightening. As they were, they made her feel warm and welcome.

Once she could tear her gaze away from Gabriel's, she noticed his skin was a burnished shade of copper, his face so lined with cracks and creases that it reminded her of a well-worn piece of leather. His hair was long and white, flowing over his shoulders in a long snowy mane, receding only a little despite his obvious age. He smiled at her scrutiny. "Sammy," he said, reaching out and clasping his friend's hand in greeting with both of his own, "I've been waiting for you, just like we agreed." Gabriel let go and turned to face Katelynn. "And this must be the young lady my friend has been telling me about lately."

"Katelynn Riley," she told him, turning to shake hands. His hand was thin and seemed fragile, but his skin was rough with years of hard work, and his grip was still surprisingly strong. She noticed that he was dressed in a pair of faded jeans and a blue chambray shirt that hung loosely on his thin frame. His feet, propped up on the end of the bed, were clad in a pair of soft suede moccasins.

"Please, sit with me, here by the window," he said, indicating several chairs that had been set up by the sliding glass door leading out to the balcony that formed most of the wall in front of the bed. "I was just enjoying the warmth of the afternoon sun."

Having been there countless times, Sam had already taken a seat, but Katelynn paused a moment to look around, taking in the austerity of the man's living space. She had glanced into several other rooms on the way up, and she knew that this was not the normal decor. The only furniture in the room besides the bed and chairs was a nightstand that appeared to have been hewed by hand from one solid piece of wood. It was rough and unfinished, but its very simplicity seemed to give it a wholesomeness that a perfectly stained piece would never have possessed. The walls were plain white plaster, unpainted, unadorned except for an intricate macramé piece that looked to her like some kind of bird rising out of a fire.

When she turned away from the wall hanging, Katelynn found Gabriel watching her. She smiled shyly, and he gestured with one hand, indicating with a smile of his own that she should join Sam and him at the window. The three of them sat together in silence for a time, letting the heat of the sun warm the chill from their bones. Eventually, Gabriel turned to her, and said, "Sammy thinks that I may be of some help to you?"

"Yes," she replied eagerly, leaning forward in her chair, anxious to get down to business. "I'm employed as a teaching assistant while I work toward my doctorate in sociology at Benton University. I've been doing a thesis on the dynamics of communities that arise from one central, familial influence. The impact of the Blake family fortune on the rise of Harrington Falls has been a perfect model. Sam tells me that your family had some association with the Blakes in the past, and I thought you might have some information that might add some local color to my work."

He nodded, a curious expression on his face. "I'd be delighted to help if I can, but most of what I know would be second- or thirdhand information."

"That won't be a problem. I've been focusing lately on the figure of Sebastian Blake, including the circumstances that surrounded his final disappearance from this area. Anything you can tell me about him would be a great help, since I've managed to uncover next to nothing." As she spoke, Katelynn delved into her bag for her notebook and pen, while at the same time surreptitiously turning on her tape recorder. She left the recorder inside the bag so as not to make Gabriel uncomfortable. When she straightened, she found the atmosphere in the room had changed, the air suddenly charged with tension. The old man was staring at her intently, a strange look on his face. She could feel that his expression was one of fear.

"Why would a pretty young woman like you want to know about a man like him?" Gabriel asked in a soft, quiet voice that somehow carried far more force than his earlier exuberance.

A sudden thrill went through Katelynn, the one that told her she was onto something. *Easy, girl*, she told herself, not wanting to ruin things by being hasty. Mindful of the old man's reaction, she answered carefully, "Well, the Blake family has had a tremendous effect on the development of this region. Since so much has been done on the other, more notable members of the family, particularly Elijah and Nathaniel, I wanted to stay away from them and choose a lesser-known figure. My early research uncovered very little information on Sebastian, Elijah's younger brother, and so I decided to find out why. The more I looked, the less I found and the more curious I became."

"And now, like a child with a lost treasure map, you just can't seem to put it down," Gabriel said gently, almost remorsefully, in reply.

She nodded in agreement.

He turned away, staring off into space, as if considering whether or not he was going to help her. His hands, idle until then, were suddenly in motion as he began wringing them together in an outward expression of some internal conflict. That went on for several long moments as Katelynn and Sam sat holding their breaths wondering what had so upset the man. Finally, he seemed to return to himself and looked over at them. Turning to Sam, he said, "Shut the door, Sammy."

Katelynn watched as Sam complied, and on his face she could see an expression of bewilderment that probably matched her own. Her feeling of excitement was growing. The old man was acting as if he was about to impart national security secrets, and that could only mean that he knew something good.

Gabriel waited until Sam had resumed his seat, then addressed Katelynn. "There is no way I can turn you from this course and suggest you choose another?"

Katelynn shook her head. *I've done too much work now as it is, spent too many hours combing dusty works in the back shelves of the library, all to no avail. Now, when I finally stumble onto something, he wants me to give it up? Not a chance!*

He nodded again, as if her answer was what he had expected. "Tell me what you know," he said.

Katelynn took a deep breath to hide her excitement, and began. "Besides the general facts like his parentage and where he was educated, not much. I do know that he was a loner, almost the exact opposite of his brother Elijah, and he got into trouble with the authorities on more than one occasion while he was growing up. He left Harrington Falls to attend school in Boston and spent many years overseas."

"Sounds fairly normal to me," Sam said.

"To an extent," Katelynn agreed. "He returned some years later a changed man, however. The wild attitude of his childhood had been replaced by an intense studiousness that seemed to please everyone. He's mentioned several times in historical documents of various types after his return, attending a town meeting here, appearing at a dinner engagement there, just as you would expect of a wealthy member of one of the town's founding families. But soon after that, the world seems to have lost track of him. Right up until the spring of 1760 he's a fairly prominent figure, but then there's nothing. After 1760, there isn't a single mention of him anywhere I looked." She sighed in exasperation.

"The various family histories seem to ignore the question of what happened to him as well. I couldn't even find a record of his death."

Unconsciously, she shivered. "It's as if he fell off the face of the earth, and no one noticed that he was gone."

Next to them, Sam listened to her litany, fascinated. It was all news to him. He'd heard the man's name mentioned once or twice in the past and seemed to remember something about there once having been a statue of him in the town square that had been torn down for some reason. He was beginning to feel the same sense of mystery that had infected Katelynn.

It was obvious that Gabriel was troubled by what she was saying. Sam had known the man too long not to recognize the subtle clues—the changed look down in the depths of his eyes, the nervous tic in his little finger. He was upset, and for a moment Sam was certain he wouldn't tell them anything. Then Gabriel turned and looked out the window, gathering his thoughts. Sam had seen the same expression whenever the old man was getting ready to tell one of his tales of the mystical past.

"Sebastian Blake," Gabriel said softly, as if tasting the words on the tip of his tongue and finding them bitter. "I haven't thought of him in many years. And with good reason; he was not the type of man one allows into his thoughts lightly." He turned to face them, and they both saw that a sadness had descended over him, a blanket of weighted sorrow that for the first time made him seem old in spirit as well as body.

He went on, "The natives of this country believe that when the Great Spirit made this world, he populated it with many strange and wondrous creatures, some good, some bad. One of these was Coyote."

Katelynn glanced over at Sam, and by the look on her face he could tell she was wondering what on earth the old man's words had to do with Sebastian Blake. Gabriel had his own way of telling a tale, and Sam had learned long before that it was no use trying to hurry him along. He'd tell it his way, in his own good time, and that was that. Besides, Sam reflected, he always said things for a specific reason, and what at first seemed trivial was often important later in the tale. He calmed her with a subtle motion of his hands.

Gabriel was still speaking, and Sam refocused his attention. "Coyote is one of the great spirits of the Indians. According to legend, he taught man many things—the use of clay to make pots, the way to make mats from the reeds that grew by the river's edge. The arts and crafts of the People that have been preserved from the beginnings have all been taught to them by Coyote, according to their beliefs. Yet, Coyote had two faces, and it wasn't long before the People realized this. At heart he was a bullying, greedy trickster. He would roam among the People in a form none could see, and he would wreak havoc whenever he found the opportunity."

Gabriel looked directly into Katelynn's eyes, and for a moment she was frightened of the old man, so forceful was the strength of his gaze. "The man you speak of was much the same way, but it took those who lived beside him much longer to recognize him for what he truly was."

It took her a moment, but she at last found her voice. "So he wasn't the Mr. Nice Guy that he appeared to be when he returned from Europe?"

"Outwardly, he was. But it's not what a man is on the outside that defines his essential nature, but what he is in here"—one long thin finger touched the center of his chest—"that makes him who he is. In the heart of Sebastian Blake, there was nothing but darkness."

The sun went behind a cloud then, as if echoing Gabriel's words. Sam was struck by the uncomfortable feeling that it was hiding, not wanting its precious light to be sullied by what they were saying. The old man must have felt it, too, for he looked toward the sky and nodded, as if the sun's behavior was entirely appropriate to the moment.

"My great-grandfather used to speak of him when I was a boy, passing on tales he had learned from his father before him. A wise man was my great-grandfather, wiser than I can ever hope to be, I suspect. From him I learned many things about the true nature of the world. But of everything he ever taught me, the most important was this: Evil walks in the world, under many faces and many forms, in sunlight or in darkness." His gaze lost its focus, as if he had turned it inward, down a road neither of them could see. "I don't think I ever really understood what he meant, until I met Sebastian Blake."

The last was said in a near whisper, and it took a moment for Katelynn to realize just what it was that he had said. When she did, she spoke without thinking. "Oh, come on! Met him? That would mean you'd have to be over three hundred years old!"

The tone of her voice brought Gabriel out of his reminiscing with a start. He appeared confused for a moment, then smiled gently. "A figure of speech, of course. Knowing about him was as close as I would ever want to come to meeting him, I assure you." His grin widened, and he winked at her. "Then again, maybe I am over three hundred years old. But I bet I don't look a day over seventy-five, right?"

Katelynn grinned back to acknowledge the joke, and relaxed. For a minute she'd feared the old man wasn't nearly as lucid as he seemed.

"Blake was a man who searched for forbidden learnings, for knowledge that was best left far from the eyes and ears of man. Instead of embracing the philosophies and teachings that had brought man out of the Dark Ages and into the modern world, he sought after ancient beliefs and legends, delving into areas of darkness, seeking the company of the Dark Ones."

"You mean the Devil?" Sam asked excitedly.

Katelynn cast him a sour look. She was there to do some serious research for her thesis, and she didn't want to waste time indulging Sam's love of the fantastic. If he wanted to think that devils and demons and things with a thousand legs haunted the dark and forgotten places of the world, that was fine, but she didn't want it interfering with what she'd come to accomplish.

He didn't seem to notice her look, and neither did Gabriel, for he turned to reply to the question.

"Not exactly, Sam. At least not in the way that you mean. You've got to remember that this was in the early days of this settlement. The people who had come here had fled the Old Country out of a desire to escape religious persecution. For them, belief in God and the Devil was not just something to indulge in when they felt like it, as so many of today's religions have become. For them, it was a question of eternal salvation or damnation. But Blake wasn't interested in that limited view of the universe. He looked beyond that, to an older and darker view of the universe, and sought to recapture the power that the ancients supposedly had through their rituals and ceremonies."

Katelynn interrupted him before he could go any further in his explanation. "Wait a minute!" she said sharply, her mild irritation at Sam's question having rapidly grown into annoyance with Gabriel's response to it. "Are you trying to tell us that Sebastian Blake practiced witchcraft?"

"Dark Magic might be a more appropriate term for it, but yes, that is what I am telling you," he answered simply, the congenial expression never leaving his face.

"Cool!" Sam exclaimed happily. When he'd agreed to bring Katelynn in to see Gabriel, he'd expected to sit through a long conversation about a guy who'd long since turned to dust and who'd led a life so boring that no one even remembered him. Now all of a sudden they were talking about something that was right up his alley—a real, live warlock, right in his own town!

Katelynn, however, was far from thrilled at the news. "I'm sorry, but I just can't believe that," she said.

"Why not?" Gabriel asked, a playful smile on his lips and a twinkle in his eye.

His expression just served to aggravate Katelynn further. He was a nice old man, and probably pretty lonely most of the time. That was why he liked making up stories to tell Sam while Sam worked the late shift, only the two of them awake so late at night. He'd probably misunderstood how serious she was, and having no real information that could help, had decided to invent some story along the lines of the ones he told Sam, thinking that was what she wanted to hear. She'd come looking for solid leads to help her, and talk of rituals and black magic was just going to put her in a foul mood. How gullible did he think she was?

"Why don't I believe it?" she answered him, the smile on her face as false as a three-dollar bill. "I'll tell you why I don't believe it. Because there is no such thing as black magic."

"Are you so sure of that, Katelynn? Has someone actually proven that such a thing does not exist?"

"Of course not. No reputable scientist would bother with such an experiment. The idea of magic completely defies what we know of modern physics. It just can't happen."

"Ahh, but remember what we are talking about here. We're not discussing modern ideas of reality but the views of those people who created this town in the late 1600s. Belief in witchcraft was a way of life back then, and in just about every small town you could find some man or woman who was considered a witch or warlock. Having those individuals run out of town or put to death by angry mobs in the middle of the night was not uncommon, especially here in the backwoods of New England. Just look at Salem. Do you really think these people didn't believe in magic?"

Grudgingly, Katelynn had to admit that he was right. When delving into the past, one had to remember that modern beliefs and attitudes just didn't belong. You had to adopt the beliefs of that particular era, or you would arrive at incorrect conclusions, just as she was doing now. *But what did all this have to do with Blake?*

Gabriel was more than happy to let her know. "Blake believed that he could gain power through the use of black magic, and much of his public demeanor was just an act, designed to deceive the townspeople into accepting him back into the fold while his research went on behind their backs. He scoured every reference he could find, tome after tome after tome, searching for just the right ritual that would put him in touch with the dark entities he believed existed amongst us, hoping to make use of their power to elevate himself into a position of dominance in the community."

"Then, in the early months of 1762, the killings began. The townspeople at first thought they were accidents, for they had been cleverly disguised as such. A wagon accident here, a sudden fall from a horse there, a child lost in the woods and found frozen to death the next day. But as the year passed, the killings became more frequent. And more violent. Random accidents could no longer account for what was happening, and the ravaged conditions of the corpses made the people begin to suspect that something out of the ordinary was going on. Then, late in 1763, the killer was discovered."

Katelynn was listening with a skeptical look on her face, but Sam was completely engrossed in Gabriel's tale, his belief in every word etched clearly on his face.

"An anonymous tip sent the local authorities to a small shack on the woods of the Blake family estate, and there they discovered Sebastian in the midst of one of his foul rituals. A small child was laid out on an altar before him as some kind of sacrifice to the powers with whom he had fallen in league. Before their very eyes, he plunged a knife into the young one's chest and cut out his living heart."

The old man shuddered, and Katelynn found herself involuntarily responding in kind. One thing she had to give him credit for; Gabriel was a great storyteller. Whether what he had to say had any basis in fact was another issue altogether.

"The townsfolk saw no need to wait for a formal trial. They formed a lynch mob and hanged him on the spot."

"So how come there is no record of any of this?" Katelynn asked, trying to trip the man up.

He had an answer ready for that as well. "Not wanting to besmirch the Blake family name, or to create a reputation for their newly prospering town, the village elders agreed to wipe any reference of the event from the records and forbade the papers from printing anything concerning the story, which wasn't difficult because they were owned by the Blakes."

"So how am I going to prove that this actually occurred?" she asked him.

Gabriel sat back and spread his hands, palms up. "I don't know. You're going to have to figure that one out for yourself. I've told you all that I know."

Throughout the story Sam had been quiet, but he finally spoke. "They couldn't have gotten to everyone, Katelynn. There's bound to be someone who recorded the events. A merchant, or a traveling minister, maybe even one of the families of the victims. At the very least you should be able to document the number of deaths that occurred at that time, right?"

Katelynn thought about it for a moment, then agreed. The town records, if they were still around, should show the death certificates for those years. If she could substantiate the deaths, she might be able to find another lead to help her prove the rest. She smiled to herself, surprised that she was seriously considering the story she'd just heard. The idea that Blake was consorting with the Devil was absurd, but proving the man had been some kind of a serial killer was not beyond her ability.

She focused her attention back on Gabriel. "Could you tell me any more about the people who were murdered?" she asked hopefully.

The well of information that Gabriel seemed to possess had apparently run dry. He didn't know the names of any of the victims, or the dates on which they had been killed.

Nothing except for the fact that it had started in early 1762 and ended in late 1763. "I'm sorry I can't help you more," he said.

"Oh, that's okay. You've given me a beginning, anyway. I'm not saying I believe it, but maybe it's worth looking into."

He smiled at her, and she gave him one of her own, the skepticism she'd felt earlier in the conversation having dissipated.

They chatted for a few minutes more, then said their good-byes. Sam had to start his shift, and Katelynn had to prepare a lesson for the class she was teaching in the morning. They told Gabriel they'd be back to see him soon and stepped out into the hallway.

"What do you think, Katelynn?" Sam asked, as they headed for the nursing station at the other end of the hall where he was assigned for the duration of his shift. "Do you think he was telling the truth?"

"I don't know, Sam. It could be that this guy actually was running around, sacrificing people in the mistaken belief that it could give him supernatural powers. It was the eighteenth century, after all. Then again, Gabriel could've just been making it all up in an effort to please you. It's obvious that he likes you, and if he felt that was the type of story you were looking for, he might just do it. He's certainly intelligent enough to pull it off."

"I don't know, Katelynn. Gabriel's never lied to me before, and he certainly understood how important this is to you."

"Only time will tell. Maybe I'll turn something up with a little more research. In the meantime, I'd better get going."

Sam handed over the car keys. "Pick me up at nine, and we'll drive to Jake's together, okay?"

"Sure thing. See you then," she replied, and headed off down the hall, throwing one last smile in Sam's direction to show that she didn't think the whole afternoon had been wasted.

Sam grinned in return and turned back to begin the day's work, but his mind was on that long forgotten evening in 1763.

At the other end of the hall, the one calling himself Gabriel sat staring into the distance, his eyes unfocused and dreamy. The voice of the beast was in the back of his mind, as it had been throughout the interview, whispering to him all the awful ends it had devised for him in its long years of confinement. It had been easier to ignore it when he had his two young friends in the room to talk to, taking his mind off what the beast was saying, but with them gone, it was harder to shut it out. He listened closely for a moment, trying to gauge if it had grown any stronger; but being unable to do so, he tuned it out. He didn't want to listen to that vile voice any longer.

He was worried. He was no longer the man he'd once been. His power was waning quickly; his body at last had grown old and tired. He'd assumed the Nightshade's prison would hold him indefinitely, but in that he'd been wrong. He should never have had that much pride in his own abilities. The beast was awake, and before long he knew it would be free as well.

Then it would come for him.

He had no doubts as to what would happen when it did.

He had one last hope, however. The seeds of his plan had already been planted. Sam was a good listener, and mixed within the stories he had been telling were grains of truth. He trusted that the boy would be smart enough to tell one from the other when the time was right.

The girl was a different story. He could tell she was skeptical of the tale he had told, and it would be questionable whether she would be able to overcome that skepticism in time to help Sam with what needed to be done. But overcome it she must, for Sam could not face this evil alone.

Gabriel decided to nudge her along the right path.

Rising from his bed, he crossed to the dresser and opened the bottom drawer. Beneath several old sweaters was a locked strongbox. He removed the box and placed it on top of the dresser.

Inside were the odds and ends that he had accumulated over the years; mementos of special moments and personal interests. One of these was a necklace of gold from which hung a crimson stone, wrapped in a piece of soft cloth. It had been fashioned years before by his enemy's ally, and Gabriel had taken possession of it following his victory over them. It was a communication device of sorts, for the right kind of individual, and Gabriel had little doubt that Katelynn fit the mold.

Gabriel reached for the phonebook and determined Katelynn's address. He then called a courier service, with whom he made arrangements to have the necklace picked up and delivered.

If he was right, it wouldn't be long before Katelynn was involved in his plan whether she wanted to be or not.

It was unfair, but necessary.

With each passing day the beast was growing stronger, coming that much closer to escaping.

Gabriel knew it would not be long.

His task finished, he began to pray.

3

BLAKE

As Jake drove his Jeep along the winding road that led from the tall iron gates marking the entrance of the Riverwatch estate to the mansion itself, he glanced out over the lake to his left. The beauty of the setting sun as it reflected off the still waters had not lost its appeal in the years since he'd first seen it.

He had arrived in Harrington Falls five years earlier, after spending almost a decade in New York City. The romance of the metropolis had long since worn away by the time he'd made the decision to leave. He'd grown tired of the crowds; tired of the press of humanity on all sides; tired of the hectic pace. He needed a cleansing of the spirit that just wasn't possible to find in the city, and one afternoon he decided he'd had enough. He sold almost everything he owned, packed his Jeep, and headed northeast. Eventually, he wandered into Harrington Falls and decided to stay.

He had accomplished a lot since then. With the help of a local bank, he started a construction company, finally putting the engineering degree he'd earned at NYU to good use. He started small, concentrating on additions to existing structures, home improvements, that sort of thing. After a time he discovered that he had a true talent, and interest, for restoring the older homes in the community, bringing them back to the vitality of their youth. He changed the focus of his business and now had a strong following in the surrounding communities. It was his success that brought him to the attention of his current client, Hudson Blake.

Blake was a direct descendant of the family that had started Harrington Falls in the late 1600s, a fact that he never let anyone forget. Jake had agreed to renovate one of the family mansions, a place known as Stonemoor. He knew the job would provide steady work for the rest of the fall and on into the winter, the period when available work usually became scarce.

Jake was beginning to regret that decision.

He hated the meetings with Blake. Held once a week, they were ostensibly to check the progress the crew was making on the renovations. Blake had always tried to make Jake feel inferior. The man was a pompous, condescending ass who wanted everything done yesterday and got verbally vicious when it wasn't.

No, this is not going to be a fun meeting.

Jake pulled into the cul-de-sac at the end of the drive and parked beside a sleek, silver Rolls Royce, circa 1937. A wide brick walkway curved across the lawn to the main door of the mansion.

He picked up the door's knocker, a heavy piece of brass molded into the shape of a lion's head, and rapped it sharply three times.

A moment passed before the butler, Charles, opened the door. He glanced at Jake's attire with clear disapproval. Jake was still wearing the jeans and work shirt he'd had on at the site. Coming across the threshold, Jake returned his best up yours stare, with a certain sense of satisfaction.

It was bad enough that he had to take such flak from Blake. Taking it from the man's servant was just too much.

Without a word, Charles turned and led the way through the first floor until they reached a set of broad oak doors near the back of the house. Having been there before, Jake knew it was the library.

"Wait here a moment," Charles said, in that toneless servant voice he had cultivated, and turned away without waiting for an acknowledgment. He knocked softly on the door in front of him before noiselessly sliding into the room. When he returned, he indicated Jake was to be admitted.

Jake stepped inside and heard the doors close firmly behind him.

Blake was seated at a desk formed from a massive piece of black stone that squatted in the middle of the room's hardwood floor like an altar erected to some particularly vile god. He didn't look up or acknowledge Jake's presence in any way. He merely continued to read through the papers held up before him.

Instead of standing there and growing uncomfortable, which Jake knew was the purpose of this little "exercise," he used the time to study his employer.

As always, whenever a few days had passed without seeing Blake, Jake was repulsed anew by the sight of his client. It wasn't that he was physically disgusting; he didn't have grotesquely scarred features, no loathsome birth defects that made looking at him a trial in itself. Nothing one could point to, and say, "There's the problem." Nothing like that. Instead, it was an odd sense of discomfort that crept into his bones, an unsettling feeling that slowly came over him. A feeling that said the heart at the center of this fruit was shrunken and black with rot. Add to that Blake's long bony frame and small evil-looking eyes set in a ferret-sharp face, and Jake figured it was pretty understandable that he felt the way he did.

Blake continued the charade for several long moments, letting the silence stretch.

Finally, "You're late," he said, in a tone that showed his own disgust, never once looking up at his visitor.

"I know," Jake replied calmly.

Blake suddenly threw the papers onto the surface of the desk and Jake found himself staring into the man's beady little eyes. "I suppose you have some kind of excuse?"

Jake still hadn't been offered a seat. He knew he wouldn't be. He chose to ignore the verbal gibe as well. "I'm afraid I have some bad news," he answered instead. "I was forced to stop work in the cellar this afternoon because of something my workmen uncovered."

The look changed in the man's eyes as his words registered, and for just a moment Jake thought he saw a gleam of excitement there before his employer's expression went carefully neutral.

"What do you mean?" Blake asked, his tone now as flat as his expression.

"After we finished pumping out the river, we uncovered the entrance to a set of stairs leading deeper underground. I went down with my foreman and followed the tunnel to a point some two hundred yards farther, where it has been bricked shut. I thought it was best if we waited to see what you wanted us to do before continuing."

"I see. . . ." Blake replied, then swung his chair around so he was facing the window, his back to Jake, so that the younger man wouldn't see the wide smile of surprise that spread slowly across his face. "And what did you do then?"

"Nothing. I sent the boys home, locked up, and came on over here."

"I see," Blake responded again.

The silence stretched for an unusually long time, with Blake staring out the window lost in thought, and Jake reluctant to disturb him and break the man's good mood, but finally, Jake felt that if he didn't interrupt, they'd be here until Tuesday.

"Mr. Blake? What do you want me to do about it?"

"Hhmm? Oh, nothing. Nothing at all."

The chair swung back around. Jake was unable to read anything behind the man's carefully blank expression. "I'm afraid I'm going to have to think about this for a while before I come to any decisions. Why don't you and your men take the next few days off?"

Then came the clincher.

"With pay, of course," Blake said.

Jake couldn't believe what he was hearing. *Days off? With pay? Has somebody turned the world upside down and not told me?* But Jake was nobody's fool. Whether he believed that Blake was really being a nice guy or if he had ulterior motives, Jake knew not to look a gift horse in the mouth. He quickly agreed with the idea, left off the paperwork he'd been requested to bring, and made plans to get back in contact with the man before the end of the week. Then he got the hell out before Blake could change his mind.

A few days off?

Hell, yes. Sounds good to me.

Climbing into his Jeep, Jake finally allowed himself to grin at his good fortune.

Once the fool had gone, Blake let a triumphant smile emerge as he pondered the implications of the news. His ancestor's journal had long hinted at a secret vault within one of the family estates, but after spending thousands of dollars and months of effort searching for it, he'd finally dismissed it several years ago as foolish nonsense.

Today's news changed everything.

There was no sense putting himself at risk to be certain, however. He'd pretend to give the situation some thought, then call the young fool back later that night. He'd tell him he'd changed his mind and give him permission to investigate further.

His smile grew wider as he realized what he had hunted for for so long might at last be within reach.

Which wasn't really all that surprising, by any means.

He was, after all, a Blake.

4

GAME NIGHT

Sam made a covert roll of his eight-sided die. Noting the result, he made an announcement to the players in front of him. "Five of the eight warriors you just killed suddenly sit back up and start rising to their feet."

"I think we're in trouble," Jake said to Katelynn, who nodded her agreement. Turning to Sam, Jake said, "Chelmar steps back and prepares to cast a sleep spell."

"Okay. And what about Alganea?"

"She stands a few feet in front of him, out of his line of sight but close enough to defend him if the things attack again."

More dice tumble, and another grave pronouncement is made: "The first ghoul reaches his feet and turns his head in your direction. His eyes seem to glow when they see you, and he slowly begins lumbering toward you, the sword in his right hand raised overhead threateningly."

"Hurry up, Jake!" Katelynn said excitedly.

"Okay, okay. Chelmar steps up next to Alganea and casts the spell, making sure before he does so that she is behind him and therefore out of the area of the spell's effect." Jake smiled at Katelynn winningly, as if to say that he had everything under control.

"Chelmar, you realize that you cast the spell properly, but it doesn't seem to have any effect on the ghouls, who are in fact undead, and therefore are not affected by mortal requirements like sleep. The first ghoul is almost close enough to strike, and looking past his shoulder both of you can see that now the other four have also climbed to their feet and are starting to move in your direction."

Both of the players knew that their characters were in real trouble. If they didn't think of something soon, they would probably die there in the dark caverns beneath Zolthane Mountain.

It was just after 10:00 P.M., and the three friends were deep in the midst of a session of Swords and Sorcerers, testing Sam's latest creation for playability. They were seated around the table in the kitchen of Jake's apartment, with Sam on one side and Jake and Katelynn on the other, their books, papers, and charts spread out before them. The lights in the room were off, the only illumination coming from half a dozen candles that cast a reddish glow across their faces, adding to the atmosphere of the game.

Loki, Jake's Akita, slept contentedly at his feet, head resting lightly on his paws, lost in his own fantasy world of dreams.

The game went on. "I reach out and yank Chelmar out of the range of the ghoul's sword," Katelynn said quickly in response to Sam as soon as she heard the magic had failed to work as they'd planned.

Another roll of the dice. "You manage to pull him back just in time, Alganea. But the ghouls close in."

The game continued in that vein for another hour or

so, with Katelynn and Jake managing to have their characters escape from the clutches of the ghouls, only to find themselves lost in the labyrinthine maze of passages that led them deeper beneath the earth, setting the stage for the next week's adventure.

Jake had seemed distracted for most of the evening, and as they were cleaning up, Sam decided to broach the subject. Jake was staring off into space, absently stroking his dog's head, when Sam said, "What's up, Jake? You usually enjoy poking holes in all my hard work. Sometimes I feel that the only reason you play anymore is to make certain I don't pull a fast one on the unsuspecting public. You're letting Katelynn do all the work tonight."

Jake laughed. "Sorry, Sam. Just distracted I guess. We had an incident at the site today, and I guess it's been on my mind all night."

He had both Sam and Katelynn's attention instantly. "Somebody get hurt?" Katelynn asked, her face showing concern, the adventure module in her hand forgotten for the moment.

"Nah, nothing like that." Remembering his first reaction to Rick's appearance in his trailer, Jake almost smiled. "My men have been working in the cellar for the last several days, pumping out the river so we can lay the wood floor, you know?"

Sam and Katelynn nodded. Spending as much time together as they did, they'd become almost as familiar with Blake's renovation plans as Jake.

"Once Rick's team pumped out the water, they found this shallow trench bisecting the entire basement. And there, at the bottom of the trench, is a set of stairs leading down into the earth." Jake looked up from where he was staring at the floor, to see if his friends were following his explanation.

They were, so he told them the rest.

About his gut reaction to the stone. About the tunnel he and Rick uncovered, and of the journey the two of them made into the darkness beneath. He told them of a phone call he had earlier that evening from Blake, and of the man's request that he and his crew break through the barrier that blocked off the end of the tunnel in order to discover what lay beyond.

"What are you going to do?" Sam asked.

"Just what I was told to do. Break down that wall in the morning to see what's on the other side."

"Want some company?" Sam asked.

"Sure. Just come ready to work. Taking down a brick wall in open air in the light of day is one thing. Having to do the same while underground in a dimly lit and poorly ventilated tunnel is another. It isn't going to be easy."

Throughout the conversation, Katelynn sat quietly, doing her best to cope with the flood of feelings at Jake's revelation. A strange sense of unease uncoiled like a snake in her belly, all cold and hungry, telling her to leave things well enough alone, not to disturb whatever it was that had lain at rest in the dark depths of that tunnel for so long. She was suddenly certain that it would do them no good to intrude.

At last she spoke up. "Do you really think it's a good idea to go down there, Jake?" she asked tentatively, not trusting her own feelings sufficiently to protest any harder.

"We checked it out pretty thoroughly this afternoon. That tunnel is hewed from solid rock. There's no danger of its collapsing on us," he replied, misunderstanding her reason for caution.

Katelynn couldn't find a way to voice her concern without looking silly and superstitious, so she let the matter drop. Mentally, she sought some rational explanation for the fear that was rapidly spreading through her, but found that none existed. Something was going to happen when they went down there, something awful. She knew it, could feel it in her bones.

While Katelynn struggled to identify her feelings, Jake and Sam quickly agreed to meet the next morning just before seven. After that, the gathering broke up quickly.

The ride home with Sam passed in silence. When they pulled into her drive, and he walked her to her door, she tried once more. "You guys really ought to just leave things alone and let Blake hire some professionals to investigate that tunnel. What if it's unsafe, and the two of you get trapped down there?"

Sam sighed. "We're not going to get trapped, Katelynn. You heard Jake. That tunnel has been standing for a long time. One more day isn't going to make a difference; it's not going to suddenly come tumbling down around our ears. You're just jealous that you can't go with us because you have class in the morning." He chuckled, not recognizing the depths of her fear. "Go on, get inside," he said. "We'll tell you all about it at lunch tomorrow. We'll be fine. You'll see." With a wave he turned away down the steps.

Katelynn was still standing there, watching, as the taillights of his car disappeared around the curve at the end of her street.

In the darkness, she shivered.

5

HALLORAN

As Jake was telling his friends about that afternoon's discovery, across town another type of celebration was going on.

Kyle Halloran was getting drunk. He sat at the bar in Mikey's Place, his oversize frame dwarfing the padded stool, his thick, meaty hands wrapped around a frosted mug of beer, his ninth of the night.

His craggy, square-jawed face reflected the emotions roiling there just beneath the surface. He sat there, dressed in the same sweat-stained T-shirt and jeans he'd been wearing all day while working under the hot sun, and let the anger swell inside him like gas in an overripe corpse.

Fuck Jake! he thought savagely. *Bust my ass all day long for the guy and does he show any gratitude? Hell, no!*

He slammed the mug up to his lips, drunkenly unaware that the glass cracked against his teeth. He took a long swallow, finishing off the drink.

The first time I ask for a raise and what do I get? "Sorry, Halloran, you're just not working hard enough for me to give you one yet," he mimicked in a high, squeaky voice.

Halloran slapped several bills down on the counter and stumbled out into the night air. The cool crispness cut through the beer-induced haze, sharpening his anger. Insisting on a raise earlier in the day had gotten him fired. Now, as Halloran stumbled off down the street, barely conscious of where he was going, his thoughts turned to how he could pay Jake back for his prejudice against him.

After considering several plans, each of which involved physical damage to Jake himself, Kyle stopped for a moment under a streetlamp, trying to discern just where he was. The sign before him read LAMPLIGHTER LANE, and it took him several moments to realize that he had wandered in the opposite direction from his apartment.

"Shit!" he swore into the darkness, turning to go back.

As he turned, the peak of a house caught his eye as it rose over the treetops to his left.

It was the Blake estate once known as Stonemoor, the very place he'd been working for the last several weeks. Seeing it brought his thoughts of revenge back into focus, and a plan began to form. He'd heard something that afternoon that he could use against Caruso.

Something about the cellar . . .

Then he had it. *A secret passage! Cantelli's crew had found a secret passage down in the cellar.* Joey Henderson had told him about it at lunch that afternoon. He'd barely heard him at the time, and he wished he had listened more closely. Hadn't he said something about it leading to some kind of secret room, a storage room, or a . . .

A treasure vault.

The idea took sudden hold. *Why else would somebody build a room underground that nobody could get to? That had to be it!*

It took only a moment for him to make up his mind about what to do with the information. *When opportunity knocks, only a fool doesn't answer,* he thought, *and I am no fool. Right here in front of me is a way to screw Caruso over and get rich at the same time.*

He glanced around, satisfying himself that no one was watching, then set off through the woods in the direction of the estate.

Ten minutes later he was crouched at the corner of the supply shed by the side of the house. A quick survey of the area assured him that the idiot, Caruso, hadn't hired a night watchman. *Just shows how stupid he really is,* Kyle thought wryly. He stepped out of hiding and over to the shed. Reaching out, he tried the door.

Locked.

No matter. He knew how to deal with the situation. Kyle wandered around to the back of the mansion to where the construction crews had been discarding the wood and metal pieces they'd been replacing inside the house, along with a few inexpensive tools. From the pile he selected a crowbar.

Halloran returned to the shed and forced the point of the iron bar into the opening between the doorjamb and the hasp of the lock. One strong heave, and the door swung open with a muffled crack. Kyle stepped inside. It took only a few moments to gather the supplies he needed: a couple of heavy-duty flashlights, a pickax, and a shovel.

The mansion's front door gave more easily than the trailer's had. Once in, he flipped on one of the flashlights to light the way. The mansion was set back a good way from the road and who in his right mind would come out there at that time of the night? It was creepy enough in the daylight, never mind after dark. Goose bumps rose on his arms the moment he stepped inside.

He found the steps to the cellar and descended into the darkened basement. He crossed the floor, damp muck sucking at his heels, darkness surrounding him, pressing in on him from all sides.

If he'd been sober, he might have noticed the heavy silence that enveloped the house in its smothering embrace. He might have noticed the sudden rush of electrical tension that filled the spaces between that silence like a living entity, making the hair on the back of his neck stand at attention.

But he remained blissfully unaware.

The dark maw of the staircase leading underground suddenly loomed in the floor before him, and he jerked to a stop, almost stumbling down the steps. The gloom from the tunnel mouth seemed thicker than the darkness around him, and he shined his light down the steps, cutting through it with the precision of a scalpel. Dust motes swirled in the beam, and he could see where the passing of others earlier in the day had disturbed the thick layer of dust on the floor.

A vague sense of unease slowly seeped its way through his pores. He had the sudden feeling that someone was watching, and he turned quickly, shining the light back across the room in the direction he'd come.

The room was empty.

For a moment he toyed with the idea of giving up his crazy scheme and going home. But visions of gold danced before his eyes, and the notion was soon forgotten. He'd come this far. *There's no stopping now,* he thought.

Taking a deep breath, he strode down the steps into the darkness below.

In Room 310, the old man lay trapped in that twilight realm that hovers between sleeping and wakefulness. He lay on his side, curled into a fetal position, a thin trail of spittle falling from his slightly parted lips to the surface of his pillow. Every few moments he was wracked by spasms that made him quiver as if volts of electricity were being passed through his body. His eyes flicked back and forth beneath the protective skin of their lids.

In his dreams, he stood in a narrow stone tunnel, a little behind and to the left of a tall, hulking man who, in turn, stood before a brick wall that sealed off the passage in which they stood. The man's emotions rolled off him in waves; he was full of rage and spite. He stood there, smashing at the wall with a pickax, determined to break through to the other side. The old man watched as the youth lifted the pick yet again, those powerful arms swinging it toward the wall with tremendous force. As the stroke fell, time seemed to slow, and he watched in horrid fascination as the pickax swung silently downward. He could see that much of the barrier had already been destroyed, and he knew that if the man succeeded in breaking through, the ancient adversary would be free to walk the face of the earth.

He could not allow that to happen.

Unwilling to admit defeat, yet knowing that he was probably too late, he screamed out in desperation, hoping against hope to delay that final blow.

"Stop!!!"

Kyle's swing faltered, the handle slipped in his hands,

and he came close to smashing his kneecap into oblivion as the heavy head of the pickax bounced off the wall before him and came rearing back in his direction.

"Fuck! You could have crippled me!" he said savagely as he turned to face the speaker, his anger overcoming his fear at being discovered.

What he saw as he turned brought his cursing to an abrupt halt, however.

The corridor behind him was empty.

"Hello?" he called in a suddenly shaky voice.

His cry echoed back at him along the length of the tunnel, ghostly whispers of sound. *Hello, hello, hello*. . . .

"Who's there?"

Who's there, there, there. . . .

"Shit!"

Shit, shit, shit. . . .

Kyle turned away. "Must have been my imagination," he mumbled to himself, dismissing the incident from his mind with the overconfidence of a drunk. He could see that it would only take another swing for him to break through the barrier and as he hefted the pickax once more, visions of gold returned to dance in his mind.

He brought the pick up and back down again in a solid swing.

The stroke was directly on target.

With a loud crash, the stones before him gave way, revealing a hole a foot or two in diameter.

"Yes!" he cried exuberantly, this time not even hearing the echoes as they bounded away in the darkness behind him. *A couple more minutes, and I'll be rich!* He dropped the pick and retrieved his flashlight from where it had been propped up on a nearby stone to provide him light.

He shined the light into the hole.

A horrible, hideous face lunged out of the darkness at him.

"Christ!" he screamed, his sudden fear making his voice high and shrill.

He dropped the light, not hearing the small sound of breaking glass as it struck the floor, and grabbed the pickax, bringing it up over his shoulder ready to strike at the thing should it emerge from its hole.

Kyle was too stubborn to run away. He waited there in the darkness for a moment, his ears straining to hear the slightest sound from the thing ahead of him. He trembled with fear yet held his ground, prepared to smash the thing's ugly face as soon as it stuck its head out of the hole.

Nothing happened.

After a few minutes, he cautiously bent down and felt around at his feet for one of the other lights he'd carried in with him. His heart racing in his chest, he slowly moved closer to the hole and shined the light back inside.

The face was there again, and he almost jumped away a second time when he noticed something he'd missed before. The eyes of the thing were coated with a thick layer of dirt and dust.

"What the hell?" he whispered.

He stepped closer, putting his head inside the hole, closer to the thing itself. He could see more clearly, and, after another minute, he started laughing softly. His laughter grew from a light chuckle to a total, uncontrolled braying, until he was laughing so hard that tears ran down his face.

The thing was a statue. *A fucking statue!* he thought to himself. *I was scared of a statue!* His laughter echoed inside the enclosed space. He failed to hear the raw edges of hysteria in its tone.

Feeling much better than he had a moment before, Kyle pulled his head back out of the hole he'd created and once more hefted the pickax. Five more minutes of work made the hole large enough for him to step through.

Shining the light around the room, Halloran could see that the chamber he stood in was little bigger than ten by ten, with the same distance between the ceiling and the floor. The statue seemed to be the only object in the room.

He moved around it, his steps stirring up small clouds of dust. The statue was made of some kind of dark, unfamiliar stone. It didn't seem to be worth anything, as far as he could tell, no rubies for eyes or anything like that. After another close look he dismissed it from his thoughts and turned away.

He was there for treasure, not some weird stone statue.

Problem was, as far as he could tell, the rest of the room was empty.

There also didn't appear to be any other way out except the one he had created.

Now what?

He stood still and thought for a few moments, eventually deciding that there must be another secret room hidden inside this one. No one would take the time and energy to carve a room out of solid rock to stick some ugly statue in it, would they?

Turning his back on the statue, he began running his hands over the surface of the walls, searching for hidden levers or switches that might activate an opening. He occasionally struck the wall roughly with the haft of the pickax, listening for echoes that might indicate the presence of an open space beyond. That was how they always did it in the movies. He figured that it might work for him as well.

After fifteen minutes of searching, he hadn't found anything, despite circling the entire room twice.

Frustrated, Kyle turned to face the statue. Suddenly the room seemed to dip and sway like an unstable boat in rough seas. He put out a hand to steady himself, only to discover that the wall seemed to be receding. That upset his equilibrium further. His feet tangled, and, before he knew it, he struck the floor heavily, knocking the breath from his lungs.

For a moment he stayed where he was, regaining his breath. After a minute or two he realized that a sharp pain was radiating from the palm of his right hand. Pulling himself into a sitting position against the base of the statue, he reached out with his other hand and dragged the flashlight back from where it had fallen when he dropped it. By its light he could see a deep cut crisscrossing his right palm.

Must have fallen on the pick, he thought to himself, and a quick glance in that direction with the flashlight showed a faint red smear along its blade.

He shifted his position, intending to climb to his feet. He only managed to pull himself up on his knees before another wave of dizziness washed over him.

His head spun, the room reeled around him, and the flashlight fell from his hand with a distant crash, shattering against the base of the stone.

The darkness that suddenly enveloped the room matched his own.

He was unconscious by the time his body hit the floor.

°   °   °

With the echoes of his shout reverberating in his mind, the old man awoke. His heart was trip-hammering in his chest like a snare drum, sending a sharp pain through his left side. For a few anxious moments he was certain the frail vessel would burst asunder.

No, he thought. *Not now, not yet,* he silently pleaded. It seemed someone heard him, for the pain slowly receded, and his heartbeat settled into a more stable rhythm. He breathed a bit easier and raised a weak hand to wipe the thick sheen of sweat from his brow.

The chill in his gut and the sudden joyous laughter that echoed in his mind told him all he needed to know about the effects of his warning.

The beast was free.

6

BENEATH THE SURFACE

Early the next morning Jake drove his Jeep into Sam's driveway and sounded two quick taps of the horn. Then he dug into the bag he'd placed on the floor behind the passenger seat, pulling out a cup of coffee and a donut.

Sam came down the steps dressed in jeans and a Benton University sweatshirt, a pair of thick hiking boots on his feet. Around his neck were slung two cameras and an assortment of lenses. A fanny pack strapped around his waist bulged with additional gear.

"What is all that?" Jake asked, as Sam climbed inside the vehicle.

"Necessities, Jake. You don't expect me to go on possibly one of the most interesting finds this town has seen in two hundred years and not bring along some means of recording the event, do you? I just wish my damn video camera wasn't in the shop, or I'd have brought that along, too."

Jake chuckled as he handed the coffee and donut to Sam and dug another donut out of the bag for himself. He couldn't blame Sam for his enthusiasm; he, too, was anxious to see just what it was that had been worth burying beneath a living river. In the short time it took to cross town and arrive at the mansion, Jake felt his excitement grow.

At the end of Stonemoor's drive, Jake turned left into the construction area proper and parked in front of his trailer, where something caught his eye.

The door to the toolshed was wide-open, hanging in its frame by only one hinge.

Jake grunted in surprise, and walked over, with Sam at his heels. Jake had experienced robberies at other sites, had even bought a pistol he kept in his desk drawer in the trailer so that he'd feel some protection while working alone at night, but he had never expected to have one at Stonemoor. For a moment he was more surprised than angry. There wasn't anything of great value in the toolshed. *What would somebody want with some old shovels and a pickax or two?* he found himself wondering.

"Why would anybody want to . . ." Jake began, then stopped, his eyes widening in sudden realization. "The tunnel!" he exclaimed.

Without a word, Sam turned to go, anxious that someone else had beaten him to what he considered the story of his lifetime, but Jake grabbed his arm.

"Hang on. You've got to help me with this stuff." He let go and turned to the shed, pushing the door aside and disappearing within. He returned a moment later with a couple of shovels, a crowbar, and a pickax cradled in his arms. He gave a shovel to Sam and kept the other for himself. Then he moved over to the trailer and, unlocking the door, went inside. He had a large ring of keys and two battery-powered lanterns in his hands when he emerged. His pistol was stuck in the waistband of his jeans.

"We're going to need them to see down there," he said, indicating the lamps. "We haven't had a chance to string any lights yet."

They crossed the yard, headed for the front door. As they walked, Jake felt his concern growing. Very few people knew of what they'd uncovered the previous day. Unless some of the crew had shot their mouths off to friends, it had to be one of his men who had caused the damage they'd seen. After all, they'd be the ones most likely to know just where the tools were kept and what they might need down in the cellar.

His suspicions that someone had been after whatever was hidden in the tunnel were confirmed when he and Sam mounted the steps, only to discover the front door standing half-open like an invitation.

That pissed him off. Blake was going to have a fit when he told him about the break-in, and Jake fervently hoped nothing had been stolen from inside. That would make matters even worse. *God help me when I find out who did this,* he thought grimly.

Behind him, Sam was taking pictures. The click of the camera sent Jake over the edge.

"Will you knock that off, for Christ's sake?" he snapped angrily.

Sam wisely lowered the camera without a word.

The same gouge marks were in the frame of this door, and on closer inspection Jake recognized them as having come from the notched end of a crowbar. Just to be sure, he hefted the one he had in his hand and laid it against one of the marks. It was a near perfect match.

Looking at the state of the aged oak that made up the doorframe, Jake ruefully shook his head. *Add another item to the list of things that need to be replaced,* he thought to himself.

He reached out to the door, intending on going inside, when Sam's voice stopped him.

"Ah, Jake?"

Jake turned, a questioning look on his face.

"Don't you think we'd better call the police?" Sam asked, nodding in the direction of the trailer and the phone he knew to be inside.

Jake thought about it for a minute, then shook his head. "Not just yet. I want to have a look around first, try to get an idea of what kind of damage has been done. See if there's anything missing." *And I want to have a look at that tunnel,* he added silently.

The open door beckoned to him.

He opened it the rest of the way with a gentle nudge of his foot, Sam's request reminding him that he didn't want to disturb any evidence unnecessarily, and stepped inside, Sam close at his heels.

The morning sun had yet to rise high enough to crest the trees surrounding the property, making the interior of the house dim and gloomy. Jake was forced to turn on one of the lanterns to see clearly.

The entryway looked undisturbed.

"Wait here a sec," he said to Sam, and stuck his nose into the rooms on either side of the foyer. Everything looked to be in its place.

Jake didn't bother going up the stairs directly ahead of him. They led to the second floor, and there was nothing of value up there anyway. Besides, for some strange reason he was certain the intruder hadn't gone up.

He'd gone down instead.

To the basement.

To the tunnel.

"Come on," Jake said, and crossed the foyer into the dining room and out through the kitchen to the door that opened onto the cellar steps.

Holding the light high before him, he descended.

Once down below he discovered that his suspicions were correct. The tarp covering the stairs leading deeper into the earth had been pulled aside. A crowbar lay discarded next to it.

Jake moved over to the steps with Sam right behind him. A hand gesture told Sam to extinguish his light, which he did, and the two of them stood there in the darkness.

No lights shone up the stairs from below.

No sound reached their ears.

Jake drew his gun and leaned close to his friend. "Looks like we're alone, but let's not take any chances. Keep your voice down and follow me. If we come upon an intruder, I'll hold him at bay while you go back to the trailer and call for help."

Sam gripped the shovel in his hands a bit tighter and nodded his agreement.

Turning on their lights and moving carefully so as to make as little noise as possible, the two started down the steps in pursuit of the intruder.

They moved down the length of the tunnel and turned the corner to find a large hole cut in the center of the wall that had previously blocked the way. Jake stopped before the hole, shining his light inside, gazing through it at the scene on the other side.

Sam stepped up to his side and added his light to his friend's.

After a moment, he lowered the flashlight and raised his camera.

Several shots later he turned to Jake, and asked, "Now can we call the police?"

Jake nodded without saying a word.

On the other side of the wall, the corpse of Kyle Halloran gazed back at them with wide, staring eyes.

7

WILSON

Damon Wilson was on duty in Harrington Falls when the call came in. As sheriff of Algonquin County, he was responsible for the safety of the inhabitants of not only Glendale, but also Harrington Falls and the other similar mountain communities within the county limits. He had two men out sick, so he was covering their shifts himself, patrolling in his Bronco.

"I'll take it, base. I'm in the vicinity."

"That's a roger, Sheriff. See Jake Caruso at the site."

"Ten-four."

Damon replaced the microphone and headed for the Stonemoor estate.

Back when he was on the force in Chicago, such calls had been a fairly commonplace occurrence. They were called into abandoned buildings and derelict lots all the time, especially during the summer months when the stench of decomposing corpses would disturb the denizens of even the roughest neighborhoods. The winters weren't so bad; a body could lie in the dark for weeks without being discovered. He'd seen his fair share; that was certain.

But here in Harrington Falls? He couldn't remember the last time there had been a violent crime. Glendale was a bit different; a little more modern, more bad apples. Harrington Falls seemed to have missed all of that, nestled as it was in the mountains. The people were quiet folk. They kept to themselves and generally obeyed the law. Aside from the occasional loud drunk or teenage shoplifter, the patrol in Harrington Falls was considered incident-free.

Making the call even more interesting.

As Damon pulled up in front of the house, he saw two men sitting on the top step of the porch, obviously waiting for him.

Jake watched as a large, heavyset man got out of the Bronco. Roughly six-foot two, he had to weigh a good 250. His hair was salt and pepper, right down to his beard and mustache. Both were carefully groomed and short in length. The man was dressed in the brown uniform of the sheriff's department, with a pistol clearly visible on his belt.

Jake and Sam rose to greet him.

"One of you Jake Caruso?" Damon asked.

Jake said, "I am," and extended his hand in greeting.

"Damon Wilson, sheriff's department." The sheriff shook Sam's hand also. Turning back to Jake, he asked, "I understand you've found a body?"

Jake nodded. "Down in the cellar."

"Mind telling me what you were doing out here in the first place?"

Jake explained to the sheriff how he came to be there that morning, going back to the events of the day before.

The sheriff listened closely, made notes every few minutes, but otherwise left Jake to tell the story without interruption. When Jake was finished, the sheriff turned to Sam and asked him if he could remember any other details.

The sheriff then suggested that Sam wait outside to direct the coroner to the scene, before asking Jake to lead him to the body.

The two climbed the steps to the house, passed through the foyer and the kitchen, and reached the stairway to the basement. The smell of mildew and decay from below reached Damon. For just a moment, he had a vivid picture of bodies lying for days in forgotten Chicago tenements, the memory of another time, another place. He quickly slammed the lid closed on that particular memory before it could escape the Pandora's box of his mind. Chicago was a long time ago, and Damon definitely wanted to keep it that way.

Jake headed down the steps, and Damon followed.

"Sorry about the stench. When we began renovations, this entire level was flooded. My men pumped out the fetid water the other night, but the smell will probably linger for a while."

"That's how you found this tunnel?" Damon asked.

"Yeah. There was a big stone slab in the middle of a small trench dug into the floor. The tunnel was underneath it."

Jake had left the lanterns behind when he and Sam went to the trailer to call the police. By their illumination Damon could see the trench where the men had been working. When they moved closer, he could see the opening to the passage itself.

Jake stopped and picked up his lantern from where he had left it beside the opening. He nodded at the heavy flashlight the sheriff was carrying. "You'd better turn that on."

The sheriff was surprised at the tunnel. It appeared to be man-made, carved from solid rock sometime long ago. The effort that went into such an undertaking had to have been incredible.

Why would someone go to all this trouble? he wondered.

He didn't have much time to think about it, however, since they were rapidly approaching their destination. Ahead, Damon could see the remains of a brick wall that had once blocked the tunnel. Jake stopped a few feet away, allowing Damon to pass him.

Damon stood just outside the chamber and gazed in at the body. He could see that it was that of a white male, in his mid-to-late twenties, lying faceup and partially on his right side. The man's face was twisted into an expression of horror. One arm was trapped beneath the body, the other hung limply across the base of the statue. In the dim light, Damon could not make out any signs of injury.

"This the way you found him?"

Jake nodded. "I went inside the room and checked his pulse, but I didn't touch or move anything."

Damon shined the light around the rest of the room. The only objects were a heavy-duty flashlight, lying against the opposite wall, and a pickax, a few feet away from the feet of the corpse. The room was otherwise empty.

Damon next turned his light on the statue. A good seven feet in height, it was carved entirely from some kind of shining black stone that gleamed like ebony oil in the beam of his light. It appeared to represent a demon, or maybe a gargoyle. Two long, curling horns jutted from its forehead. Its strikingly reptilian mouth was open wide, revealing a double row of razor-sharp teeth. The creature's torso was humanoid in form, but covered with thousands of tiny scales like the flesh of a miniature dragon. Wicked-looking talons jutted from its four-fingered hands and feet. Batlike wings swept outward from the center of its back. The craftsmanship was superb, giving the creature a sense of life. To Damon it seemed as if at any moment it might leap off the small pedestal on which it stood.

"It's certainly ugly," Damon said. Jake didn't answer. The statue might have been easy enough to handle if that was all it was, ugly. But there was something more, something near indefinable about it that instantly put Damon on guard. It was more a gut feeling than anything else, a sense of wrongness about the thing that disturbed him on some deep, primitive level.

Damon felt the short hairs on the back of his neck start to rise and quickly turned his attention to the body on the floor. It took him a moment, but he finally recognized it as that of Kyle Halloran. Kyle had been one of the bad ones, constantly getting into fights at the bars down in Glendale. More than once Damon had had to toss him in a cell for the night on charges of drunk and disorderly. Kyle had been the type to stay out of trouble for a month, maybe two, then end up back in a cell on similar charges.

Aside from the expression on his face, there were no obvious signs of violence. Damon could not detect any evidence of a disturbance in the dirt around him, either.

Drugs were the first thing that came to mind. That would explain the lack of injury. The theory might also explain the man's expression. *Who knew what one might encounter in their own drug-induced hallucinations?*

"Recognize him?" the sheriff asked.

Jake nodded. "Kyle Halloran. Hired him last week as a temp. Bit of a loudmouth. My foreman said he was slacking on the job, so I let him go yesterday."

"Any idea what he might have been doing down here?"

"I couldn't even tell you how he found out about it. He wasn't on the detail that was working down here."

The sheriff nodded. It seemed pretty obvious to him. Halloran had heard about it from another worker, figured there might be something valuable hidden in the tunnel, and decided to check it out for himself. He'd probably been pumped to the gills with whatever he'd been on that week and taken on more than he could handle.

Damon took out his notebook and jotted down his impressions and general facts about the scene. He'd learned long ago to make a record of everything at a crime scene; you never knew what was going to be important later. When he was finished, he stepped inside the room for the first time.

Jake watched the sheriff make a careful inspection of the body. Damon squatted next to the corpse and felt for a pulse on the man's neck. He sat back on his haunches and visually inspected the corpse, taking care not to touch anything else. After a few moments he jotted down some notes and even sketched a quick diagram of the situation. Jake recognized the hallmarks of a methodical and patient man. Once the sheriff had finished with the corpse, he turned his attention to the statue above it, going over it with the same care and diligence he'd shown with the body.

Jake didn't want to be in the room with either the statue or the corpse. His earlier excitement had quickly died when he and Sam had discovered Kyle's body. Now all he wanted to do was retreat back up the stairs into the bright sunshine and forget about what he'd found.

He stepped back into the passage, a glimpse of movement catching his eyes as he did so.

He turned in the doorway, staring at the statue, watching its eyes, watching its hands.

Must have been the sheriff.

Statues don't move.

The sheriff called out to him as he turned away.

"Where does this go?" Damon asked, pointing behind him to something that Jake could not see because of the intervening statue.

"Where does what go?" Jake asked. He stepped to his left and gaped in surprise at the doorway visible on the other side of the chamber.

"Where the hell did that come from?" Jake asked.

Damon watched Jake examine the door and knew he wasn't faking it. He really hadn't known it was there. The iron door had been coated with a thick layer of dust and dirt, causing it to blend with the wall in the dim light. In the horror of finding the statue looming over Kyle's body, it had been overlooked.

The sheriff intended to let the forensics team open the door once they had thoroughly checked the chamber. He hadn't counted on Jake's curiosity. Before the sheriff could stop him, Jake placed his hands against the door and pushed with all his strength.

The door swung outward with a groan.

Sunlight flooded the chamber.

Without a word Damon stepped over to stand next to Jake.

The two men stared out the doorway onto the carefully trimmed green of the Forest Green Cemetery.

"Holy shit," Jake said under his breath.

The sheriff agreed. *Holy shit is right. We must have traveled a couple of hundred yards underground, clear off the Blake property and onto the adjoining one.* He hadn't realized they'd gone that far.

He stepped out into the sunshine with Jake at his heels. As one, they turned to face the doorway.

The door proved to be the entrance to a white marble mausoleum that was built into the side of a small hill. Across the lintel of the doorframe was carved a name.

SEBASTIAN BLAKE.

8

RESURRECTION

Inside the tomb.

Movement.

It began as nothing more than a subtle shifting in the darkness, a change in the rank air that filled the buried structure, a stirring sense of motion that was more felt than seen, as if the air pressure had suddenly lowered.

Gradually, as the moments passed, the motion became more substantial until at last it could be seen with the naked eye, had anyone been watching.

A patch of darkness, darker than even the heavy gloom filling the tomb's every nook and cranny, detached itself from the shadows in one corner and drifted like a curtain of mist into the center of the chamber. It churned about in rich, lazy spirals, a bubbling, seething witch's brew that whirled and spun about itself.

The mist became a haze; the haze became a fog, and still it writhed and rolled. With each revolution it slowly gathered substance from the darkness around it. When the cloud was several feet in diameter, it slowly wrapped the statue in its inky embrace.

The murk began to adhere to the finely wrought stone,

slowly at first, then faster, as the intelligence guiding it gradually awakened from a long sleep, its senses progressively becoming more in tune with physical reality.

The human blood shed earlier acted as a catalyst, providing the ingredients required for him again to assume a corporeal form. The dark union of forces that had sustained him for so long did the rest.

A light sparked about the statue, a tiny flash of crimson the size and shape of a cigarette ember, located somewhere near the center of the thing's chest. With each pulsation it grew slowly brighter, bit by bit, until it reached the intensity of a carefully contained fire. There was no heat. The strange light seemed to give off an unnatural chill that wafted forth and turned the air inside the tomb several degrees colder than it had been moments before. The bloodred light flickered across the face of the statue, causing its teeth to gleam eerily in the glow.

The cloud pulsed and swelled as it coalesced about the figure, until it was a semisolid mass of churning black, mated to the stone, covering every exposed inch of its surface.

The light flared suddenly brighter, so bright that it would have blinded anyone in the room in its gory red glow.

But no one was there, and so the change went on.

Unheeded.

Unhindered.

Unnoticed by all but the one who'd triggered it and the other who'd sought so desperately to prevent it.

A smell suddenly filled the air, a stench like the cloying reek of sulfur. With it the light flared in a flash that lasted for several long moments.

When the light died down and the darkness returned, the beast that had been hidden for centuries stood in the center of the room where the statue had been just moments before.

In the darkness, yellow eyes gleamed brightly.

The beast remained where it was for a moment or two, rejoicing in its newfound freedom. The rush of the stolen blood in its veins brought a rhythmic pounding to its ears, and after the ages of silence even that slight, internal sound was like thunder.

It reveled in it. It was alive.

The creature once known as Moloch walked toward the door, eager to escape the confines of the dank, stone structure where he'd been imprisoned. He moved with steady deliberation; the first steps were slow and awkward, the joints in his knees and hips seemed rusted tight with disuse. After a few more steps the tissues began to remember and established the proper rhythm.

Where his movements had at first been disjointed, jerky, they gradually became fluid, composed and filled with a savage, feline grace. He walked the circumference of the room. Once, twice, three times, each step renewing his familiarity with physical motion and the laws that governed it.

As he walked he worked his arms, swinging them back and forth at the elbows and rotating them in their shoulder sockets, flexing the muscles of his biceps. He clenched and unclenched his fists.

Moloch opened and closed his jaw several times, snapping it shut to hear the sharp click of his teeth with force enough to crush bone to a pulp.

He delighted in the tension and release of the muscles

in his back and legs. The sound of his claws scraping the rough stone underfoot sent a shiver of pleasure through his frame.

Moloch strode across the chamber. With a shove from one muscle-laden arm, he swung wide the door. It crashed against the outer wall with a loud metallic clang. He was barely aware of the sound, so entranced was he with the sight through the open door.

There, just steps away, lay freedom.

Sounds were assaulting him from all sides; the whisper of the wind, the trip-hammer of tiny hearts in the shrubbery.

He laughed, the sound welling up from the depths of his throat in manic glee and echoing into the night.

It was a sound that was less than human.

Lights gleamed off in the distance. Spying them, the beast's thoughts turned to the terrible, gnawing hunger that had awakened deep inside. Too long he had been locked inside that stone, imprisoned and left to die alone in the darkness. Too long he had existed in that twilight between this world and the next, his life extended by the dark forces that had imprisoned him there.

Now he was free.

Free to act.

Free to feed.

He extended his arms. The leathery wings that lay smoothly against the surface of his back extended with them, rustling in the breeze like the sound of a quickly snapped sheet. Bunching the muscles in his scaled legs, Moloch gave a powerful downward shove and cast his body upward into the dark night.

9

A DEATH EXPLAINED?

Edward Strickland, medical examiner for Algonquin County, stepped into the chill confines of the morgue and switched on the lights. Though it was late in the evening, Strickland was preparing to perform one last task for the night, a task he had saved until the end, so that other duties would not prevent him from giving it his complete attention.

Strickland was an agreeable man in his early sixties, and had been ME for sixteen years. Despite his constant joking that the only reason he'd been able to retain his post was due to the fact that nobody else wanted it, he was a competent professional who got the job done and got it done right the first time. He was nearing retirement, but was in no way ready for it.

His work was a constant puzzle to him, and he pursued it with an almost fanatic devotion. To find him working far into the night, as he planned on this occasion, was not an unusual occurrence. The silence in the morgue after hours was deep and peaceful, soothing, vastly different from the hectic pace that enveloped the facility during regular hours.

Brilliant fluorescent lights illuminated the room in which he was working, washing across the institutional green walls and slick linoleum floor. A body lay on the mortician's table before him, its flesh a sickly shade of gray, the color of death. A wide white tag was tied to the big toe on the corpse's left foot, giving the deceased's name, age, and presumed cause of death. Strickland gave the tag a quick glance.

"Halloran, Kyle, Caucasian male, age twenty-six, probable overdose," he read to himself, humming aloud to the strains of Mozart that wafted through the room from the speakers set in the ceiling above, just loud enough to be heard.

His rubber-soled shoes made barely a sound as he circled the body before him, carefully looking it over for any obvious injuries, dictating his findings aloud so the microphone above the table could pick them up for transcription.

When he thought he'd seen all there was to see, he moved to the tray of instruments set up alongside and picked up a scalpel. The cool metal of the blade glinted sharply in the light.

"Now, my dead, young friend, " he said to the corpse as he reached out and made the first incision in the slightly rubbery flesh, "let's see what secrets you're hiding."

Three hours later he was finished. When he'd first read the tag, Strickland had expected the postmortem to be a rather straightforward piece of work. But now he realized that this was anything but a straightforward case. He discovered a number of things that just didn't make any sense, and while they bothered him, they also sparked his professional curiosity; something that didn't happen all that often anymore. In over thirty years of forensic medicine, he thought he'd seen it all. The body on the table before him proved him wrong. Determined to get to the bottom of things, he dialed Sheriff Wilson's office extension.

"Hello?"

"Damon, it's Ed. Figured I'd find you there. Don't you ever go home?"

Wilson laughed. "Sure, right around the same time you do." The two men had known each other for years, from before Damon had gone off to Chicago. They'd gone to the same high school together, had even dated some of the same women. Their friendship had picked up again once Damon had returned home.

"What's up?" Damon asked.

"I just finished that autopsy on the young fellow you pulled out of that crypt over on the Blake family plot."

"Halloran. Kyle Halloran."

Ed grunted. "Yeah, that's the one. Thought you should know that it wasn't your everyday, run-of-the-mill experience. Some of the results I got are pretty strange."

"Strange funny or strange weird?"

"Strange weird."

"Like what?" Damon asked. "Hell, it' an open-and-shut case. Witnesses said the guy had been drinking and snorting enough cocaine earlier in the night to flatten an elephant. Too much physical exertion after all that, and you end up in cardiac arrest."

"Well, for one thing, it wasn't an overdose that killed him."

Damon laughed. "Yeah, right. Try telling that to his heart and respiratory system. They're still trying to figure out what hit them."

"That's just it, Damon. The toxicology tests showed high traces of benzoylecganine, so the guy had been doing cocaine earlier that night, enough to send most people straight to the moon. Combine that with a blood alcohol level of 1.8, and you can be damn sure he was as high as a kite when he went. Probably didn't feel a thing. But it wasn't the drugs or the booze that killed him." Ed paused, then said, "He bled to death."

"What?" Damon asked, shocked.

"You heard me," Strickland replied. "He bled to death."

"But that's not possible, Ed. There were no wounds on the body, and we certainly didn't find anything to indicate that at the scene. For a guy that size to lose enough blood to kill him, we should have found a lake of the stuff. We didn't; the place was as dry as a bone."

"Didn't you tell me the floor of that tomb was just dirt? Could it have simply seeped into the ground and whoever was at the scene just missed it?"

"C'mon, Ed. My men are better than that. Besides, I'm the one who answered the call. There wasn't any blood. *Nada*, nothing, zippo. Catch my drift?"

Ed sighed. "Yeah, I hear you. It's been bothering me, too. But it gets worse. I can't figure out how it happened. There weren't any wounds on the body, nothing but a fairly shallow cut on the palm of one hand. It probably hurt like hell, and bled a bit, but certainly not enough to kill someone."

"Shit, Ed, this is not good." Damon shook his head in bewilderment. It sounded like the case was going to be one bitch of a headache, and he just didn't need that just then.

Then Ed said something else, and it was so weird that Damon thought he hadn't heard him correctly.

"Run that one by me again?"

"I said, this guy didn't just lose enough blood to kill him, he lost all of it."

Damon felt goose bumps suddenly rise on his arms. "What do you mean *all* of it?"

"Just what I said. All of it. You know how it works. Once the heart stops, the blood will normally pool in the lowest portion of the corpse, giving the flesh there a dark purplish coloration. Except, in this case, that didn't happen. I couldn't find any evidence of postmortem lividity anywhere on the body. If you hadn't told me the position he had been found in, I wouldn't have been able to figure it out. And when I cut him open, I didn't even have to drain him. I could have done the whole procedure on my kitchen table and eaten off of it afterward. He was that clean."

While listening, Damon had involuntarily stiffened in his seat. Something wasn't right; that much was obvious. On some deeper, more primal level, Damon was suddenly certain that things were going to get a lot worse.

"Hey, Damon, you there?"

"Yeah, yeah. I'm here. Got anything else, Ed?"

"Sorry. That's it, I'm afraid."

"Okay, thanks for the call. I appreciate it. And listen, keep this one from the press for a while, will ya?"

"Sure thing, Damon. Talk to you soon."

For the first time in his long career, Edward Strickland found that he didn't want to be alone with a corpse.

Damon hung up the phone and leaned back in his chair, his gaze resting on the far wall but not really seeing it. His thoughts were elsewhere.

Bled to death?

How?

The whole thing was absurd. The pickax they found was several yards away from the corpse. There was no way he could have hurt himself. *Even if he had, how do you bleed to death from a cut on the palm of the hand?* It just wasn't possible.

He thought back to the events of that morning, picturing the scene in his mind. The corpse had been sprawled in that dark, little room at the base of that ugly statue with little evidence anywhere that there had been any kind of confrontation or struggle, one small wound on the body. That was why he'd been so positive that it had been an overdose or a heart attack. All his years of police work had pointed him in that direction.

Did I miss something?

He didn't think he had. The forensics team had shown its usual diligence going over the scene once he'd called it in, and he had even stayed behind to supervise. He was positive the job had been done thoroughly and professionally.

Nevertheless, he had a nagging feeling that he hadn't seen everything he should have, that he had overlooked something important.

Damon was a cop who believed in hunches. More than once during the course of an investigation he'd gotten a feeling about a certain aspect of the case. Nothing more than that, just an impression, a blind, gut reaction not founded on anything he could put into a logical sequence. He learned to pay attention to them, more often than not discovering that he was right. He knew such a reaction was simply his unconscious mind tying things together in a way that his conscious mind had overlooked, and his "hunches" were just its way of telling him to perk up and pay attention.

Something about the mental image of the crime scene was bothering him—something he couldn't put his finger on, and so, instead of going home as he'd been about to do before Ed phoned, he went to his filing cabinets and pulled out the case file. He pulled out the photographs of the crime scene. He stared at each of them slowly in turn, scrutinizing them for something he might have missed.

The pictures looked the same as they had before. The cemetery, the tomb, the corpse. Nothing more.

He picked up the few photos that were solely of the statue itself, staring at the face carved into the stone with a strange mixture of admiration and revulsion. He had to admit it really was a marvelous piece of work, if you happened to like that sort of thing.

The detail in the work was astounding. Every little detail was rendered precisely, from the scales that covered the face to the curved claws that extended from the feet. All in all, it was a stunning piece of work.

Damon just didn't like it. Remembering how he'd felt beneath its stony gaze still made him uncomfortable. If he didn't know better, he would have sworn the damn thing had been watching him the whole time he was down there. Looking into its eyes in the photographs, that feeling returned. The beast seemed to gaze back at him, the glint of an evil intelligence in its stony orbs.

Something was there in the pictures, something important that he was overlooking. He just wasn't seeing it.

But what?

Tired and more than a bit frustrated, he returned the

photos to the file and put them away in his drawer. He'd had enough for one day; staring at the photographs for another couple of hours wasn't going to get him anywhere. It was time to call it a night.

As he crossed the parking lot to his car, Damon had the uneasy feeling he wasn't alone.

He glanced around.

Beneath the dirty yellow light of the sodium-vapor lamps, nothing stirred.

The lot was empty.

He shrugged, dismissing the feeling. Too much work and an overactive imagination, that was all it was.

Yet in the back of his mind an image lingered.

A pair of stone eyes, watching . . .

10

A DEATH IN THE NIGHT

"**B**ring me another piece of that cake, would ya, honey?"

In the kitchen, Martha Cummings looked through the interior window that connected to the next room. Her husband George was seated in his favorite recliner in front of the television. Her gaze was full of affection as she took in his slightly overweight body and the little round bald spot on the top of his head. She shook her head in mock dismay at his request, but happily complied with it nonetheless.

Martha was in her late sixties and quite happy with her lot in life. Time had been good to her. A large, buxom woman, not particularly pretty by modern standards, but filled with an inordinate amount of kindness, she had married her present husband, after two unsuccessful marriages, at the age of thirty-five. She had a nice home, an affectionate husband, and enough money to keep the two of them happy for the rest of their lives. That was more than most could say, and for that she was thankful.

Of course, there were her cats, too.

Martha's pride and joy, the cats had proven to be an acceptable substitute for her inability to have children. She lavished on them all the care and love and attention she might have given her own children. They were a constant nuisance to her husband, although he was sweetly tolerant for her sake. The felines had free run of the house and yard. She had lost track of how many of them there actually were, having stopped counting somewhere after sixteen. Originally there had been only five, each with a separate name, but before long she'd given up trying to keep them all straight and begun referring to them all now simply as Kitty. They didn't seem to mind, and it was much easier that way.

She brought the cake to her husband, along with a tall glass of milk. "Here you are, dear," she said, giving him a quick peck on his bald spot. That flustered him a little, since he was self-conscious about the loss of his hair, but his eyes let her know that it was all right.

Back in the kitchen she decided to start an apple pie that she would bake the next day and was deep into the process when George announced he was going up to bed.

"Are you going to stay down here all night or will you be joining me?" he asked, a suggestive leer on his face.

She blushed. Despite their advanced age, the two of them enjoyed a good grope in the dark more than once a week, as if they were a couple of hormone-crazed teenagers. It didn't matter that nine times out of ten the machinery didn't work. It was the desire that counted, and lately it seemed to be increasing. It made her feel wickedly sinful to know that her husband still wanted her after all these years, and that alone was worth all the trouble.

She leered back at him. "I'll be up in just a few minutes. If you're still awake when I get there, old-timer, maybe we can find something to keep us awake a while longer." She waved her hands at him. "Now shoo and let me finish or I'll just sleep on the couch for the night, and you won't get anything."

George gave her a quick kiss and disappeared up the stairs in a hurry, muttering to himself about domineering women as he went. Martha turned back to her baking.

Her pace was quicker than it had been a few moments before.

Half an hour later, just as she was placing the pie into the refrigerator where it would stay until she had a chance to slip it into the oven in the morning, she heard a long, thin wail coming from the front yard.

Martha stopped in midmotion, bent over in front of the open refrigerator door, pie in hand, her head cocked to one side.

The house around her was silent, the only sound the ticking of the grandfather clock in the living room.

After a few moments of intent listening, she decided the noise had only been in her mind. A product of the late hour and her restless imagination.

You've been watching too many of those horror films, Martha old girl, she told herself good-naturedly, and slid the pie onto the shelf. She straightened up and closed the fridge, turning back to the sink to get a sponge to wash the countertops.

That was when the scream came again, a high-pitched shriek that reflexively made her pull her head down into the crook of her shoulders in response.

She took a step toward the window above the sink overlooking the front yard, but hesitated, the action uncompleted. *What's out there?* she thought, frightened, visions of ax-wielding psychopaths swimming through her mind. She suddenly wasn't certain she wanted to discover the origin of that cry. What if it was just a trick to get her near the window?

What if I look out, only to find someone looking in?

As soon as that particular thought crossed her mind, she was struck with the uncanny feeling that someone *was* out there, watching her.

Watching.

And waiting.

Martha turned and quickly made her way to the staircase, wanting to be anywhere but alone in that room. She intended to go upstairs and wake George. He'd know how to handle the situation. He'd know just what to do.

She was halfway up the stairs when another cry reached her ears, and this time there was no mistaking its animal origin.

The image of a blood-smeared feline loomed, and in the rush of motherly affection that accompanied it, her fear dissipated.

One of her babies needed her.

Boosted by her concern for her feline charges, Martha got herself under control. *Go on, old girl*, she said to herself. *March right out there and see what's going on. No need to stand cowering in the kitchen. After all, when was the last time the police actually had to work to earn their pay in this sleepy little town?* The crime rate was so low that the town council had considered tearing down the auxiliary police station to make room for a new supermarket a few months ago, and had only decided against it when a better location was discovered.

Ax-wielding psychopaths? Not in Harrington Falls.

Reassured by her logic, Martha calmly crossed to the hall closet, glancing down at her housecoat and slippers as she went. It wouldn't do to have the neighbors see her snooping around the front lawn like that, so she drew on a long trench coat and searched for her shoes. After a moment, she remembered she'd left them by the bed upstairs. In order to retrieve them, she'd risk waking George.

"Slippers will just have to do," she said to the pink bunnies on her feet, and wiggled her toes inside their confines, giggling at the thought of how silly she would feel if any of her neighbors caught sight of her.

She withdrew a broom with a thick wooden handle from the rack on the closet door. Holding it aloft like a baseball bat, she moved to the entryway.

"Don't worry, Kitty," she said softly, "Mommy's on her way."

Outside, the beast dropped the cat's corpse to the ground, then licked the blood from its claws, savoring the bittersweet taste.

Suddenly, a noise caught its attention.

It stopped its grooming and peered through the branches. From where it was seated in the large, old elm that dominated the front yard, it had a clear view of the house. It watched as the front door opened and a woman stepped into view on the porch that extended the length of the house. She was holding something long and slender over one shoulder.

The beast's eyes widened in anticipation.

Now that the appetizer was out of the way, the main course conveniently made its appearance.

Deciding it wanted to have a little fun before indulging itself, the beast slowly lowered itself to the ground.

In the darkness, Moloch smiled.

Martha stood on the front porch, peering into the darkness before her. The night was quiet. A soft wind was blowing, rustling the leaves of the nearby trees in a whispering chorus. The moon had not yet arisen, and the darkness around her seemed thick and total.

She didn't like it.

She reached back inside the doorway and flicked the switch to turn on the porch light, but nothing happened. She tried again, with the same result.

Bulb must have blown, she thought. *What a time for it, too!* Her thoughts turned to the idea of waking her husband, but she quickly stifled them.

She could handle this herself.

"Here, Kitty. Here, Kitty, Kitty," she called softly as she took a few steps farther out onto the porch.

The old wood beneath her feet groaned weakly.

"Here, Kitty, Kitty. Come to Momma."

Only the wind answered her.

Martha crossed the porch until she stood at the top of the steps. The front lawn spread out before her, a giant carpet cloaked in dark shadows.

The night was oddly silent, the usual symphony of tree frogs and crickets absent. The fact that she could no longer hear that earlier shrieking only served to heighten her anxiety.

She peered into the gloom ahead of her.

Lights from the neighboring homes occasionally pierced the thick foliage, causing shadows to dance on the edge of her sight. Several times she thought she saw movement, but when she looked directly at that spot, nothing was there.

As she descended the few steps to the stone walkway that led to the drive, a low, furtive rustling reached her ears. She stood still, listening.

After a moment she heard it again. It was coming from a stand of bushes off to her left.

Cautiously, she moved a few steps closer.

"Here, Kitty," she called softly.

The bushes rustled again.

She stepped closer, to just a foot or two away, feeling the cool moisture from the dew-laden grass that had soaked through the material of her slippers onto the soles of her feet.

The rustling came again, this time accompanied by a plaintive meow.

The sound made Martha smile, and she lowered the broomstick in response as relief surged through her system. It had been one of her cats, after all.

Poor baby's probably trapped in the hedges and can't get out, she thought. Laying the broom on the lawn, she softly crept forward the last few feet, not wanting to scare the little darling, and reached out with both hands.

"Easy, baby," she said. "Momma's here to help you."

Very gently, she parted the bushes and pushed her head into the space she'd created.

She didn't even have time to scream.

When Moloch was finished, he hefted what was left of the corpse under one arm and turned toward the house.

His meal was not yet complete.

There was another human inside. He could hear the loud thumping heartbeat in his mind, and from its resonance could tell it was a male.

The sound made him eager.

As he started walking slowly toward the still-open front door, his body hunched so that the corpse's heels dragged along the lawn after him, and he began to laugh.

A low, chilling laugh.

A laugh that would have sounded only partially human, had anyone been around to hear it.

11

LEGENDS FROM THE PAST

Later that evening, Sam found himself finishing his rounds at the nursing home earlier than usual. The patients were quiet that night, their requests relatively few, so that when he was done with his rounds he made his way down the hall to the last room on the left, eager to tell Gabriel the events of the morning.

Gabriel was expecting him and Sam quickly took his usual seat by the window. This time their roles were reversed as Sam told Gabriel of the morning's events with Jake. Gabriel listened quietly throughout the telling, never interrupting, though he did lean forward with a surprising amount of interest when Sam was describing the condition of the statue they found in the tunnel. He shook his head sadly when Sam mentioned finding Kyle's body, and for just an instant Sam thought he saw the wet glisten of impending tears in Gabriel's eyes.

"Pretty amazing, don't you think?" Sam asked, when he finally ran out of steam.

"Yes, indeed, Sammy. Quite a tale. Tell me, what do the police intend to do now?"

Sam thought about it for a moment and realized that he

really didn't know. *Had the sheriff told Jake to stay away from the mansion, or was his friend intending to resume work on the renovations in the morning?* He didn't remember hearing any discussion about the issue, but figured that since it was a crime scene, the work would have to be suspended for at least a few days, and told Gabriel so.

"Seems you had quite an exciting morning, my young friend. So exciting that my story seems so dull and uneventful in comparison that I think we'll just forget about it for tonight, don't you think?"

Sam shook his head. "Not a chance, Gabriel. We have practically all night to talk, and there's no way I'm going to miss one of your stories." Every time Sam came to Gabriel's room, the old man had a tale to tell, and they were always so incredibly interesting that Sam sometimes found himself looking at his own works with an air of resignation, his own story lines seemed so uninteresting in comparison.

Gabriel watched closely for a moment, as if gauging the sincerity of Sam's reaction, then agreed with a smile.

"Tell me, Sammy, how do you think it was that man left behind the life of a wanderer and began to settle down in one location, changing from a society of hunter-gatherers to one of agriculture and domesticity?"

That was an easy one. Sam had learned the answer years before in secondary school. "As the great beasts began to die out, and man's numbers started to swell, a more constant food source was required to survive. It became impractical to move large groups across such vast distances while following the herd animals, so they turned to a more stable food supply in the form of whatever crops they could grow."

"And how did they learn to do that?" Gabriel asked.

"Well, ah, I suppose they just figured it out."

It was a weak answer, and Sam knew it, but it was the only one he had. He'd never considered the question before, having taken the stock answer his schooling had taught him and leaving it at that.

He looked over at Gabriel, his eyebrows raised questioningly.

"I'll tell you how they did it, Sam. They had help."

"Help?"

"Yes, help. Help from a race of people who had come before them, and had learned to do it on their own. You see, your history books only tell you the basics. Of how man slowly adapted, leaving his ancestral ways behind. But that's not really what happened. Did you really think humanity managed to do it all on their own?" Gabriel asked, and for the first time Sam heard something besides simple good cheer in his friend's voice. For just a moment, he thought there was a touch of arrogance there, too.

"Long ago, before man ascended from his primal beginnings, there was another age, the Age of Creation it was called, and in this time other beings ruled the land. The wisest, gentlest of these were known as the Elders. They were the most important link in man's transition from brutality to civilization. The Elders were human in appearance, so much so that if you were to pass one on the streets today you would see no difference. Your mind and your soul might notice something, for the Elders *were* different. They were more civilized, more at peace with themselves and the world around them than any other race from then until now. If you were not completely anesthetized by the wonderless world in which you now live, you would recognize the differences between our races."

Gabriel paused for a moment and in the silence Sam was struck by the odd notion that Gabriel was speaking of himself, that he had lived and walked among the Elders.

"They used harmony to create a vast civilization that spanned the globe. They raised cities of wonder, full of joy and light, whose sparkling towers reached for the heavens above with grace and spirit, and let all who saw them know that these were a people to be respected. A people to be loved.

"Some of the Elders took a liking to the apelike creatures that were man's ancestors. Slowly their confidence was won with offers of food and other gifts. The Elders began to teach them, discovering early on that several of these beings had a rudimentary intelligence different from the other creatures of the wild. It quickly became a mission of the Elders to raise these creatures up from the level of the beasts around them and give them something more."

Gabriel turned to face Sam, his eyes shining with intensity. His hand shot out from under the bedclothes and grabbed Sam's wrist. "Think of it, Sam! A whole race devoted to bettering the lives of another. What hope they must have had! What joy! What a wonderful world to have lived in!"

His grip loosened, and Gabriel slumped back against the pillows. "That was to prove their undoing, their downfall."

Sam was eager to hear more. "What do you mean, 'their downfall'?" he asked. "Did man turn against them? Destroy them?"

"Not directly. You see, there was another race competing with the Elders for supremacy. These winged, vaguely reptilian creatures were the antithesis of the Elders, full of cruelty and rage, but no less intelligent. They preyed on the lesser races. They called themselves the Na'Karat, but it was their habit of swooping down out of a dark night sky to attack their prey that earned them the nickname, 'Nightshades.' They hunted many different kinds of creatures, but enjoyed hunting primeval humans more than any other type of game. Man had more intelligence, and therefore had a richer, deeper notion of fear, and it was fear that the Nightshades were after. They fed on the meat, but it was the fear that sustained them, fear that fulfilled their warped sense of spiritual need.

"Where the Elders sought to help the humans, the Nightshades wanted nothing more than to allow them to wallow in their primitiveness. They were cattle, nothing more, and the Nightshades treated them as such, herded and corralled and hunted for the sustenance they could provide."

"So, what happened?"

"War happened, Sam. War. The Elders couldn't sit idly by and watch this occur. They went to arms against the Nightshades and swore the conflict would not end until the humans were freed and allowed to prosper as befitted an intelligent race. Where once was peaceful coexistence, now was racial hatred. Vast armies marched out of our great cities."

"Armies led by those who would later become legends—Michael, Uriel, even Gabriel—marched onto the fields of battle. Down out of the sky came the 'Shades to greet them, in numbers so vast the brilliant blue above was blotted out by their forms."

Sam could see it all in his mind's eye, his writer's imagination filling in the details. He saw the armies of the Elders marching off to war, their raiment golden in the sunlight. He imagined heroic stands against incalculable odds, the armies of good triumphing over those of darkness, conveniently forgetting that war is never that simple or bloodless.

He realized suddenly that it had gone quiet. Gabriel was sitting and studying him. Sam felt uncomfortable under the intensity of that gaze, but he wanted to hear the end. "Who won?" he asked.

Gabriel smiled a tight, bitter smile in response. "No one won, Sam. Battle after battle raged, the best of both races lying to rot in the bright sunlight of fields strewn with the dead. Cities crumbled under the onslaught and the dark caverns of the Nightshades were taken and destroyed. The numbers on each side dwindled. Yet still they fought on in their stubbornness, the war continued not for the noble reasons it had begun but out of pure hatred and vengeance for all those who had fallen before. Every man, woman, and child on both sides joined in the struggle. Before long, what had once been a glorious civilization was a decrepit ruin. The few surviving members on either side saw the destruction and mourned for what had passed from the world. They kept on fighting until there were too few remaining for the races to survive. Both the Elders and the Nightshades dwindled in number, bled into extinction by their own foolishness. Out of the ashes of their conflict came man, for he had watched and learned as the battle raged. Freed from the one predator that had effectively culled their numbers, humans multiplied rapidly. The wisest of them remembered the lessons that the Elders had taught them and slowly led the others in that long climb toward civilization."

At that moment Sam's beeper went off, signaling that another patient somewhere on the floor needed him.

"Damn!" he swore, not wanting to leave.

As if sensing Sam's thoughts, Gabriel smiled, and said, "Go on, Sammy. It's all right. I'm sure we'll speak of this again some other time."

Sam thanked him for the story and slipped out the door, his thoughts on the Elders and the sacrifice they might have made for mankind had the tale been true.

Behind him, in that last, lonely room on the left, the final member of an all-but-forgotten race smiled another tired smile.

It was done.

The seeds had been sown.

All that was left was to see if they bore fruit.

After all that had happened that day, Jake didn't feel like being alone. Sam was at work, so hanging with him and talking it all over was out of the question. While Sam was allowed visitors, especially during the night shift when no one else was around to tell him differently, Jake didn't feel like making the forty-five-minute ride into Glendale.

A quick glance at his watch told him Katelynn would be home by then, so he turned his Jeep in that direction and drove across town to her place.

As he neared the top of her walk he realized that she was sitting in the large swing on her front porch.

"Hi. You look tired," she said, as he sat down next to her.

"You have no idea," he replied. "Hey, is that new?" He

pointed to the red gemstone she wore on a gold chain about her neck.

"Sam's friend, Gabriel, sent it over this afternoon with a note saying it was his way of saying thanks for spending time with him this morning. I called and told him I couldn't accept something so obviously expensive, but he sweet-talked me into keeping it." She smiled. "So what the heck. How did the morning go? What happened when the cops showed up?"

"That's the weirdest part, Katelynn. The sheriff answered the call himself. Turns out he is a pretty decent guy. After taking down our story, he asked me to lead him underground to where we had found the body. We climbed through the hole Kyle made in the wall and found ourselves in a large stone chamber. Inside, Kyle's body was lying at the feet of this massive stone gargoyle. Ugliest mother I've ever seen." Jake shivered, remembering. "While the sheriff was looking at the body, I poked around and found another door on the side of the chamber. The whole situation must have gotten to me, because I opened it without even thinking about the fact I was disrupting a crime scene. The door led into the cemetery nearby. It turns out that the brick barrier in the tunnel was actually the rear wall of a mausoleum that belonged to Sebastian Blake, and the door I'd found was the outside entrance."

Katelynn's eyes gleamed with interest. "How do you know it is Sebastian's tomb?"

"His name was carved right over the doorway."

Katelynn thought about that for a few moments, trying to put it into perspective with what she already knew from her research. The wild story Gabriel had told her reared its head again, but she wasn't ready to believe something that crazy.

At least not yet.

"A secret tunnel from the house leading to the family crypt? Sounds like one of Sam's novels, Jake."

"No kidding. The sheriff was ticked that I opened the door, but he got over it pretty quickly. I think he was as spooked as I was over the whole thing."

"What do you think happened to Kyle?"

"I don't know." Jake chuckled. "Sam would probably tell you that an ancient curse had just arisen to claim its first victim."

The two talked on for another hour before calling it a night, never realizing how close to the truth Jake's comment had actually been.

12

BLOODSTONE

The dream begins innocently enough.

In her sleep, Katelynn moves through an amusement park with Jake at her side. Sights and sounds slip past in a kaleidoscope of activity. Flashing lights, turning wheels, the harsh bark of a carny's voice. They ride the Tilt-a-Whirl, then the Viking Longboat. Jake wins her a teddy bear by knocking down milk bottles with a softball. It is a typical dream, skipping from scene to scene with no real continuity, yet somehow making sense just the same.

Suddenly, a flashing red light intrudes from the other side of the carnival. A light so sharp, so insistent, that Katelynn is drawn irrevocably toward it. Jake fades into obscurity behind her as she moves out of his reach. The light draws her forward, and the cacophony on all sides slips away into oblivion as all of her attention is tied up in chasing that insistent beacon.

In reality, Katelynn tosses and turns beneath the sheets, the ruby red stone about her throat pulsing with light.

She sleeps on, and the carnival fades away, replaced by a thick gray haze that swirls around her in lazy spirals, shifting and churning. The light shines before her, even closer, hidden somewhere in the depths of that mist.

Katelynn stumbles in after it.

The haze shifts, and Katelynn finds herself standing before the light as it hangs motionless in the air before her. It shines vividly, cutting through the murk, pulsing with an eerie life. Katelynn watches as her arm lifts of its own accord and reaches to touch it . . .

She soars high above the ground, carried aloft like a glider tossed into a storm. The wind is cool, flickering across her flanks in a silken caress. The sky around her is dark with heavy rain-laden clouds extending out to the horizon, shutting out the afternoon light, for which she is thankful.

The storm comes on fast, without warning, and she rejoices in the opportunities it could bring.

She drops lower, riding one of the storm's savage currents in a swift, sickening drop that plunges her several hundred feet in seconds, the air screaming past her ears with a shrill, bestial shriek. She recovers easily, swooping along just above the treetops, following the trail she sees below her, knowing that it was often used by those she sought.

Movement catches her attention.

She shifts lower, descending to mere feet above the ground, and angles off to the left in order to intercept whatever it is. A moment or two and the thing comes into view.

It is an antelope, with long curving horns atop its head and a brown-and-golden coat. It is part of a herd, which comes into view as she sails over the head of the first animal. Her presence starts them milling about, nervous but not panicked. As a group they collectively wait to see what she will do, watching her closely with upturned heads.

She has better sport this night, however, and she glides over their heads without giving them another thought.

She regains some altitude and uses the warmer currents to glide and detect movement on the plain beneath. A dark, scorched section of earth can be made out to the west, and she notes it with a sort of grim satisfaction. Her enemies once lived there, in a great sprawling city that stood as a fortress against her kind, but had finally fallen in a glorious battle. The streets of that city had flowed red with the blood from those fed upon that night.

Not long after she passed the city, she spotted what she was looking for. A thin column was moving along the path, at her height little more than specks in motion. She had hunted there before and knew that she had found her target.

She swooped closer, and counted fourteen of the herd moving in tandem the way the Elders had taught them. They found a certain level of protection in this fashion, occasionally managing to fend off an attack with the help of the four-legged animals that traveled with them. It didn't happen often, but it also didn't hurt to assess the situation before attacking.

Another of the Na'Karat was trailing the same group, she noticed, a large male, hanging off to the side, watching just as she was. From the haste of the group below, they had obviously seen him, and were trying to reach a sheltered location before he attacked. *The fool,* she thought. *He allowed himself to be seen too soon and is now simply compounding the error. He will lose his chance if he doesn't engage soon.*

She decided to make her move before he could.

She flew overhead and began to circle the group. Below, the cattle swiftly pulled in their ranks, moving to form a large circle with the weakest in the center and the strong on the rim, just as the Elders had taught them.

It would do them no good.

She spotted a straggler, an offspring by its size, tens of yards away from the group and moving slowly. She smiled, her tongue flicking across her teeth. That would be the one.

She folded her wings and dropped toward the earth.

Her victim was twenty feet from the group when she struck.

Unfolding her wings, she used the resistance of the wind to slow her descent abruptly, so she seemed to appear out of nowhere directly in front of it. As expected, it froze in place for a moment.

That was all the time she needed.

She swung one of her arms around in a blinding fast arc, the talons on the end of each finger extended.

She shrieked with satisfaction as flesh tore, blood flew, and the stench of pain rose into the air . . .

Katelynn awoke screaming in her bed.

She knew instantly she'd had a nightmare; her heart was thundering in her chest, and her body was soaked with sweat.

She had only a fleeting recollection of what it had been about, however, and that quickly slipped away as she tried to get herself under control.

She got up and went into the bathroom. Using a face-cloth soaked in cool water, she wiped her upper body down and splashed some water on her face. Her heartbeat slowly returned to normal.

By the time she climbed back into bed, the dream was no more. It had slipped away as swiftly as the morning dew under the summer sun.

Five minutes later she was fast asleep.

It had been the first of the dreams, but it would not be the last.

Across town, the beast turned in its sleep, its dream disturbed by an unwanted presence.

It lasted no more than a moment, however, and the creature never fully awoke, preferring to sink back into its memories of another time and place.

It gave the presence not another thought.

13

GRUESOME DISCOVERIES

The ringing of the phone jarred him awake.

"Wilson here."

"Sorry to disturb you, sir. But we've got a bad one."

Damon listened for a few moments and hung up. He was dressed and out the door in less than ten minutes, using both the sirens and lights as he climbed the hills into Harrington Falls. As he made his way down Chestnut Street, it was easy to see the activity that surrounded the house at the end of the block.

The house was a beacon, shining in the darkness, calling out to him, demanding the justice he could supply, commanding him to avenge those who lay still and silent inside.

Though he was still half a mile away, he could see the house clearly. It stood out from the rest because it was the only one on the block with every window bathed with electric light, like a blazing torch in an empty field, and he moved toward it reluctantly.

The unspeakable had occurred. For the first time in over twenty years, there had been a murder in Harrington Falls.

Damon didn't want to see what lie waiting inside those four walls, didn't want to smell the freshly spilled blood or see the wounds, didn't want to stare into lifeless eyes and wonder what they had seen in those last few precious moments before death.

Despite his resignation he continued on, if for no other reason than it was his job. There was no one else to do it.

He'd only gone to sleep moments before the call had come, and as he put down the receiver he realized he hadn't been surprised to learn that someone had been killed. All evening since leaving the office he'd been nervous, watchful, unable to relax and settle down the way he usually did after a day's work, his conversation with Strickland playing over and over again like a Top Forty record in his mind. It was almost as if he'd been expecting something to happen.

When he arrived, he could see that the house was set back from the street on a thickly wooded lot. In the drive were several police cars, their blue lights flashing, giving the house's white paint a sickly glow. Two ambulances were parked at the curb.

The house was a split-level, as were many of the others in the neighborhood, though some work had been done subtly to alter its appearance. There was a small addition, probably a den or TV room, jutting out from the rear left corner, and from it a wide latticed porch extended around to its opposite corner on the front. The original windows facing the street had been taken out, and two large bay windows had been installed in their place, looking to Damon like the bulbous eyes of some giant fly.

The sheriff looked away, suddenly uncomfortable.

For just a moment, he was struck by the uneasy feeling that he was being watched.

His attention turned to the thick row of hedges that lined the path from the front door to the drive, and the manner in which the pines in the backyard crept across the rear of the property. Both areas would provide fine places for concealment for anyone trying to approach the house undetected, and he made a mental note to have the boys check them for any sign that the killer had indeed been there.

Deciding he couldn't postpone the inevitable any longer, Damon resigned himself to what lay ahead and walked to the front door.

Inside was chaos.

The living room was in shambles. A recliner had been overturned, its leather upholstery slashed. Cushions from the sofa and love seat were strewn about the room, ripped as well, their white foam interiors spilling out around the jagged tears. It looked as if someone had taken the same knife to the heavy drapes too, as they hung in ragged strips. The floor was littered with chunks of ceramic and glass; all that remained of what Damon guessed had once been a pair of table lamps.

Two technicians were moving about the room, pausing now and again to scoop some object into one of the many clear plastic envelopes that jutted from their pockets.

One of them looked up and waved a hand in the direction the hallway was leading, and Damon followed it to a stairway that led to the second floor.

At the top, Deputy Frank Castiglioni stepped out of the shadows to greet him. Frank was a ten-year veteran of the department, and one of Damon's most hardened and experienced officers.

"Sheriff," he said in greeting.

"How's it going, Frank?" Damon noticed that his fellow officer was pale, his voice slightly off key. Behind the man's back, where he obviously hoped Damon wouldn't be able to see it, Castiglioni's right hand was shaking violently.

"Is it bad?" he asked.

The other man swallowed once, hard, and nodded. He tried a weak smile but failed to bring it off.

Damon laid a comforting hand on Frank's shoulder, then moved past him. He stopped at the entrance to the room just beyond, his bulk framed in the narrow doorway.

What he saw in front of him made the bile rush to the top of his throat, and for a moment he thought he might be sick at a scene for the first time in many years, but after a moment or two the sensation passed.

"Holy Mother of God."

What he saw was far, far worse than what he'd expected.

The room was a slaughterhouse.

Blood was splattered everywhere; on the floor, on the ceiling, on the walls. It was as if someone had taken buckets of the stuff and merrily splashed it around.

Pieces of bloody human flesh were likewise cast about, scattered across the floor and atop various pieces of furniture.

A hand, with only three fingers intact, its missing digits ripped off at the first knuckle, dangled from an open dresser drawer.

A foot, still clad in a bloodstained slipper, lay in the middle of the floor; the shinbone was shining whitely through the torn and bloody flesh.

Many of the other pieces were unrecognizable as to what part of the body they had originated from, a fact Damon found increasingly disturbing as his gaze kept returning to them repeatedly, his mind trying to discern what they once might have been, so as to give order to the chaos.

What he took to be glistening lengths of rope dangled about the curtains that concealed the surface of the king-size bed, reminding him of the tinsel he used to decorate his Christmas tree every year.

Curious, he stepped closer, only to realize with rapidly escalating horror that they were actually human entrails.

In the back of his mind an evil little voice began singing, *"A Slinky, a Slinky, a wonderful, wonderful toy, a Slinky, a Slinky, they're fun for a girl and a boy."*

Vomit surged back up into his throat, and he barely managed to choke it back down, leaving a foul taste in his mouth that matched nicely the reek of death that hung in his nostrils.

In all his years of police work, he had never seen anything so vile.

So twisted.

So undeniably evil.

Conflicting emotions ran through him as he stared down at the carnage before him, the sickness he felt warring with his need to study the scene and understand just what had happened.

Anger reared its ugly head, and he let it come, knowing it would help calm nerves that were dangerously close to the breaking point. Anger would get him past his revulsion, would allow him to look at the situation objectively. He clung to it, wrapping it around him the same way a child might envelop itself in a comforting blanket on a cold winter's night.

I'll make the bastard who did this pay, he vowed to himself, and felt a little better for the thought.

For the first time Damon noticed a police photographer in the room with him; he had indeed been clicking away the whole time Damon had been standing there, ignoring his presence, wanting to finish up and get the hell out of there.

Damon didn't blame him.

"There's more, boss," a voice said from behind him. "The rest is worse, if that's possible to imagine."

Damon didn't trust himself to speak, so he just turned to look at Frank. *The rest of it? Worse? What the hell can be worse than this?*

Castiglioni motioned the sheriff toward the bed, and Damon followed, his feet as heavy as cement blocks. He didn't want to get any closer, didn't want to see what his fellow officer had to show him, but duty compelled him to follow. Frank ducked under a low-hanging piece of intestine and drew back the dangling curtains, exposing the bed itself and what lay atop it.

Damon felt the breath sucked from his lungs at the sight.

A human corpse was on the bed, and from its musculature Damon could tell it had been a male. From its chest gaped a savage wound, and it was from there that the internal organs had been pulled and stretched forth to the canopy around them. If that wasn't enough, the body had also been dismembered.

And beheaded.

The sheer brutality of the act was sickening. Damon

hoped to God that the victim, whoever he had been, had been dead long before the killer had performed his grotesque artistry. To even contemplate what the man might have endured had he been alive was unthinkable; his mind balked at the very concept.

When he had recovered sufficient breath to speak, Damon asked, "Where's his head?" He noticed that his voice trembled when he spoke, and wondered if Frank had noticed it, too.

Frank laughed, a strange eerie chuckle. Wilson instantly recognized it for what it was; the type of laugh you make to chase away the willies when you're alone in an empty house in the dead of night. It was the sound of a man doing his best to reassure himself.

And miserably failing.

It was anything but comforting.

"In the bathroom," Frank replied. He hesitated, clearly considering how much to say, then decided against saying anything at all, for he merely indicated once again that Damon should follow. The two of them crossed the room, to where a door stood next to the bureau.

It was not the extravagant master bath Damon had expected. An oval mirror hung over a marble sink. A toilet stood to his left, a claw-foot tub to his right.

Frank nodded at the open toilet.

Damon stepped over and looked down, peripherally aware that Frank had moved back out of the room.

The man's missing head was stuffed in the toilet bowl, the once-blue-tinged water a sickly purple hue from the blood that had been spilled into it from the leaking neck.

The man's white hair writhed about his head like living seaweed. His ghastly dead face was frozen in an expression of horror, his mouth open wide in a silent scream of pain, his empty eye sockets still leaking blood.

For just a split second, Damon's mind told him it wasn't real.

But it was.

And deep down inside, he knew it.

He turned away, unable to face that eyeless, accusing stare a moment longer, only to find he could still feel its gaze burning into his back.

"You poor bastard," he muttered under his breath.

Numbed by all the destruction, he stood there for a moment, seeing himself in the bedroom mirror, his eyes reflecting the questions that were rushing around inside his head.

This was worse than anything he had imagined. That he was the best man to be in this position was beyond a doubt; the rest of the men on the force had never dealt with any type of violent crime. They were good, yes, but something like this was beyond the scope of their experience. They were deputies in a small town, and things like this just didn't happen in a place like Harrington Falls. In the city it was different, and Damon knew that from too many years of personal experience.

Now he wondered if those years would be enough.

And then another, more chilling thought occurred to him.

What if the bastard killed again before they could stop him?

The thought of bodies piling up around him while the investigation floundered sent a stream of sweat rolling down his back, dredging up all the old concerns and self-doubts. The mountainous weight of responsibility settled about his shoulders like a leaden cloak, and he was suddenly more scared of failure than he'd ever been.

What if my best just isn't good enough? he asked himself.

What then?

He forced his doubts away, knowing he needed to concentrate in order to get the job done. Frank was waiting for him in the bedroom.

Now that the initial shock had passed, Damon found he could think a bit clearer. He asked the first, obvious question, "The radio call mentioned two bodies. Where's the other?"

Frank glanced away, uneasily. "Look around," he directed, waving his hand about the room.

Damon did. All he saw were bits and pieces of flesh everywhere.

The implication of his officer's words sank in slowly.

He turned to face him. "You mean . . ."

"Yeah. There's not enough flesh missing from the male's corpse to account for all this mess, so most of it had to come from the guy's wife. We can't find the rest of her body, though, so we think maybe whoever did this took it when he left."

"We got an ID on the body yet?" Damon asked.

"Yeah, but it's still unconfirmed. Some of the pictures in the house match this guy here, near as we can tell. George Cummings. We have to wait until the coroner does the prints to be sure, but I'd bet next week's pay on it. We've got an APB out on the wife, just to be sure she isn't the cutter and that it wasn't some young bimbo that got chopped up with him."

"Anyone call Strickland?"

"Yeah. Should be here any minute now."

Damon nodded approvingly. His men were doing their jobs despite the atrocity around them, and of that he could be proud. "Okay then, let's get out of here and let the techs do their jobs." He waved Frank out of the room before him, and the other man seemed more than happy to oblige. Damon didn't blame him; if he had to spend another moment in that room he thought he might scream. Back downstairs, the two of them gathered the other deputies who weren't currently involved in securing the site from the crowd that was beginning to show up, and assembled them in a loose huddle by the patrol cars.

Damon began giving out assignments, doing his best to get the situation under control and the investigation rolling. There was no time to lose. He knew the cardinal rule of homicide investigations; most killers would be caught in the first forty-eight hours of the investigation, if they were going to be caught at all. When he was finished, one of the men raised his hand.

"What do we do about the press?" the deputy asked. "The local papers have got people already out there, mixin' with the crowd and tryin' to get inside. The TV crews can't be that far behind."

Damon swore under his breath. He knew he couldn't contain this for long, but letting it out now would just cause panic in the streets. He thought hard for a moment. "Okay, listen up. I want all of you to keep your mouths shut on this one. If they get one hint about what we got upstairs, I'll come down on every one of you, you got that? At the moment we're the only ones who know how bad it is, and we've got to keep it to ourselves until the county executives can assemble a press conference in the morning. We don't know if this is a one-timer or not, and we don't need any other loony out there starting to act like a copycat. Keep the details to yourselves. If anyone asks, let 'em know we got a suspicious death and leave it at that. If anyone gives you any trouble, you send 'em direct to me, got it? Questions? Okay then, get to work."

The men moved off to follow their orders, leaving Damon alone for the moment. He slumped against the side of his vehicle, suddenly drained. He stood there and stared out into the night, wondering about the killer.

Who is he? What does he look like?

More importantly, where is he now?

At the moment, Damon didn't have any answers.

But he would discover them in time.

He had to.

14

A SUMMONS IN THE NIGHT

Midnight.

The night was still.

Hushed.

Expectant.

The moon hung low on the horizon, looming there as if poised on the edge of a long drop. Since it was early in its ascent, it filled the sky, a vast ball of incandescence that punched a hole in the night's blackness.

Standing on his balcony, the smooth flagstones beneath his feet damp from the evening's chill and glistening with the silvery blue light of the moon, Hudson Blake gazed out into that darkness, watchful and vigilant.

As he watched the darkness, he felt it watching him in return.

He sensed it was hungry.

Turning away, he reentered his study through the set of French doors that led to the balcony and crossed the room, picking up the withered journal that lay open on his desk. The book's leather binding was stiff and laced with cracks, its pages fragile, yellow with age and neglect.

He read aloud the entry written on the open page.

"To summon the Beast, one must make a true and worthy sacrifice. An offering of that which is most precious to the denizens of the pit must be made swiftly and without hesitation. Once the blood has been shed, if ye be of sound mind and valor, ye must take up the Bloodstone in both hands, cupping it between the palms, with the left hand, the Hand of Vengeance, above the right, the Hand of Righteousness. Repeating the words of the unholy incantation contained herein, reach out with the very essence of thy now damned soul and call forth that which thou desirest."

He'd read that passage more than a hundred times, and the words fell from his lips with the ease of long familiarity.

Having made a substantial study of ancient, mystical traditions, Hudson dismissed most of the text as bullshit. Such rituals were mainly for show, to bolster the performer's image in the eyes of the uninitiated.

But as the best lies often contain a kernel of truth, so, too, did the description of the ritual contain the clues needed to bring it to its proper fruition. And in this instance, Blake was certain he had correctly identified them.

The remarks about the crystal were the key.

Carefully laying the book back on the desk, Hudson reached up under the collar of the shirt he wore and removed the necklace hanging about his neck. The dark stone that dangled on the end of the chain spun in the air like a pendulum, sending off tiny flashes of crimson whenever it was touched by the room's light.

This was the crystal to which the journal had been referring.

The Bloodstone.

He stared at it now, wondering as always where his ancestor, Sebastian, had obtained it. Years earlier Hudson had shown it to several prominent jewelers. None of them had been able to identify the type of stone or its country of origin. Ever since, it had held a particular fascination for him, and he'd often gazed at it for long periods of time, attempting to unlock its secrets.

What he did understand was that it was the stone itself, not the ritual or its flowery incantations, that would allow him to communicate with the beast his ancestor had known as Moloch.

He held it up to the lamp, shining the light on its ruby surface. Deep inside the stone, he thought he could see movement.

His eyes narrowed as he looked closer.

There! Something had shifted position deep within its depths.

But what?

While he yearned for the answers, he knew they were really not all that important. Only what the stone would allow him to do was.

He leaned over the desk and reread the vital line in the journal.

". . . reach out with the very essence of thy soul and call forth that which thou desirest."

At first, the line had confused him. *How does one reach out with the essence of one's soul?* But after a time he came to realize that he was seeking a deeper meaning than necessary, that the words needed to be taken in the literal sense. Medieval writers had seen the mind and the soul as one, so the passage was actually referring to the mind. Thus, reaching out with his soul really meant reaching out with his mind.

He believed that somehow the crystal channeled his thought patterns, much the same way an antenna will channel radio signals.

All that he had to do to reach Moloch was think about him.

It should be that simple.

He'd tried it before, however, without success. His failure with the stone and his inability to find the hidden vault had caused him to dismiss the entire legend of his ancestor's winged familiar as so much fantasy.

But now that the vault had been found, he was convinced that the journal's contents were true.

Maybe it was my doubt all along that prevented the connection.

The discovery of the body in the basement of Stonemoor had added fuel to the flames of his beliefs, and after getting all the information from Caruso that he could, he decided that there was only one possible explanation.

The journal was true; the beast did exist.

And with the death of that vandal, it seemed to have returned to the world after hiding itself for so long.

Not that he cared about the fool who had been killed; that wasn't important. What was important was the fact that at last he'd be able to prove the family legends that had intrigued him all of his adult life. The end of his search was finally in sight.

His fingers itched to seize the power in their bony grasp.

He first learned of the beast's existence when he'd found the journal years before, hidden in a niche in the fireplace in one of the mansion's unused rooms. Upon reading it, Hudson scoffed at the information it contained, but later found himself irresistibly drawn back to its musty, yellowed pages again and again, his mind alight with the possibilities he saw there. It was in the journal that he also learned of his ancestor's pact with the beast, and the awesome powers it employed for him. Dreaming of possessing such knowledge for himself, he set about to learn if what the journal contained was true.

Tonight he would finally know.

It was time to begin.

Dangling the crystal from one hand by its slim gold chain, he moved to the center of the room.

On the floor at his feet rested a number of objects. Considering what he was about to do, he decided to take certain precautions.

Blake was not a deeply religious man and never had been. When he was younger he scoffed at the idea of God and his army of heavenly hosts. Likewise, if there was no God, then there was no Satan, and no demonic army with which to corrupt man from the salvation that supposedly awaited him.

As he'd grown older, he discovered the power that a religious leader can hold over his followers, particularly religions of a darker nature. He joined one after another, studying the craft, learning from those above him before ruthlessly replacing them, taking their power for his own. All those years had slowly but surely convinced him that there was some truth to what the leaders preached. He had become convinced that there was another realm of reality separate from our own, which could be tapped into with the right methods. It didn't matter what you called it; the supernatural realm, the astral plane, the Other Side, whatever. It was there. Waiting to be made use of. Of that he was certain. Once he made this concession, it was only a short step to believe that this other realm was populated by beings of which man has little knowledge. Hudson felt it was encounters with creatures from the Other Side that had led man to invent religion. After all, what was religion but the attempt to explain that which man feared and didn't understand?

Although he still scoffed at the old rituals with their trappings of mysticism and their elaborate schemes to protect the summoner from the very powers he sought to invoke, he did not abandon them entirely. After all, what if there was some validity to them? Could he take the chance and leave himself vulnerable to the very creature he sought to summon and harness for his own use?

No.

That would be foolish, and Hudson Blake was anything but a foolish man.

He replaced the crystal around his neck so that he would have both hands free. Shedding the long, black robe he was wearing, he carefully folded it and laid it aside. He took up a small clay bowl in both hands and moved to the open floor space immediately in front of the French doors.

He held the bowl upright in front of him at arm's length as if in silent supplication, remaining that way for several long moments.

Lowering his arms, he dipped his left hand inside and took up a handful of the fine white salt that filled the bowl. He knelt on one knee and slowly began to let the mixture fall from his grasp to form a smooth, unbroken line on the floor. Once his hand was empty he repeated the process, inching backward as he went, bit by little bit, until a circle was laid out around him.

Satisfied, he stepped out of the circle, carefully avoiding making contact with the powder so its integrity as an unbroken circle would remain intact, and returned to the small pile of objects a few feet away.

Bending, he picked up a small cage and a leather-wrapped parcel of considerable length. A large black cat lay curled inside the cage and hissed warily as he lifted the cage, watching him with liquid green eyes that accused without words.

Blake grinned.

He hated cats. Always had. He went out of his way to use them in his rituals, taking a sadistic delight in ridding the world of as many of the foul little beasts as he could. With the two objects in hand, he reentered the circle, again carefully stepping over the boundary, and moved to the center, setting the cage at his feet.

He unwrapped the second object, tossing the covering it had been wrapped in outside the circle. The sword swept free of its scabbard with a soft reptilian hiss, and the sound of the steel scraping against the leather sent the blood quickening in his veins. This was the part of the ritual he liked best, and so he waited a few minutes, letting the anticipation he was feeling build until it was a raging river surging against the mental dam of his will.

When the time was right, when his excitement had reached the proper fevered pitch, he straightened and raised the weapon aloft.

Naked, with the moonlight rippling across the silver-blue steel of the blade and a light breeze stirring the edges of his hair like the touch of unseen phantom fingers, Hudson Blake began to sing.

The song started as a low murmur, the sound of the wind whispering through the river reeds, but it built with power as he went, getting louder, stronger, until it grew into the roar of a thousand voices all crying out at once.

In the midst of this, he withdrew the cat from its cage. It hissed and spat at him, scratching his forearm with its claws, but he ignored the attacks. He made certain he had a firm grip beneath its forelegs and held it out at arm's length, away from his body, still singing all the while.

He drew the sword over his shoulder until he could feel the soft kiss of the blade against the bare flesh of his lower back.

Suddenly, abruptly, he stopped singing.

The silence was thick with tension, the air in the room seeming heavier than when he'd begun, filled now with a vibrant energy.

The cat met his gaze with its own.

Understanding passed between them.

The sword came whistling down, cutting through the air with an eerie shriek.

The cat's severed head fell at Blake's feet with a soft, wet sound.

Blood sprayed from the stump of its neck; a hot crimson fountain that splashed Hudson's face and upper body.

Moving quickly, he held the sword beneath the cat's upended corpse, turning it like a spit on a barbecue so that the entire blade was covered with blood before the river stopped. When the blood ceased to flow, he tossed the corpse across the room.

With the dripping blade he unhesitatingly traced a pentagram inside the boundaries of the circle he had created earlier. According to custom, as long as he remained inside the symbol he would be safe from harm.

Not being the type to risk everything on one toss of the dice, however, Blake stepped clear of the circle and retrieved the last object he'd left on the floor. The Smith & Wesson felt satisfyingly heavy in his hands.

He hoped he wouldn't have to use it.

Returning to the circle, Blake laid the pistol down between his feet. With his other hand he thrust the sword point first into the floor in front of him so that it stood upright without any support.

He knelt and meditated for several moments, clearing his mind of all extraneous thought.

When he was ready he reached up, cupped the Bloodstone between both palms, and called out with his mind into the dark night, summoning the beast to his side.

15

A WITNESS IN THE DARK

On the other side of town, something stirred.

Moloch awakened slowly, ponderously, like a dragon aroused from its enchanted slumber.

He blinked his yellow, catlike eyes, once, twice, three times.

A voice was calling to him in his mind, a voice he didn't recognize.

If it had been the old man, he simply would have ignored it, having already decided he would deal with the old fool when the time was right. But this wasn't the Elder, nor one of his own kind.

So who then?

As far as he knew, the old man and he were the only survivors of the Age of Creation.

Therefore, it had to be a human.

The notion filled him with mild amusement.

Curious, he closed his eyes and relaxed, sloughing off the earthly restraints imposed on his body, sending his awareness soaring out into that dark realm that separates this world from the next; that place out of time, out of space, where the physical laws of reality no longer have any meaning.

In that realm he was free to travel wherever he willed, and he used the summons as a beacon, homing in on it, following it to its source.

What he saw there surprised and delighted him.

It also aroused his hunger.

Taking to the sky, he headed in that direction.

In her dream, Katelynn was standing in the cemetery.

It was late at night.

The moon was hanging in the sky, a baleful eye in the darkness. Its cold blue light touched the edges of the gravestones around her, sending their long, solemn shadows across the dew-wet grass in perfect rank and file, reminding her of an army standing watchful and still.

A grim, motionless army.

The air was heavy with their silence.

Feeling this silence all about her, Katelynn grew afraid.

Without knowing why, she began to run, slipping in and out between the gravestones as she raced desperately across the wet grass. Her heart was thumping wildly, and the need to scream rose dangerously in her throat.

She managed to stifle it in time, knowing that if she let it loose, he would hear her.

That thought startled her and brought her up short in her headlong flight to lean against the nearest tombstone.

He'll hear me? she asked herself, with a moment's rational thought. *Who will hear me?*

She didn't know. But she did know he was there.

Behind her. In the darkness.

Coming for her.

She had to get away!

A whimper of fear escaped her lips as she pushed away from the headstone and began running again.

The silence behind her changed, became the silence of fear, thick and lazy.

The air grew colder.

She had the unmistakable feeling he was closer by then, relentlessly closing the distance between them, and she glanced around frantically, knowing he was out there but unable to find him.

And then she fell.

The night grew still.

Even the trees seemed to be holding their breath, standing immobile, frozen in place.

The light breeze that had been blowing moments before suddenly died.

The crickets stopped their singing.

From where he knelt in the middle of the floor, Hudson Blake opened his eyes and looked around the room.

He was alone.

But he didn't expect to remain that way for long.

The beast was coming . . .

The feeling that someone was nearby, watching, struck him suddenly, and he instinctively cringed, reacting to the presence on a primal level, intuitively aware of the nearness of danger.

Coming . . . coming . . . coming . . .

His mind screamed at him to run, but he remained where he was, believing he was safe as long as he stayed within the confines of the protective circle he'd created. He grasped the stone tighter between his hands, his knuckles leeched white from the effort, and re-

peated the name again and again in his mind, calling
out to him.

Moloch . . .

Moloch . . .

Moloch . . .

Abruptly, he realized he was no longer alone.

The warmth of life slowly seeped from his frame as he
saw the shadow that fell on the wooden floor, the shadow
of the large hulking beast that crouched on his balcony
rail, its wings swept wide in the moonlight.

Blake could only mutely stare as icy terror swept over
him with the swiftness of a cyclone, but it was too late for
thoughts of escape.

Moloch had arrived.

The dream shifted, wavered, then coalesced.

No longer in the cemetery, she found herself standing
on a railing. Behind her a thirty-foot drop over the balcony
stretched away to the ground below. A pair of open French
doors faced her, and through them she could see an older
man kneeling naked in the middle of the floor. His chest
and face were stained with a dark, crimson crust.

Dried blood, she realized, as its tangy aroma reached
her nostrils. Her mouth twisted into a wide, cruel grin.

Her tongue flicked forward, caressing her upper inci-
sors, feeling their length and sharpness.

What the hell? a distant part of her mind wondered.

A voice not her own spoke, and a chill ran up and down
her spine at the icy menace in its words.

"Give me the stone," it said.

A hand, her own but not her own, reached forward and
uncurled its fist.

She saw with growing horror that it wasn't human.

There were only four fingers, each one tipped with a razor-sharp claw, and when they curled into the palm and back out again, gesturing, she heard them clicking together like the rasp of steel on steel.

Her breath caught in her throat as she tried to scream . . .

She awoke, gasping for air, the sound of her scream still ringing in her ears. Something clutched at her out of the darkness, twined itself in and out of her legs, and she screamed again, thrashing her limbs frantically, fighting off whatever it was with strength born of desperate fright.

With a start she realized she was merely tangled in her bedsheets, the material clinging to her sweat-drenched skin.

"Oh, my God!" she said, her chest heaving as she fought to control the wild beating of her heart.

"It was a nightmare, just a nightmare," she mumbled as she slumped back against the headboard, drained and exhausted.

Unlike most dreams, this one stayed with her, most of the details etched firmly in her mind. It had been shockingly real and frightening. She couldn't imagine what had caused it; she hadn't had such a vivid dream in years, certainly not one so violent.

Or so strange.

She sat up and glanced at the clock.

Three-thirty.

Hours before daylight yet.

She lay back down, willing her body to relax. In time her shaking finally stopped, and her breathing lost its ragged edge, returning to its normal rhythm.

Though she hadn't expected to return to sleep that night, her exhaustion worked to her advantage. Eventually the gentle sounds of her own breathing lulled her to sleep as easily as a child listening to a mother's lullaby.

At her breast the red gemstone shone brightly with a crimson light all its own.

16

PREMONITIONS

Katelynn awoke the next morning with a nagging suspicion that something was wrong. The dream remained with her still and all through breakfast images flashed before her, reminding her of the horror she'd seen. The face of the man she'd seen from the balcony kept playing itself over and over again, haunting her, until she knew she would have to do something about it.

Although she was reluctant to admit it to herself, she knew that face in her dreams.

She saw the scene again in her mind.

The open balcony doors.

The symbols etched out on the floor.

The man standing in the center of the room, blood covering his face and chest, a sword held in his right hand.

She'd seen both eager anticipation and sudden fear in his eyes.

Katelynn couldn't deny it any longer. There was absolutely no doubt in her mind that the man in her dreams had been Hudson Blake.

She saw enough in the local news and had even gone to his estate to try and interview him at the start of her thesis. She could still recall his butler's haughty dismissal of her request and the way he'd slammed the door in her face.

What was Blake doing in her dreams?

Katelynn ate her breakfast, mulling it over, then picked up the phone and called Jake. She told him that she had something important to speak to him about, something that she had to do in person, and asked if they could meet. Jake agreed and told her he'd be at her place within the hour.

Good to his word, Jake arrived just on time. She let him in, and the two of them walked through the kitchen and out onto the deck, where they took seats next to each other on the patio chairs. It was a gorgeous morning, but the heat of the sun did nothing to thaw the chill in Katelynn's bones.

"I want to go over to Riverwatch."

Jake could see that she was agitated. "Why?"

"I want to try again to get Blake to give me an interview for my thesis. I thought maybe you could help out."

Jake laughed. "Hell, Katelynn. The man can't stand me. You'd probably have better luck going without me."

"No, I don't think so. He hired you, didn't he? Maybe with you there he will be more apt to say yes."

Katelynn didn't like lying to Jake. He was a friend and deserved better, but she knew that if she told the truth, he would laugh in her face. Jake was too firmly rooted in reality to believe that something like premonitions could exist outside their weekly Swords and Sorcerers sessions. She wanted him there because she had a nagging suspicion that something would be horribly wrong when they arrived at the Blake estate. Jake had always been level-headed in a crisis, and she needed that rock-solid support if it turned out that she was right.

He protested for several more minutes, but eventually Katelynn wore him down. He had the day off because of the continuing police investigation at the Stonemoor estate. He had yet to hear when they would be resuming work, so he could use that as a pretense for going to see Blake. Reluctantly he agreed, if for no better reason than the fact that he enjoyed her company and had nothing better planned for the morning.

Jake waited while she cleaned up her breakfast dishes, then they went out to the Jeep. Loki was waiting inside and Jake let him out to greet Kate for a moment before they all climbed back inside.

The ride to Riverwatch passed in companionable silence, with an occasional chuff from Loki at a passerby on the street whom he found particularly interesting. It was a sunny morning, and Jake was feeling pretty good about things in general. He had time off from work, money in his pocket, and good friends. He did his best not to think about yesterday's events, not wanting to ruin the beginning of a potentially great day.

When they arrived at the estate, Jake pulled into the drive and down to the front of the house. He parked directly in front of the entrance, knowing that it would probably irritate Charles, which was okay by him, and got out of the Jeep. Katelynn did the same. Before she could shut her door, however, Loki pushed his way past, shot up the front steps, and began barking furiously at the door.

"Shit!" Katelynn exclaimed.

"Don't worry about it." Jake said, shutting his door. "Just leave the door open a minute, and I'll get him back inside." He called to the dog, fully expecting him to return. He'd trained the Akita well, despite the aggravation and the time it had taken. Having such a large dog made the training mandatory in Jake's view, and since being trained Loki had always obeyed him. This time was no different. The dog stopped barking immediately and trotted back to Jake's side. But instead of climbing back into the car, Loki stood close to Jake, his attention fixed on the mansion's front door, growling low in his throat.

Jake had only seen him act this way on one other occasion, and that had been when a burglar had tried to break into his home. Something was wrong, that was clear.

Jake squatted down next to the dog. "What is it, boy? What's in there?"

The Akita looked at him, then turned back to the door, growling once again. He took a step or two forward, looked back at Jake, and growled a third time.

"Something's wrong, Katelynn. He never acts like this. I think we should go."

"Go?" Katelynn asked. She hadn't taken her eyes off the dog since he'd leapt from the car. A heavy, suffocating weight was slowly settling on her shoulders as she realized that her suspicions had been correct. Something was terribly wrong there, and Katelynn had a hunch she knew just what it was.

"We have to go inside," she heard herself say. It sounded to her like her voice was coming from a distance, and she wondered if she'd even said it aloud.

Apparently she had. "Inside? What the hell for?" Jake replied.

"Someone might be hurt, Jake. We can't just leave."

"The hell we can't. If it's got Loki this upset, I'm not

going inside." He turned toward the Jeep, intending on doing just what he'd suggested, when Loki made his own opinion known. The dog dashed back up the steps and jumped up, putting his front paws against the door.

Much to everyone's surprise, the door opened beneath him and dumped the dog into the foyer. With a cacophony of barking, the Akita disappeared inside.

"Oh, shit!" Jake exclaimed as he chased after him.

Katelynn followed.

Loki must have gone straight upstairs because once he was inside Jake could hear barking from somewhere above. He raced up the steps to the second floor. Loki's barking became deeper, more strident, and Jake knew that the dog had found whatever it was he had been looking for.

Back in the foyer, Katelynn glanced around.

Instinctively she knew the house was empty. She knew it with a certainty that surprised her, and it only served to heighten her discomfort. She was frightened for both Blake and his servant, beginning to think that what she had seen in her dreams had been a premonition of harm for them both.

Somewhere above, the dog's barking became more urgent.

Katelynn glanced into the closest rooms. If anyone had been in the house, they would have heard the commotion and come to investigate, but every room she checked was empty. Satisfied that her observation had been correct, Katelynn returned to the entryway and started up the steps to the second floor.

❖   ❖   ❖

As Jake reached the second-floor landing, he glanced down the hall to find the dog standing in the entrance to the very last room. Loki stopped barking and stared at him, obviously waiting for permission before entering.

Jake was not going to give it.

"Come, boy," he said firmly.

The dog stood his ground.

"I said, come."

Loki paced back and forth, whining in his throat. It was clear he was not going to obey the command.

"You're going to regret this," Jake said through clenched teeth, his anger rising. The last thing he needed was to be caught in his employer's house with his dog. He would be out of a job quicker than he could blink. Shaking his head in frustration, he started down the hall.

As soon as Loki saw that Jake was coming toward him, he turned back to face the room, but did not enter it.

When Jake reached the door, he saw why.

Katelynn came up the stairs, calling their names. She reached the second-floor landing and saw Jake and Loki down at the end of the hall. "What's going on?" she called.

Jake jumped, then turned to face her. "Stay there, Katelynn. You don't want to see this."

"Don't want to see what?" she asked, ignoring him.

She started down the hallway, her fear growing with each step.

Jake came forward and tried to stop her, but she slipped by his grasp, needing to know, needing to see.

The room was just as she'd seen it; the bookcases, the symbols drawn on the floor, the sword standing upright in the center of the room, except now the room seemed to have been splashed with blood. It was everywhere, and the stench of it must have been what drew the dog. Across the room, Katelynn could see the body of a small animal in the far corner. Through the open patio doors the lower portions of a man's legs could be seen lying on the balcony.

Loki growled softly.

"Is he . . . ?" She couldn't bring herself to finish the question.

"I don't know."

"We've got to find out. What if he needs help?" It was the right thing to do, but in her heart Katelynn knew the man was already beyond help.

Jake nodded and started forward.

Katelynn watched as he made his way across the room and out onto the balcony. He disappeared from view behind the partially opened door and emerged a few moments later. He saw her looking at him and shook his head, letting her know there was no help to be given.

"It's Blake's butler," he said, when he rejoined her. "We'd better find a phone and call the police."

Taking hold of Loki's collar, Jake led the way back down the stairs and into Blake's study, where he knew he would find a phone. He gave the details to the 911 operator and was told to wait outside until the sheriff arrived.

Back in the Jeep, Jake thought about what he'd seen upstairs. He hadn't really needed to go into that room, hadn't really needed to discover if the man they'd seen on the balcony had been dead or alive.

He'd already known.

Once you've seen death up close, he thought, *you can recognize it anywhere.*

Despite the sun shining high overhead, the day was no longer as bright and beautiful as it had been when they'd left Katelynn's.

It had gotten considerably darker.

In the backseat, Loki looked up into the sky and growled low in his throat.

17

RIVERWATCH

Damon spent his first twenty minutes on the scene interviewing Jake and Katelynn. After telling them he'd be in contact shortly to follow up, he let them go home and turned his attention to the scene itself. He had had a lurking suspicion that they'd missed something at the first two crime scenes, something that would provide that one important clue he so desperately needed. This time he intended to take no chances.

If it's here, he thought with grim determination, *we'll find it.*

He ordered the deputies to take up watch at the gates to the estate with the command that they admit no one but the ME and the state police forensic squad. Officers searched the house thoroughly looking for any sign of the owner, to no avail. Hudson Blake was quickly put at the top of the sheriff's suspect list, and an APB was put out on him with a "wanted for questioning" alert.

It wasn't long before Strickland arrived, alerted personally as he'd been by Damon via radio just after the call came in. Ed came up the drive in a hurried walk, his black doctor's bag in one hand and his crime scene kit in the other.

Damon turned toward the house and matched his stride, filling Ed in on the details as they went in.

On the second floor they stopped at the entrance of the room before entering, letting initial impressions sink in. Roughly sixteen feet per side, the square room looked to have once been a study. A desk was pushed flat against the wall off to the right, next to a small table. Bookshelves partially lined two of the other walls. A glass-shelved display case, filled with medieval weaponry, stood between the bookshelves. The fourth wall, directly opposite the doorway in which they were standing, was split in the center by a set of open French doors.

In the middle of the room a large circle had been drawn on the polished wood floor with some kind of white powder or sand. In the center of that circle, a second design had been similarly laid out, but outlined in a dark substance. A bejeweled sword was thrust point first into the floor inside the latter. A dark stain coated the blade's surface and a section of the floor several feet wide surrounding the tip of the blade. The light from the morning sun coming in through the open balcony doors glistened off the precious stones set in the weapon's hilt and cast a long, cross-shaped shadow across the floor in their direction.

Beside him, Damon heard Strickland whisper, "What in the name of God . . . ?"

Once Damon tore his gaze from the strange tableau in the center of the room, he noticed what had sparked Strickland's outburst.

Small amounts of blood were splashed in odd places throughout the rest of the room: on the spines of a book, on the front of the desk, on the gossamer-like curtains that blew in the slight breeze coming through the open doors. The headless corpse of a small animal, possibly a cat, lay in one corner, as if carelessly tossed there. A small gilded cage lay discarded in the center of the room. A revolver rested nearby.

A man's lower legs jutted out from behind one of the open balcony doors.

Thinking of the other recent crime scenes, Damon found himself hoping there was a body attached to that leg.

"Ed," he said aloud, pointing out the limb to his companion, who was still staring in amazement at the condition of the room. The two men made their way to the balcony, being careful not to disturb anything as they crossed the room.

On the balcony they discovered the mutilated body of a middle-aged man. Like the Cummingses, large chunks of flesh were missing from the corpse. However, this time the killer had added a new twist. Several weapons, obviously taken from the weapons case in the next room, had been thrust violently into the body and left there, reminding Damon of pins in a pincushion. One corner of Damon's mind began absently cataloging the weapons; *that's a broadsword, and an epee, and a dirk. . . .* He shut the voice off quickly.

"Recognize him?" Strickland asked.

"No, but we've got a positive ID."

Partially splashed with blood, the man's face was twisted in a savage expression of fear and pain. Damon told Strickland that Jake had provided a confirmation that the man was Charles Turner, Blake's butler.

Strickland set his bags down on a clean section of the

balcony and opened one up. Withdrawing a pair of thick rubber gloves, he pulled them on and knelt next to the body to begin his examination.

Damon gave him a few moments to do the prelim, and asked, "What do you think?"

"No question it's the same killer. Exterior soft organs gone; eyes, tongue, etcetera. Chest cavity penetrated, probably find a few organs missing from there as well once I open him up on the table. What I can't figure are these weapons."

"Pre or post?" Damon asked, referring to whether or not the weapons had been used while the victim was still alive.

Ed gave it some thought. "At a guess I'd have to say he was still alive when they were used. There's some evidence of bleeding around the wounds themselves, though it is hard to be sure. From his facial expression there is no question the poor bastard suffered." Ed shook his head in frustration. "Then again, they could all be postmortem. Wounds of that type should have bled one heck of a lot, yet the floor beneath him is practically blood-free." He looked up at Damon. "I can't say either way until I open him up."

When Ed bent again over the body, Damon left him to his task and walked back into the room. He surveyed the damage, then headed over to the dark stain in the center of the room. As he got closer to it, several details became clear.

The stain was obviously blood; that was immediately apparent. And though the shape was partially obscured by the blood, Damon could see that the design laid out on the floor was actually a pentagram enclosed by a circle, drawn first with salt or colored sand and then retraced with blood. It reminded him of the Hopi sand paintings he'd seen once on a trip out West.

The symbolism troubled him. A pentagram inside of a circle was not all that common. He didn't like the implications. Back in Chicago he'd encountered the symbol once before, during a rash of cult-related homicides. The killer had been deep into the occult, the murders took place as sacrifices in the midst of a black mass. *Is that what happened here?* Damon wondered. *Is Turner the sacrificial victim in some occult ceremony? Did his death take place here, inside the room, and his body was dragged out onto the porch once it was no longer needed? If so, why?* Damon gritted his teeth in frustration. This one was like all the others; too many questions and not enough answers. *Starting to be the story of my life,* he thought.

Being careful to avoid disturbing anything, Damon moved closer to get a better look at the sword. The blade, most of which was stained with blood, was roughly three feet in length. The weapon's hilt was covered with what looked to Damon to be precious stones, though they might have been fake; he certainly wasn't one to tell the difference.

All in all, it was an impressive weapon. As were the others in the room. *Blake must be quite a collector,* Damon found himself thinking.

The thought froze him in place.

Damon stood and moved over to the display case. Some weapons were still in their proper places, but the majority lay in a reckless heap on the floor in front of the case. He looked them over carefully, taking his time, examining the setup. He counted those he could see, then did his best mentally to place them in their proper places with the help of the identification tags inside the case and his own knowledge of ancient weapons. He did this three times, each time arriving at the same result. If he included the sword in the center of the room and those still in the corpse outside, he came up one short. Another sword of approximately the same length as the one in the center of the room was missing.

Had the killer taken it with him?

Damon moved around the room, bending to look beneath the furniture and the bookshelves, making certain he hadn't simply overlooked it. Beneath the shelves closest to the display case something glinted in the light from his flashlight. Something red.

Damon withdrew an extendable pointer from his breast pocket and used it to fish the object out into the light.

It was a necklace. A gold necklace on which hung a ruby red stone of considerable size. The chain itself was broken and stained with more dried blood. Damon guessed that it must have been torn off and flung aside during a struggle, and wondered whose it was. *Blake's? Turner's? The murderer's?*

He used the pointer to push the necklace into a clear plastic evidence bag he withdrew from another pocket and marked with his pen, noting the date, time, and location he found it.

At that point Strickland came back in from the balcony. "Okay. Here's what we've got. Turner's wounds are definitely consistent with the other killings. Rigor has set in, but hasn't left yet, so we know that his death took place sometime in the last twenty-four hours. There's no sign of postmortem lividity on the body. A full autopsy should provide more answers, but for now my guess is that he was killed in this room and moved out to the balcony afterward."

The sound of Damon's radio interrupted him.

"Wilson here."

"Nelson, sir. The CSC team is here. And, uh, so is the press."

Shit.

"Send up the team. Hold the press at the gate; do not, I repeat, do not let any of them onto the property. We've got a crime scene to protect here. Tell them I'll be right down to talk to them personally."

He replaced the radio on his belt and looked over at Ed.

The coroner nodded, a grim smile playing across his face. "Have fun."

"Yeah," Damon responded dryly, and went downstairs to face the music.

18

TO PROTECT AND SERVE

"**I** hate this," Deputy Steve Bannerman mumbled beneath his breath.

In the seat next to him, his partner, Deputy Charlie Jones, nodded in silent agreement. He knew without asking just what it was that Bannerman was referring to; the fear they both felt, fear bred from constant hours of uncertainty. A week ago, night shifts like this one were considered an easy ride. A few cruises around town in the patrol car, a little time spent at the station house doing paperwork, an extralong dinner break over at Rosie's Truck Stop on the west edge of town. They were simple and hassle-free tours.

Until the killings started.

Now these shifts were the worst.

Knowing that somewhere, out there in the darkness, was a killer who operated solely at night and whom they knew next to nothing about was not a reassuring thought. It made them constantly edgy, always looking over their shoulders, wondering if he was behind them, waiting, watching, choosing his next victim.

It did not make for a relaxed evening.

"Did you hear the latest?" Jones asked his partner.

"No, what?"

"They found a scene right out of a black mass this morning at Hudson Blake's mansion."

"You're kidding me."

"No. Pentagrams inscribed on the floor, a bloody sword, even a decapitated cat. Never mind the hunks of flesh missing from the corpse of Blake's butler."

"What?"

Bannerman never got the chance to reply. As he opened his mouth to speak, something dashed out of the darkness and into the road directly in front of them. He reacted instinctively, wrenching the wheel in an effort to avoid whatever it was and sending the car into a long, uncontrolled slide.

For just a second, Bannerman thought he'd been successful, that they'd missed it.

Then came the thud of impact as the back end slewed around in response to the motion of the front, and there was no mistaking that sound.

The car traveled for several more seconds before the deputy could get it under control and pull to a stop.

Bannerman got out and looked back.

The body was about a hundred yards behind them, lying near the left shoulder of the road.

It wasn't moving.

From this distance he couldn't see enough detail to determine what it was. For all he knew, he'd struck a hitchhiker who'd run into the road to catch his attention.

Drawing his weapon, Bannerman moved forward.

Behind him, he could hear Jones getting out of the cruiser. He knew his partner would assume the standard position several yards behind him and off to one side, in order to be able to provide backup without having his line of fire blocked by Bannerman's movement forward.

The body did not move.

As he got closer, Bannerman could see that the body had four legs, not two. Blood stained the road around the carcass, black and glistening in the moonlight.

Bannerman breathed a sigh of relief when he was close enough to realize what it was that he had hit.

A deer.

It was a fair-sized male, judging from the rack of antlers and the overall size of the carcass. Somewhere in the neighborhood of 125 pounds, was his guess. There was no doubt that it was dead; its tongue lolled out the side of its mouth, and its eyes stared glassily across the road.

"What is it?" Jones called out nervously.

"Deer," Bannerman called back, tactfully ignoring the quaver that he heard in Jones's tone. "Big one, too. I don't think he felt much."

Bannerman lowered his weapon, staring in remorse at the animal he had killed. Remembering how swiftly the creature had charged out of the undergrowth, he guessed it had never even known the car was there. Something else, something in the woods behind it, must have spooked it enough to force it to charge out of the undergrowth in a blind panic.

These thoughts ran through Bannerman's mind in a matter of seconds, and he came to his conclusion right about the same time that Jones started yelling. Bannerman jerked his head up in surprise at the stark panic in his partner's tone, and was astonished at what he saw.

Jones was brandishing his gun in the air as he ran straight toward him!

Bannerman fumbled for his own gun, thinking Jones had finally cracked under the pressure of the recent murders. He got it halfway out of its holster when he was struck violently from behind. He hit the ground hard, and heard the snap of his wrist clearly as it was trapped between the weight of his body and the hard surface of the ground. The sudden pain almost made him pass out.

Gunshots split the night air seconds later, and Bannerman jerked his head up in surprise.

Jones was standing in the middle of the road firing his revolver into the sky above, using all six cylinders, then immediately reloading. Only once he had ammunition back in his weapon did he run over to check on his partner.

Pain suddenly overwhelmed Bannerman.

His back was on fire, a white-hot forge full of molten lead, the pain searing at his body. As Jones squatted down beside him the full force of that pain became acutely clear, and he screamed in agony.

"Oh Jesus, Oh God," Jones said, when he saw the condition of his partner's back.

It was immediately obvious that he was seriously hurt. A softball-sized chunk of flesh had been torn out of his body in the area of his kidneys, and Jones could see pieces of internal organs extending from the wound. Blood was flowing in copious amounts, a small dark river pumping its waters onto the road beneath.

Bannerman screamed again in pain.

"Christ," Jones swore. "What do I do? What do I do?"

The decision was taken from him.

A whistling sound filled the air, and Jones knew that the thing that had attacked his partner was coming back for another strike. Realizing he was dead if he didn't move, Jones dived to the left, away from Bannerman.

He had a momentary glimpse of a dark, winged shape roughly the size of a man and the flash of claws in the moonlight, then it was gone back into the darkness above as quickly as it had come.

"Shit, Steve! We've got to get out of here." He crawled back over to his partner and bent to help him up, knowing he had to try and get him to safety even if the effort seemed fruitless.

He needn't have bothered.

A fresh, thick stain of blood was pouring out of a second wound high on the man's back, and Jones could see that a good portion of the man's neck had been torn free during the attack.

Bannerman was beyond pain.

Jones didn't hesitate any longer.

He leapt to his feet and ran for the car, his head tucked low in the hollow of his shoulders, acutely aware of his present vulnerability. He kept his eyes fixed on the car ahead, believing that he could find protection inside its steel frame if he could just reach it in time.

He almost made it.

He was roughly fifteen feet away when the Nightshade struck for a second time that evening. The beast came at him from behind the vehicle, skimming low over the rooftop. He exploded out of the darkness, a dark shape that hurled forward on wide-stretched wings, resembling a Dantean demon straight from the depths of Hell. As the beast crossed the distance between them in the blink of an eye, Jones flung himself forward and down in a face-first slide that got him beneath the reach of the Nightshade's wings and saved his life. He could feel the closeness of the passage of the thing's claws as they sliced through the hair atop his head, carving a thin furrow across the surface of his scalp but penetrating no deeper.

Instantly he was back on his feet, crossing the remaining distance to the car in a half walk, half crawl, yanking open the door and falling inside. He slammed the door closed, locked it, and grabbed for the radio with his free hand, his revolver miraculously still held tight in the other.

All of his careful police training was forgotten in his fear and need to get help as quickly as possible. He depressed the transmission switch and started yelling into the mike. "Help! I need help! Bannerman's dead and this thing is . . ."

The car door was torn violently away. The beast reached in and grabbed the deputy by the arm. Jones screamed in horror and turned to look.

For the first time he got a close look at what was attacking him.

The light from the patrol car's interior fell on a long, narrow face with wide, upswept ears and a mouth full of several rows of needle-sharp teeth. The thing's yellow, catlike eyes glared at him, full of hunger and hatred. One thick, misshapen hand was clasped tightly around Jones's upper arm as the beast dragged him out of the car. His head smacked the steering wheel, a hard, painful blow, then hit the ground as the beast dragged him free of the patrol car.

Jones was dizzy and disoriented from the blow to his head, but could still feel the reassuring weight of his weapon in his hand. He lifted his other arm and pointed it in the general direction of the thing that was holding him.

His revolver found its voice, speaking out into the night in a succession of thunderclaps. So close, he couldn't possibly miss.

Jones watched as each bullet struck the beast in rapid sequence, knocking it backward into the road. Its claws gouged a long furrow down his arm as it did so, tearing through his uniform and the soft skin beneath with little effort. Jones could feel the sudden pain and the warm gush of flowing fluid, but he ignored both, his attention riveted on the spectacle of the six-foot winged beast before him. Blood splashed onto him, a deep purple in color, and fountained up into the night in a dark spring running from the creature's wounds. For just an instant their gazes locked, then the beast was knocked to the ground and the connection was broken.

His training reasserting itself, Jones whipped open the breech of his revolver and quickly slipped in another set of six rounds, never once taking his eyes off the beast.

When he was finished, he tried to stand and discovered he was already getting dizzy from loss of blood. The beast hadn't gotten back up and he didn't expect it to; nothing short of a grizzly could survive that much damage. He stumbled back toward the cruiser in order to radio for assistance again.

When he reached the car, he steadied himself against the doorframe and slipped into the front seat.

Jones had just picked up the mike when a sound caught his attention.

Her turned his head.

The beast was sitting up, looking at him. Fury churned

in those yellow eyes, and a double-forked tongue shot from between its lips to hiss at him in anger. Jones was not concentrating on the creature's face, however, because as he watched, the six lead slugs he had fired into the beast were slowly reversing their course, working themselves free of the creature's flesh with soft pops and thin drizzles of blood, which quickly stopped flowing as each slug fell free to the ground.

As Jones watched in horror, the thing climbed to its feet and shrieked a challenge into the night air.

Jones's bladder let go suddenly, filling the air with the sharp scent of urine.

The beast seemed to smile in response.

It spread its wings, looming above him like some kind of avenging angel.

Its piercing, yellow eyes held Jones's own for a moment, and Jones found he was completely paralyzed with fear, the gun in his hand forgotten.

The beast pounced.

Jones screamed then, a long, shrill scream of complete terror as the beast seized his leg in its iron-strong grip and hauled him bodily back out of the patrol car.

Back at the sheriff's office, the dispatchers could hear Jones's screams through the open mike.

Eventually, they stopped.

Only to be replaced by something far worse.

The sounds of a large animal feeding.

19

WARNINGS

While the two officers lay dying on the other side of town, Sam was seated in his swivel chair behind the nursing station with his dog-eared copy of Stephen King's *IT* in his hands. He was halfway through his shift when he heard a faint scream.

He leaned forward so he could see over the countertop and looked down the hall.

It was empty.

Silence lay thick in the air, a brooding, physical presence.

He sat there for a moment, listening, and had just convinced himself that he'd only heard the sound in his mind, a result of King's ability to bring the written word to life, when he heard it again.

Except it didn't stop. This time it continued in one long wail, a desperate sound of anguish and terror that rose in volume until it was impossible for him to believe it was anything but real.

For a split second, Sam was paralyzed by the horror he heard in that cry.

Then his training took over and he was up and running,

his rubber-soled shoes slapping against the cold linoleum floor, his book forgotten on the counter behind him.

The screaming continued.

He felt the cold dead hand of fear grasp his gut and twist it savagely.

Nausea threatened.

His mind raced ahead of him, doing its best to come up with a medical emergency that would cause a person to scream in such a fashion.

When it failed, his imagination took up the slack, conjuring up visions of dark little demons that had crossed the barrier from the Underworld, hell-born fiends that ripped and tore at frail, unprotected flesh; their razor-sharp teeth glinting wickedly in the dim lighting of the rest home.

He was halfway down the hallway by then. Only a few seconds had elapsed since he'd hurtled out of his chair, but as that scream rose and fell in his ears, every second felt like an eternity. Time became an exercise in slow-motion cinematography, and Sam was cast as the show's male lead. He felt like he was swimming through a river of molasses and barely making headway against the current.

His mind urged him to run faster.

The scream went on and on.

His heart was in his throat, beating a rapid-fire rhythm.

His hands were slick with sweat.

A strong urge to clamp his hands tightly over his ears to block out that chilling cry came to him then, but he ignored it. *Jesus,* he thought, *make it stop, please, God, make it stop!*

But God either didn't care or wasn't listening because it didn't. It just went on, echoing off the stark institutional walls.

Sam was passing individual rooms now—301, 302, 303, 304 . . .

With a jolt he realized the sound was coming from the last room on the left, the one that stood all alone around the far corner of the hall.

Number 310.

Gabriel's room.

As he swung around the corner, his feet sliding on the slick tile, his arms thrust against the walls to maintain his balance, time returned to its normal pace, and for one awful moment Sam thought he'd black out as his senses rebelled against the illusions his mind was creating. But then he regained a minimum of control on his body and the grayness that was looming just behind his eyes receded.

He skidded to a stop in the doorway of the room.

In the split second in which he first glanced inside the room Sam thought he'd been right; gremlins from Hell had indeed paid Gabriel a visit. The old man was thrashing wildly in his bed and Sam saw with horror that there was something crouched on the man's chest, a small dark form he was beating with his fists. The room was filled with the sound of screaming.

As Sam's eyes adjusted to the dimness inside the room, he realized the truth.

Gabriel was having a nightmare.

The object on his chest was nothing more than his own pillow. His thrashing was a result of being entangled in his bedsheets.

Relief swept over Sam like the touch of a cool ocean wave.

Sam crossed to Gabriel's side and tried to awaken him.

The old man's efforts were only making the situation worse, as each new tossing of his limbs twisted the sheets tighter around him, so that he must have felt like a fly caught in a spider's web.

The screaming suddenly stopped.

In its place came a whimpering cry that filled the room, the cry of a rabbit caught in a snare, and Sam felt the hair on the back of his neck stiffen at the sound.

His mind balked at the terror the man must be experiencing to reduce him to such a state.

"Gabriel! Wake up! It's just a dream! Wake up!" Sam yelled over the noise. It took some effort to pin one of the old man's arms to the mattress after grasping hold of it, and Sam was surprised at the man's wiry strength. He made a grab at the other arm and missed, getting a fist in the mouth for his trouble.

"Gabriel, wake up!"

This time his voice was of sufficient volume to cut through the terror of the Gabriel's nightmare and reach him. He awoke with a start, and Sam held his arm tighter as he saw the sudden fear that surged in the man's eyes.

"It's okay, Gabriel. It's okay. It's Sam. You were just having a bad dream, that's all, just a dream." He spoke in soft gentle tones and gradually the fear he saw in the man's wrinkled features receded, to be replaced by a look of utter exhaustion.

"Oh, sweet mercy, Sammy," the older man croaked in a weary voice as he slumped back against the pillows.

"It's okay now, Gabriel. You were just dreaming. Take a few deep breaths and try to relax."

"He's out there, Sammy. I know he is. I can feel him. He's out there waiting for me."

"Nobody's out there. It was just a bad dream."

"No, Sammy. You don't understand! He's out there and he knows I know it. He escaped, he's gotten free. But I'm too weak now Sammy, too weak. I can't stop him this time," he said.

Sam watched as Gabriel turned his head to stare out the window into the night's darkness. He seemed to be searching the sky for something and seemed more than a little relieved to see that whatever it was wasn't there. He turned back to face Sam.

"He knows. Knows where I am. He'll come for me, too. You mark my words, he'll come for me. And this time he won't be the one who loses."

"Come on, Gabriel. There's nobody there. No one is going to come after you. You were just having a bad dream." Sam was growing nervous himself, Gabriel's agitation like some kind of infectious disease, quickly spreading.

Relax, he told himself. *The old man's starting to lose it upstairs. Had to happen sometime, right?*

Sam sighed. He genuinely liked Gabriel. He was a quiet patient, never needing much but a few kind words now and then, but old age was bound to have caught up with him at some point and it looked like it finally had.

"Tell you what, Gabe. I'll just sit right here next to you and keep you company. That way no one can get to you without going through me, okay?" he said, smiling to show there was nothing to fear as he pulled a chair up next to the bed. The old man's hand sought his own, and Sam held it gently without saying anything, calmly waiting for Gabriel to fall back asleep.

Fifteen minutes later, just when he got up to leave,

positive that the old man was sleeping peacefully, Gabriel spoke out of the darkness in a thin, whispery tone.

"Watch the sky, Sammy. When he comes, it will be on night's velvet wings, as swift as the darkness itself. It will be too late to save me but not too late to save yourself, as long as you watch the sky . . ."

He sounds so certain, Sam thought as he stepped to the door, and for a moment considered going back to question Gabriel more closely to see if there was any substance behind his talk. But then the man's gentle breathing reached his ears across the short space of the room, and he changed his mind.

He's asleep now. If you wake him up, he'll only be frightened again and may not be able to get back to sleep so easily a second time. It's better to just let it go. He probably won't even remember it in the morning, Sam thought to himself.

That was when he looked toward the window and saw the dark, hulking shape perched on the balcony just outside.

"Oh, my God!" he said in a frightened whisper, his arms falling limply to his sides. He was suddenly too scared to move.

It's here, he thought. *The thing Gabriel's afraid of is really here! It's come for him, just like he said it would!*

But after a moment or two, when whatever it was didn't move, Sam began to doubt what he was seeing.

What's your problem? he asked himself irritably, willing his body into motion. *There's no such thing as flying demons or whatever the thing is supposed to be. It's probably just a chair someone forgot to take back inside, that's all.*

Keeping that idea foremost in his mind, Sam marched across the room and flipped on the light switch on the wall next to the sliding glass door to the balcony. The lamp hanging on the wall outside came on, flooding the balcony with light.

He'd been right.

It was only a chair.

Feeling more than a little foolish, Sam turned the light off again and slipped quietly out of the room. He returned to his station at the other end of the hall and sat back down. He picked up his book, intending to return to the place where he'd left off, but found that he didn't have the heart for it anymore. Not after Gabriel's nightmare and his own scare moments later. *I've been frightened enough for one night already, thank you very much.* Tossing the paperback aside, he grabbed a stack of files and began updating the charts.

He never saw the dark form that returned to the balcony of Room 310 just moments after he'd left the room, never knew it spent the rest of the night staring in through the window at the old man lying peacefully in his bed.

More than once Sam found himself glancing up from his studies to peer out the windows into the darkness, searching the night sky for he knew not what.

There was never anything there, but for some reason that didn't make him feel any better.

20

FORENSICS

Damon sat staring at the forensic reports in short-tempered silence. The interviews earlier that morning hadn't produced anything useful, and these reports seemed to be a dead end as well. The scientific team had examined the bullets recovered at the scene. Ballistic tests proved that all of them had come from Jones's sidearm. The flattened condition of each bullet proved they had struck their target, a conclusion bolstered by the presence of blood samples on each. So far, the technicians had been unable to match the blood to any known species, however, making them come to the conclusion that the samples were somehow contaminated. Further tests were being conducted.

What a damned mess.

Glancing at his watch, Damon realized he'd have to get moving if he was going to be on time for his meeting with Strickland. The sheriff left the station house and drove over to the medical examiner's office. He rode the elevator down to the hospital basement with three surgeons; his manner hard and grim, the two dead officers very much on his mind, the physicians enduring the ride in silence, studiously not looking in his direction. At the lower level Damon stepped off the elevator and moved briskly down the hall until he came to the morgue.

The room was starkly lit with bright fluorescent lights. Three autopsy tables were spaced evenly, a bank of movable lamps hanging within easy reach over each one. Large drains dotted the floor. Two of the tables were occupied, their contents covered with white plastic sheets. Around the lip of the drain beneath the table containing the larger bundle, Damon could see a thin pink froth left over from when the floors had been hosed down after the morning's work. His shoes squeaked as they crossed the still-damp linoleum.

Strickland was at one of the sinks, washing up.

"Hello, Ed," said Damon, entering the room.

"Sheriff."

Ed dried his hands and moved to close the morgue's doors, assuring them of privacy. "I've spent the last ten hours doing multiple autopsies, first on the Cummings couple, then Blake's butler, Turner, and now on your two officers."

Damon's jaw clenched at the thought of his murdered men, but he did not interrupt the other man.

"In each and every case, I found the same types of evidence, the same confusing issues." He moved over to one of the autopsy tables. A body lay on top of it, covered by a clean white sheet. Reaching up, he switched on the bank of lamps above it, then pulled the sheet down to unveil the remains of George Cummings.

"The reason I called you down is simple." Strickland hesitated, took a deep breath, and said, "Whatever killed this man wasn't human."

Damon stared at his friend for a moment in silence, then said, "Come again?"

Ed looked down at the corpse before him, an expression of honest bafflement on his face. "In all my years of pathology I've never run across something as strange as this. Every time I think I'm getting somewhere, I find something else that completely shatters my current theory. I haven't finished all the tests I intend to do, but I've got the feeling that once I do, I still won't know any more than I do right now, which is practically nothing. There's only one thing of which I am positive." Strickland looked up and met Damon's disbelieving gaze. "Nothing human killed this man."

The words hung in the air between them.

Maneuvering the lights down closer to the body, Strickland tried to explain. "First of all, the man's head wasn't cut off his body. It was torn off."

He bent over the corpse. "See this ragged tear here?" he asked, pointing to what was left of the man's neck. The flesh at that point rose and fell in uneven peaks and valleys. "If the killer had used a knife or some other sharp object to sever the head, we'd see a relatively smooth cut."

"What about a saw?" Damon asked. "That wouldn't leave a smooth edge, would it?"

"No, but it would be a uniform tear. This is too uneven to be a saw blade." He paused and looked up to make certain Damon was following his explanation. When he saw that he was, Strickland continued. "Do you remember a game we used to play with dandelions when we were kids? Something about Momma having a baby and her head popped off?"

"You're not saying . . . ?"

Ed smiled a strange and bitter smile. "Yes, that's exactly what I'm saying. Something pulled this man's head from his body as easily as we used to flip those flowers off their stems."

Damon stared down at the corpse with a whole new sense of horror.

"It gets worse. With the exception of his eyes, still in the head you recovered from the toilet and the intestines you found strung all over the bedroom, all the other soft organs in the body have been removed."

"Removed?" The slight tremor in Damon's voice suggested he already knew what Strickland meant by the euphemism.

Again the smile. "Removed. Eaten. Devoured. Call it what you will. As far as I can tell, the beast, whatever it is, got his heart, his kidneys, his liver, even his tongue and testicles."

"Oh, God," said Damon, as he fought to make his mind accept what he was hearing.

"My thoughts exactly." Strickland flipped off the lights and covered the body.

Damon finally got his thoughts in order. "How come you're so certain it's an animal? Couldn't a human, albeit a very sick one, have done the same thing? Look at that guy Dahmer. He was certainly capable of something like that."

"Sure, I guess it would be possible. But not in this case. No human left the teeth marks I found."

"Teeth marks?" Damon echoed. He was starting to feel a little slow on the uptake.

Ed moved over to the other table. Turning on the lights and drawing back the sheet as he had before, he exposed Cummings' head and limbs.

"The bones had been deeply scored at the point of separation from the rest of the limb. My first hunch was that the marks were caused by some kind of tool, maybe a tire iron or an ax, but on closer examination I realized that they were really the imprints left when the beast crushed the limbs between its jaws. Its teeth are curved inward, at an angle, so when they cut through the skin and hit the bone, they leave evidence of their passing"—Ed turned the foot so Damon could see the exposed cross section of the bone—"and if you look closely, you'll see that the marrow has been sucked out as well. While the creature had less time with Bannerman and Jones, their bodies showed many of the same results."

"Jesus! What kind of animal are we talking about here, Ed?"

The medical examiner shrugged. "Damned if I know. Something big enough to tackle a full-grown man. Something that's not only not afraid of him, but also happens to like how he tastes. But I'm afraid there's more. I found the same strange lack of blood with this body as I did with Halloran's corpse."

"You're kidding me, right?"

" 'Fraid not. No blood, and the veins themselves collapsed throughout the entire system. I can't explain it any more than I could when I talked to you yesterday. I've never seen anything like it."

"So what you're saying is that whatever killed Halloran also killed the Cummingses as well?"

"It appears that way."

Damon was perplexed. "Why didn't it feast on Halloran, too? Why just the older couple and my men?"

"Who knows? Could be for a variety of reasons. Maybe

it was just thirsty the first time." Strickland's weak attempt at humor blew right past Damon. For all he knew, it might not be a joke at all.

"You ready for the rest?"

"There's more?" Damon asked him, incredulously.

Strickland picked the head up off the table and turned it around so Damon could see the fist-sized hole in the back of the man's skull.

"It ate his brain, too," Strickland replied.

21

CONFRONTATION

Later that night, Gabriel lay quietly in his room, thinking about the past. Once he'd been young and powerful, but that time had long since faded into dust. His end was approaching, he knew that, and in certain ways he welcomed it. He lifted one frail hand and stared at it, remembering how it had appeared long ago, smooth and strong, a power to be reckoned with, not liver-spotted and weak as it was now. The years had, at last, taken their toll on his physical form.

His mind was as sharp as ever, though, and he decided to make use of its powers one last time before he moved on from this place. Settling back against his pillows, he gathered his strength and, with a sharp mental shove, cast his consciousness out beyond the walls of the facility in which he lay to the crisp, clean air of the summer night. While the Na'Karat might have the physical power to fly, Gabriel's kind flew in other, truer ways, and he wouldn't have traded it for the world.

He soared above the buildings, reveling in his freedom, then swooped down toward the forest floor below.

As he did so, a rabbit jumped out of the undergrowth and stopped to feed on a patch of clover.

What would it be like to exist as you do, my little fellow? he asked it silently. *To have no responsibilities, no worries, to sleep at night without the burden of suffocating doubts that plague you like a leprous disease rotting you away from the inside out? What would it be like, to think only of the present moment, with no thought or consideration to the future or the past?*

The rabbit stiffened suddenly, as if sensing his presence, and with a sudden burst of speed it spun to the right and disappeared into the undergrowth.

Gabriel watched it go, following its passage into the woods by listening for the tiny thump of its heart. He wished his furry friend good fortune, then sent his presence soaring high above the ground to view the world once more in the fashion of his youth, before the coming of man and the war that destroyed his people.

Once his "eyes" had seen enough, he returned to his body and lay there in the darkness of his room, waiting.

Instead of concentrating on the confrontation he knew would soon occur, his thoughts drifted.

An image of a woman formed in his mind. She was beautiful, a golden-haired goddess with eyes of emerald green and cherry red lips.

Ah, Mira, my beautiful Mira! How long has it been? he thought sadly. His heart ached for her just as it had in ages past, when they had walked hand in hand beneath the golden spires of their fair city. He loved her as strongly as he had in the days of his youth. If anything, that devotion had grown stronger with the passage of time, until he felt close to bursting with his longing for her. He could remember her face as clearly now as if he'd seen it only yesterday; he could trace its soft, gentle curves in the air with his eyes and feel the heat of her breath on his lips. He knew it wouldn't be long before they were reunited, and he secretly longed for his journey through the ages to be over so that he could join her in the afterlife.

Gabriel watched the ticking hands of the clock and wished they'd move faster.

Eventually, he drifted off to sleep.

He awoke a short while later, and knew immediately that he was no longer alone.

The sliding glass doors to his balcony hung open, the stiff breeze coming through causing the curtains to billow out into the night.

At the base of his bed stood the Nightshade.

They stared at each other.

To Gabriel, the beast was as foul as the day he had locked it away beneath the earth. The Elder was dismayed to see that it looked as powerful as it had on that long-ago night, as if sealing it off from reality had let it gather strength in some mysterious fashion instead of crippling it as he'd intended when he'd created its prison. The beast's muscles rippled beneath its hide, and its eyes gleamed with cunning intelligence.

Gabriel was suddenly worried that he had waited too long.

There was no way Sam and his friends would be able to defeat it if it was as strong as he feared.

Moloch stared at the Elder. Rage and hatred rose in him like a rain-swollen river. Here was the one who had pursued him through the ages. Here was the one who had sought to imprison him forever without shape or substance in a timeless void deep beneath the earth.

Here was his enemy.

The beast almost laughed. The Elder was nothing more than a pathetic husk of what he'd once been, and certainly no match for Moloch's own powers. *Killing him won't be an effort, it will be a favor.*

Gabriel broke the silence, speaking in the old tongue.

"You will regret coming here." He kept his voice firm, but suspected that the beast had already seen his dismay at the other's apparent strength. He would give no more away than he had to, however.

"I think not."

The Nightshade's voice was thicker, more guttural than he remembered, and Gabriel found himself wondering if it had sustained some permanent damage from its confinement.

"You will not succeed. The humans are stronger now, more able to face the challenges that life lays at their feet. They will use their technology to destroy you."

Moloch laughed. "I have not been idle since my release. I have watched the cattle. I have seen what they are capable of. I have also learned that they do not believe in anything besides that which they can lay their hands upon. They have forgotten the past and rely too much on the future. I will show them what it means again to be hunted, and they will once again remember their fear."

Gabriel had been gathering his strength during the beast's speech. As the final syllables were falling from its mouth, Gabriel lashed out with the force of his mind in a vicious mental attack.

The Nightshade stumbled under the sudden onslaught. It had been caught off guard, unsuspecting, and the Elder's mental barrage began to knock down its internal defenses, threatening to kill it by sheer force of will. It was actually forced backward, away from the bed, by the power of the attack.

Gabriel realized that he had the upper hand, and threw more of his reserves in behind the attack, hoping to overwhelm the beast and destroy it before it had a chance to retaliate.

The end was not to be that easy, however.

The beast quickly regained control, snapping its shields into place, protecting itself, locking out the power of the attack. Gabriel tried vainly for several long moments to breach the shields, but to no avail.

At last, exhausted, he was forced to drop the assault.

Shaking his head, Moloch stepped back over to the bed and stared at Gabriel anew. He did not look damaged in any way by the attack, and despair washed through Gabriel for the first time in many years. He had to face the truth; he was no longer a match for the beast.

Unless Sam and his friends could destroy it, the Nightshade was going to win.

Katelynn was in the library, reading, when it happened. One moment she was engrossed in the record of life in the 1700s; the next, the world seemed to shrink inward on her, a black haze obscuring her sight. She fought to remain conscious, but it was too late.

She lost herself in the darkness.

When she came to again, she was no longer in the library.

She stood in Gabriel's room at the nursing home. He was sitting upright in bed, staring at her standing at its foot, an expression of fear and revulsion on his face. He was obviously exhausted, but he seemed to summon his strength as she watched, as if preparing for a confrontation.

Katelynn did not understand what was going on.

What am I doing here?

Gabriel watched the Nightshade recover from his attack. The beast's tongue flicked out over its teeth, and the Elder knew the end was near. He had exhausted his strength in that last-ditch effort to destroy the Nightshade, and knew he would not survive long at the creature's hands. That Moloch intended to make him suffer as long as possible was entirely too clear.

Gabriel had no intention of allowing that to happen.

As the beast stalked closer, Gabriel summoned what little strength he had left. He did not have the energy to project another attack at the beast, but there was another way out, one he'd longed to use for centuries.

Moloch moved closer, coming around the side of his bed.

That close, Gabriel could smell the stink of his fetid breath, and hear the rasp of claws on the linoleum floor.

The beast's long forked tongue flicked out, tasting the air, searching for the fear that should have been coming off its opponent in waves.

Gabriel waited patiently, letting the beast think it had won, letting it gloat in its success, for by doing so he gained another moment to prepare.

He had to be certain he had the strength to succeed

with his plan. If he did not, he would be too weak to do anything more. He would be helpless in the hands of his ancient enemy.

Katelynn moved closer to the bed, and glanced down as her hands found the safety rail. She was shocked by what she saw. Her hands had changed; had become hideous. They were scaled like a lizard's and a dark gray-green in color. Each one had four fingers; three rising together from the top of the palm, the fourth opposing them, much like the talons of a bird. Each finger, in turn, had four swollen, misshapen knuckles the size of walnuts, topped with long inwardly curving claws that shone like ivory in the room's dim light.

Katelynn's mind whirled at a frantic pace, trying to explain what her eyes were seeing. Then, like a dash of ice-cold water thrown in her face, her subconscious dragged from its depths the memory of her other dreams, making her accept what was happening.

With a small gasp of horror, she understood.

She was no longer in her own body, but had somehow been transported inside something else and was looking out through its eyes instead of her own!

While she could feel her madly accelerated heartbeat, she could also feel that of the creature in whose body she rode, a heartbeat that was deeper and more powerful than her own, one that beat at a much slower rate.

If she concentrated, as she did now, she could dimly perceive the other's thoughts as well.

A wave of hatred so vile that it made her want to retch rolled out of the form she was inhabiting. That Gabriel knew her in this form was beyond a doubt; there was hatred and recognition in his eyes. As her mind struggled with a thousand questions, she felt herself speak, the voice in her ears like crushed gravel.

"Time to die, old fool," she said.

Leaning close, Moloch opened his mouth to reveal the many rows of scalpel-sharp teeth.

Using the last of his strength, Gabriel reached deep inside his body and simply ordered his heart to stop.

He died with a smile on his face, knowing he'd cheated the Nightshade out of the final victory.

Katelynn felt her mouth stretching impossibly wide, felt her tongue flickering across the tips of monstrously long teeth as sharp as surgeon's knives as she leaned closer to Gabriel.

Noooo! she cried mentally, but was helpless to stop the sudden descent of those awful fangs.

As the teeth ripped pitilessly into the fragile flesh of the old man's neck, Katelynn's mind mercifully found the strength to flee, and she came to herself again, lying on the floor beside the table she'd been working on in the library. A long shrill scream was bursting from her lips. She felt someone grasping her limbs, and fearing that whatever it was had followed her, she thrashed wildly, terrified that she was about to die.

A sudden pain flared on her right cheek, bringing her back to reality. The middle-aged librarian who had administered the slap was crouched beside her, one hand in the air in preparation of delivering a second slap should it prove necessary. Two students were pinning her arms and legs to the floor. The lips of the one at her feet were red and rapidly swelling, and Katelynn realized with shocked sympathy that she must have kicked him in the face during her struggles.

"Settle down," the older woman said. "You've had some kind of an attack. Just lie still for a moment. The health team is on its way." The woman smiled at her, but Katelynn could recognize the woman's fear and apprehension.

Probably thinks I'm ready for the psycho ward, Katelynn thought.

With growing dismay she realized that the woman could be right.

Suddenly, she desperately wanted to get out of there, and assuring her rescuers that she was fine, got to her feet, quickly gathered her books, and went out into the night, ignoring their protests.

Her nightmares from previous evenings crowded in on her, spurring her fear. She finally accepted that they were more than simple nightmares, knew that the connection she had made while in that twilight realm had followed her into the real world.

Lord only knew what might happen next.

As he realized that his enemy had taken his own life before he could enact his vengeance, Moloch lost control. He tore into the fresh corpse, ripping the limbs from the body in his frenzy, delighting in the way his claws sliced into the weak flesh as if it were butter. He shrieked his rage and frustration, uncaring if any of the humans heard him. If they were foolish enough to investigate, then he would tear them apart as well.

Later, once his anger was spent and the corpse was barely recognizable as having once been human, Moloch left the way that he had entered, leaving the sliding glass doors open behind him as he soared off the balcony into the night.

As he returned to his roost, slipping easily through the night's inky blackness, he pondered the evening's events.

Just before he had killed the Elder, he'd felt the presence of another being there in the room with them.

Yet he was positive the room had been empty with the exception of the Elder and himself.

So how did he explain the sensation that someone had been watching them? Or the scream he had heard as his teeth had ripped out the old fool's throat?

He didn't know.

But he was determined to find out.

For the time being, though, he could wait. With his hunger sated, Moloch felt heavy, bloated, full. The quiet oblivion of sleep and his own sweet dreams beckoned to him. He decided he would rest before he sought the answers to those questions.

After all, with his oldest enemy now dead, what did he have to fear? He was once again ruler of the night, and nothing stood in his way. The human fools would again learn to fear the darkness, and he would rule over them in his rightful place as king.

And, oh, how much fun I am going to have, the beast thought gleefully as it winged its way home.

22

A MESSAGE FROM BEYOND

Earlier that evening, around seven o'clock, Jake sat in Sam's apartment waiting for his friend to finish dressing. Sam had swapped shifts with a coworker earlier in the week so that he could go to a celebration being held for Dana Sandings, one of his friends, and Jake had reluctantly agreed to come along. While sitting around with a bunch of literary types might not be Jake's first choice for a night out, it certainly beat being home alone.

The party was in full swing when they arrived, with people filling the apartment and spilling out onto the deck in back. Jake slipped through the crowd in search of the bar, while Sam grabbed a Pepsi from a passing tray, said hello to those he knew, and spent some time mingling with those he didn't.

After a while he felt someone come up behind him and punch him lightly on the shoulder. He turned to find Jake standing there.

"Come on, you've got to see this," his friend said.

Jake headed back into the crowd, making his way toward one of the back rooms. They reached a closed door, which Jake opened softly, gesturing for Sam to precede him through the door.

The room they entered was almost completely dark, four candles being the only source of illumination. By their soft light, Sam could see five or six people seated in a loose semicircle on the floor in the middle of the room, facing two others. These two in turn sat facing each other with some kind of game board between them.

It took Sam a minute to realize it was a Ouija board.

Will you look at this? he thought to himself. He'd always wanted to try a Ouija board but had never had the chance. He moved closer.

In the dim light, Sam recognized one of those in the group as Dana, their hostess. That wasn't surprising. Sam knew she practiced such things as spirit-trances, fortune-telling, palm reading, and what she described as communication with the dead; all a result of having a Romanian gypsy for a mother, she'd say.

While he watched, Dana began speaking.

"The spirits are everywhere, they see and know everything. They are always around us; in the air we breathe, in the smoke from the candles, in the light of the flames, forever present but cut off from us owing to our skepticism about their existence. One must overcome this if a message is to be received."

Sam realized suddenly that Jake had sat down on the outskirts of the circle and moved to join him. The others noted their presence but did not speak to them. No one wanted to interrupt Dana.

"In order for us to contact someone on the other side, we must all wipe our minds clean of doubt. The spirits are constantly trying to communicate with us on this plane;

with our help, they will be able to. If you can't believe but wish to stay and witness their presence among us, you must wipe your mind of all negative thoughts. Think only positive thoughts. It doesn't matter what they are, just as long as they are happy thoughts. The spirits will use the energy you produce to help them break through the barrier to our side."

"Whom should we talk to?" asked a dark-haired man.

Dana asked, "Are there any particular requests?"

A number of names were called out: John F. Kennedy, Jim Morrison, Ben Franklin, Adolf Hitler, Ted Bundy. Dana held up her hands for silence, and when she got it, looked over at Sam. "Choose someone," she said.

Sam was at a sudden loss. *Whom did he want to talk to?*

Jake spoke up. "What about that Jesuit who supposedly haunts the library on the Benton University campus, Father Castelli?"

Sam agreed. He was as good as anyone else.

"Okay. Father Castelli it is." Dana turned her attention to Jake. "Why don't you come over here and help me work the board?" she asked.

Jake was about to decline when Sam elbowed him sharply. "He'd love to," Sam replied for him.

Jake got up and crossed the room, sitting Indian-style in front of Dana with the Ouija board between them.

"Have you ever done this before?" she asked.

Jake shook his head. Sam could see he was doing his best to stifle a grin.

"Okay, then. Rest your fingers on the planchette. No, that's too heavy. Do it lightly, so that you're just barely touching it." As Jake complied, Dana said, "Good. That's much better." She closed her eyes and took several deep breaths. Sam glanced around and saw everyone else staring intently at the board. He exchanged a humor-filled glance with Jake and was about to follow the others' lead when Dana said, "Sam, why don't you come over here and take my place? I don't have to be using the board in order to provide a spirit channel for them to work through. I know you and your friend are most likely skeptics. This way neither of you can claim I was moving the planchette myself."

Sam enthusiastically agreed.

"Do I have your word that neither of you will consciously move the planchette?"

"Sure," said Jake.

Sam nodded as well.

"Okay. Everyone close your eyes. Clear your minds of all extraneous thoughts; let the outside world wash away. Pretend your mind is a television set, and the only thing you are receiving is static. When you feel you've reached the proper state of awareness, you can open your eyes again. Casey, why don't you read out the letters as the planchette lands on them?"

The woman seated to Sam's left agreed.

Sam let his eyes slide shut and tried to follow Dana's instructions, a little thrill of excitement growing in his stomach. *Imagine if we really manage to contact someone*, he thought to himself. *Wouldn't that be something?*

Someone gave a small gasp, and Sam opened his eyes to find Jake and everyone else in the room staring in Dana's direction.

Sam followed suit.

Dana's eyes had rolled back in their sockets, so all that was visible were the whites of her eyeballs.

Neat trick, Sam thought, a bit disappointed at the theatrics.

Voices murmured somewhere on the edge of the room.

"Silence," Dana hissed, and quiet instantly returned. In a soft voice that was oddly lilting, she began speaking. "Is anyone out there? Can anyone hear me?"

Sam started to close his eyes again. As he did so, he caught a glimpse of the clock on the wall and noted in the back of his mind that it was one minute to twelve.

"Is anyone out there? We are trying to reach Father Castelli. Can you hear me, Father?"

Suddenly Sam felt two things happen at once. Across from him, Jake stiffened, and the planchette twitched beneath their fingers. Sam glanced up at Jake, but his head was lowered, and he wouldn't meet his gaze. *Did Jake move this thing?*

"Is anyone out . . ." Dana paused, and in a whisper spoke to the group. "I can feel the spirits. They are all around us, clamoring to speak to us. I sense a great urgency among them. Everyone concentrate on reaching out to Father Castelli. Let him know we wish to speak to him. Casey, would you please read the letters off the board once contact is made?

"Can you hear me, Father?" she continued.

Beneath his fingers, Sam felt the planchette move again. He eased up on the pressure, until his fingers were barely touching it. He wanted to make sure that he wasn't causing it to move. He saw the rest of the group leaning forward eagerly to watch the proceedings, and this time he kept his eyes open like the rest of them.

"Father? Are you there, Father Castelli?"

The planchette began making slow lazy circles around

the board, and Sam felt a slight tingle in his fingertips, as if a mild current was passing through his flesh. The planchette began to move quicker, then abruptly slid across the board to the top left hand side, centering itself over the word "YES."

The group gasped collectively.

"Who are you?" Dana asked aloud.

The planchette swirled aimlessly for a moment and then dropped to the double row of letters in the center of the board.

"M," read Casey, and then "A . . . T . . . T . . . H . . . E . . . W." The planchette paused and so did Casey. After a moment, as if to signal the start of a new word, it continued. "C . . . A . . . S . . . T . . . E . . . L . . . L . . . I."

"This is Father Castelli?" Dana asked, just to be certain.

The planchette immediately moved back to the "YES."

Dana said, "The contact is strengthening now. The spirits have broken through the barrier, and their message will be clearer to us."

Before Dana could ask her next question, however, the planchette began spinning aimlessly around the board for a moment before moving on to spell another new word.

"B . . . E . . . W . . . A . . . R" Casey called out in response, her voice shaking slightly.

Stupid spirit can't even spell, Sam thought to himself.

As if she'd heard him, Dana said, "Often a spirit will misspell something, it's a pretty common occurrence, especially if the subject has been dead a long time."

"Is that your message?" she asked the board. "Beware?"

YES.

"Beware of what?" she asked.

A cool, whispery chill ran lightly up Sam's spine.

The planchette was moving faster, as if guided by an unseen hand filled with urgency. Casey called out the letters in a voice filled with excitement. "E . . . V . . . I . . . L. —E . . . V . . I . . L.—E . . . V . . . I . . . L. It's repeating the word "evil" over and over again."

The planchette came to rest in the center of the board. Sam shifted his position slightly to get more comfortable.

"Don't remove your hands, Sam! You'll break the contact," said Dana.

Her warning was unnecessary, however. Sam was too engrossed in what was happening even to consider it.

Dana went on. "What is evil? Can you tell us what evil we are to beware of, Father Castelli?" Her voice was a quiet whisper in the otherwise silent room.

Immediately: B . . . L . . . A . . . K . . . E . . . S . . . B . . . A . . . N . . . E.

"Bane?" someone asked.

This time it was Jake who answered, his voice low but steady, "It means a cause of death or ruin."

Another voice could be heard from the back of the room. "It says Blake. Do you think it means Hudson Blake?"

No one had an answer.

Dana decided to ask for clarification. "Can you tell us what that is, Father?"

The planchette fell still. Dana repeated her question twice, slower each time. After what seemed an age to Sam, the planchette moved again. This time it was different instead of the smooth, circular motions, it moved in fits and starts, spasmodically jerking across the board.

"B . . . E . . . W . . . A . . . R . . . I . . . T . . . C . . . A . . .
N . . . S . . . E . .," Casey called out for those who couldn't
see the pointer.

Sam stared down at the board. The planchette was
still moving helter-skelter across its surface, jerking left
and right like a puppet on a string. The tingling in his
arms had become almost, but not quite, pain. He
wanted to tear his hands away and break the contact,
but something compelled him to keep them in place.
He tried to reassure himself. *Jake must be doing this,* he
thought. *Jake's just spelling out messages to scare everyone.*

"Father Castelli? Are you still with us, Father?" Dana
asked. A strange expression ran across her face then, part
grimace, part bewilderment. "Who's there?" she asked.
"Do you wish to speak with us?"

Beneath his hands, Sam felt the planchette slow down,
then move with deliberation.

He watched in shock as it spelled out a message directed specifically at him.

R.E.M.E.M.B.E.R.M.Y.W.A.R.N.I.N.G.S.A.M.M.Y.

Sam sat there, stunned. The others around him who
could see the board gasped in surprise, then looked at him
rather oddly, as if they had just discovered something mysterious in their midst.

The planchette began moving again.

GOODBYE, SAMMY, it read.

That whispery touch of fear turned into a fist clenched
savagely around his spine.

Then, with the suddenness of a striking snake, the
planchette spelled out another message.

FOOLS! NEITHER YOU NOR THE OLD ONE

CAN STOP ME NOW! I WILL SLAUGHTER YOU LIKE THE CATTLE YOU ARE.

Seeing this message spelled out in front of him, Sam jumped, almost breaking the contact. After what happened next, he wished he had.

Dana moaned.

Sam looked at her and recoiled in shock. She was shaking fiercely, as if a high-voltage current were running through her veins. Her teeth were chattering, and the sound quickly filled the room, making it seem as if a herd of skeletons were charging past. The hand on his spine squeezed tighter.

There's no way Jake is causing her to do that, his inner voice said.

Everyone in the room was frozen in a state of shock.

No one moved to help her.

Over her shoulder, Sam was surprised to see Katelynn staring across the room in their direction, her face as pale as a ghost. He had been so engrossed he hadn't even noticed that she'd arrived.

Beneath his fingers, Sam felt the planchette begin to move again with slow, deliberate speed.

In a voice shaking with fear, Casey read the message aloud.

"SAY GOODBYE TO DANA."

As if in response, Dana suddenly screamed. The sound of her cry broke the paralysis that had held everyone in its grip. Sam jumped away from the board as if it were alive. Jake grabbed Dana. She was still shaking, more violently now, her heels drumming in a frenzy on the floor.

"She's having a fit!" someone yelled.

"Hit the lights!"

A moment later the room was filled with electric brilliance as someone complied with the request.

Sam recovered his wits and moved to help Jake. He held Dana's feet steady. Someone else, he thought it might be Bill, pinned her arms.

Blood was flowing from her mouth, and Sam realized she'd clamped her teeth down on her tongue. *Probably bit the damn thing nearly in half.* He watched as Jake clenched the sides of her jaw at some hidden nerve point and forced her mouth open. Inside it was a mess; blood and saliva mixing into a crimson froth that kept them from seeing how much damage she'd done to herself. Trying to find a way to prevent her from tearing herself up further, Jake forced his wallet between her jaws, then let go of his hold. Her teeth immediately clamped down on the wallet's leather surface like a spring-loaded vise.

Katelynn pushed her way over to them. "Someone call the hospital and get someone up here quick," she told the crowd. She turned to Jake. "Is she going to be okay?"

"I don't know. Does anyone know if she's epileptic?" he asked.

No one did.

Another minute passed. The convulsions slowed, then stopped altogether. Dana lay in Jake's arms, limp but still conscious.

Katelynn removed the wallet from her mouth and tried to reassure her. "Take it easy. You've had some kind of a seizure. Help is on the way, just lie still."

Her gaze rolled around the room, wide and vacant, not really noticing any of them around her. Then she saw Jake. She stiffened in his arms, her eyes growing almost comically wide. Her left hand shot up and gripped the front of his shirt and pulled, dragging his face down close to her lips. She said something to him, but Sam was too far away to hear.

Jake blanched in response.

The mobile emergency team hustled into the room then, and everyone moved back to allow them some space to work in. Sam, Jake, and Katelynn backed away as well, noticing as they did so that the party had rapidly broken up around them. Only a few people were still in the apartment.

Katelynn stood at Sam's side, her face pale. "What happened in there?" she asked.

"I'm not sure. We were using the Ouija board, and she suddenly went nuts, threw a fit of some kind." He shivered. *Jake was moving that planchette*, he kept telling himself. *Just Jake, no one else.*

That small voice spoke up again. *Why don't you ask him*, it said, and he decided to do just that.

The medics loaded Dana onto a stretcher and carried her down the stairs. Jake, Sam, and Katelynn followed the emergency team out of the building and watched as Dana was loaded into an ambulance. Lights flashing, the vehicle roared off toward the complex's gates.

Jake turned to face Sam.

One glance into Jake's eyes and Sam felt his fear grow. His blood ran cold and sluggish through his veins. He wrapped his arms around his chest in an unconscious attempt to warm himself.

Jake's scared, he realized, recognizing the look in his friend's eyes.

That frightened Sam more than anything that had happened that night. *If Jake's scared*, he told himself, *then I should be terrified*. Abruptly, he realized that he was.

What Jake said next made things worse.

"Were you moving that thing, Sam?"

The question froze him where he stood. Numbly, Sam shook his head. He didn't want to hear what he knew was coming next, but there was no escaping it.

"I wasn't either, Sam. I swear it."

Next to them, Katelynn said, "If it wasn't you, and it wasn't Sam, then who . . ."

Jake could only shake his head in reply to her question.

But Sam thought he knew. There was only one person who called him Sammy. *Gabriel. Something must have happened.* He turned and began pushing his way back through the crowd, desperate to reach his car, his sudden fear so overwhelming that he didn't bother telling his friends where he was headed.

The two of them stood there for a few minutes as the crowd dispersed, each of them lost in his own thoughts, until Katelynn broke the silence.

"What did she say to you, Jake?"

Jake hesitated, then answered in a subdued tone. "She said that someone in the room was going to die soon."

In the distance, the ambulance siren shrieked like a banshee into the night's darkness.

23

PUZZLE PIECES

Not wanting to be alone, the two of them walked over to The Hemingway, an all-night coffeehouse and Internet café on the other side of campus.

The café consisted of one long room filled with odds and ends of furniture, tables and chairs, mismatched sofas and love seats, even a few booths from a now defunct diner, really anything the students could get their hands on. A small stage stood to the left of the bar, and throughout the night the poets and writers who typically haunted the place would get up to read selections of their works, while others listened attentively or carried on conversations amongst themselves in muted tones. The walls were fashioned of unfinished wood, decorated here and there with posted notices of poetry readings and flyers from a variety of political and artistic groups.

They took a seat in the back, away from most of the other tables so that they could talk freely without being overheard. Katelynn was the first to broach the subject.

"What's going on, Jake?"

"Damned if I know," he answered gruffly, still disconcerted both by what had happened at the party and by Sam's odd behavior immediately thereafter.

"Come on, Jake. I'm serious."

"So am I, Katelynn. I don't have a clue. It's bad enough that I find a corpse every time I turn around. Adding Ouija boards and communication with the dead does not make me feel any better. Never mind Sam's rushing off like that." Jake poured himself another beer from the pitcher on the table before him. While he wouldn't admit it, he was scared. Getting drunk seemed a good solution, and he fully intended to put his plan into motion without delay. "What the heck were you doing at the party anyway? I thought you were studying tonight."

"I was. Something happened."

She took her time, explaining the dreams that she'd been having and her "attack" at the library. She told him about the odd sensation of looking through another's eyes and about her increasing belief that what she was seeing was not imaginary but real.

Jake had had enough weirdness for one night, however. "Come on, Katelynn. You can't really believe that."

"Why not?"

"Because its crazy, that's why," he retorted sharply, but upon seeing her expression he decided to take another tack. "Look," he said more gently, "just think about this rationally for a minute, okay? You've been under a lot of stress, everyone has. This killer is making everyone nervous."

"So it's making me see things, is that what you're saying?"

"Yes. I told you yesterday afternoon about the body we found at Stonemoor and that night you dreamed about

Hudson Blake. It stands to reason that your subconscious would twist what you learned earlier into your dreams at night as you slept."

"But something happened to him, just as I saw it in my dream."

Jake shook his head. "Not really. Think about it. In your dream you say you saw Hudson Blake, yet we didn't discover Blake's body at the estate, we found his butler's. And tonight you saw Gabriel, but as far as we know he is perfectly all right. We don't know that anything has happened to Blake—he's just disappeared. It's just your subconscious taking the things you know and twisting them up with your fear and your nervousness over the fact that the police haven't caught the killer yet."

Katelynn wasn't convinced. "How do you explain tonight then?" she challenged him.

"What about tonight?"

"How do you explain the Ouija board or what happened to Dana."

Exasperated, Jake replied, "It could have been any number of things. Sam could have been moving that pointer purposely. He could have been lying when he said he wasn't, just to pull our legs. Or it could have been moving on its own, a result of a buildup in static electricity between Sam and me. Hell, there are a thousand reasons it could have been moving around. And the least likely one is that we were really speaking to the dead. It was simply coincidence that Dana suffered an epileptic attack when she did. It was probably brought on by all of the excitement of the party."

"So what happened to Sam? Why did he rush off like that?"

"I don't know. Maybe he just freaked out over Dana's fit." Finding the pitcher empty, Jake half turned in his seat, searching for the waitress.

"Come on, Jake. Doesn't that all sound just a bit too pat to you?"

Without stopping his attempts to signal a waitress, Jake answered, "Nope. It certainly sounds far more reasonable than that garbage you're spouting."

Katelynn had had enough. Whether it was her fear or her annoyance at how much Jake had drunk in such a short time, she was less tolerant than usual. Having Jake brush her off so cavalierly infuriated her. She slid out of the booth, grabbed Jake by the chin, and turned his head to face her. "Do you know what a shithead is, Jake?" she asked, then continued without giving him time to answer. "I'll tell you. A shithead is someone who can't see the truth even when it's right there in front of him. Thanks for your help. I guess I'll figure it out on my own."

Jake could only stare. *Just what the hell is wrong with everyone tonight?* His beer-addled mind just couldn't put two and two together.

Without another word, Katelynn turned and stormed across the room, disappearing out the door.

For a moment Jake considered following, but quickly decided against it. She probably wouldn't talk to him, and if she felt like being a bitch, then it was best if he just left her alone. She'd cool down after a while.

And then maybe she'd talk some sense. He went back to trying to signal a waitress and did his best to forget about what had been happening lately.

It was more than he wanted to think about at the moment.

24

THE LAST OF A NOBLE RACE

Something terrible had happened to Gabriel.

Sam was certain of it and as he sped through the streets, his fear grew with every mile passing beneath his wheels.

Sam could see the flashing blue lights as soon as he turned onto the long, tree-lined drive that led to the main building of the complex. His heart froze at the sight. As he drove closer he made out the forms of the individual sheriff's cars that were parked haphazardly in the small cul-de-sac fronting the building. An ambulance was also there, its rear doors thrown wide, its red strobes mingling in eerie symphony with the blues.

Sam jerked the car to a stop, jumped out, and was running toward the front door even before his engine had grown silent. A uniformed deputy saw him at the last minute and tried to prevent him from entering, but Sam ducked beneath the man's outstretched arms and pushed through the glass door.

The main lobby was full of residents, most of them from the third floor, each in an assortment of pajamas. Deputy sheriffs were milling here and there amongst the

patients. It seemed to Sam as if the sheriff's men were trying to interview some of patients, but for what reason he
couldn't guess. Most of them were senile and would prove
of little or no use in whatever investigation they were con-
ducting.

The confusion in the room had brought him up short
just inside the door, and when he realized he was no
longer moving, Sam cast an anxious glance back over his
shoulder. He was relieved to see that the deputy he'd
sneaked past was still outside, prevented from following
him by a sudden swarm of spectators who were likewise
trying to get inside.

Ignoring the masses of people moving all around him,
Sam walked over to the elevators, his thoughts on Gabriel.
The presence of the police and the emergency medical
team confirmed what he'd previously only suspected.
Something had happened there that night, and he was all
but positive it had something to do with Gabriel.

A sense of evil lingered in the air, like a gas that had
been only partially dispelled. He wasn't the only one who
felt it; others in the room were constantly looking over
their shoulders as if they, too, could sense some presence
in the room—a grim shadow that crouched behind them.
In that instant Sam knew the object of Gabriel's fears had
come for him. All that was left to do was to find out if the
old man had survived.

Sam had a hunch he already knew the answer to that
question and had to force himself to keep moving forward. He had forcibly to ignore the reluctance that suddenly settled about his shoulders like a mantle of lead,
threatening to bend his back beneath its great weight.

He was afraid.

Afraid of what he would find upstairs.

As he reached out for the elevator call button, a hand landed on his shoulder, startling him.

"Sorry. Elevators are off-limits. Nobody leaves the lobby until we're finished," a gruff voice said from behind him.

Sam turned and found himself face to face with another deputy. The man glared at him with eyes as hard as stones and heavy with suspicion.

"Oh," Sam said, a bit flustered by the man's sudden appearance. "I'll just use the stairs then." He moved to step past the man.

The other's broad bulk blocked his path. "Are you deaf?" he asked with ill-concealed hostility. "I said nobody's allowed upstairs."

"Look, Deputy. I work here. These people are more than my responsibility. Many of them are my friends. If something has happened to one of them, I've got to do what I can to help."

"You can help out by staying the hell out of the way of the professionals."

Sam willed himself to stay calm. *Humor the guy,* an inner voice said.

"Okay, okay," Sam said in a resigned voice, and moved off into the crowd again. Several minutes later, when he was certain the deputy was no longer watching him, Sam drifted slowly to his right in the direction of the stairwell.

Damn! he thought, once he had the stairwell in sight. Another deputy was stationed there, blocking the way to the upper floors. He was stuck. There was no other way to the upper floors unless he came through the walkway that connected the nursing home to the rest of the hospital complex, and if they had this end covered, Sam was certain they would have that guarded as well.

Now what?

Then fate provided him with the opportunity he needed. Several members of the press arrived outside and were attempting to force their way past the deputy guarding the front door. The man guarding the stairwell noticed his partner's plight and moved to help, leaving the door to the stairwell unguarded.

Sam took advantage of the opportunity and calmly walked over to the door, opened it, and slipped quietly into the stairwell. He took the steps two at a time, his heart thumping madly in his chest. There might be more guards at the top, but for now he didn't care. His only concern was the fate of his friend. He had to discover if Gabriel was still alive!

He emerged onto the third floor at the opposite end of the hall from Gabriel's room. The small corridor before him was empty, but he could hear a good deal of commotion coming from the main hallway around the corner.

Sam took the chance.

The main corridor was filled with people, most of them uniformed deputy sheriffs. A few men were dressed in dark suits and ties. Sam took them to be detectives. Two ambulance attendants sat in the plastic chairs that lined the hallway with decidedly queasy looks on their faces. An empty stretcher was pushed up against the wall next to them.

While Sam was standing there trying to decide what to do, he heard a familiar voice call his name.

"Sam! Over here!"

He looked to his left and saw Jerry Peters, a coworker.

Jerry was sitting at the nurses' station, a uniformed cop at his left elbow. An open notepad was in his hand, and he frowned as Sam walked over to join them.

"What a fuckin' mess, Sam! Last time I switch shifts with you!"

His friend's face, normally ruddy with a glow bestowed from the flask of Dewar's he kept in his pocket, was so pale as to seem almost bloodless. Dark circles drooped beneath his eyes. Sam watched Jerry's hands shake as he took a drag from the cigarette he was smoking. The ashtray in front of him was filled with butts.

"Tell me about it, Jerry. What happened?"

Before he could receive an answer the cop spoke up, "Who are you?"

Jerry answered for him. "It's okay, Deputy. He works here. This was supposed to be his shift."

The deputy looked questioningly at Sam.

"Yeah, that's right. I had the night off but came in for some things out of my locker and saw all the commotion. I came up to see what was going on," Sam replied.

Deputy Collins hesitated. His orders were to make sure no one left the floor; nobody had said anything about keeping anyone out. For all he knew, the guys downstairs had sent this guy up here. After giving it a moment's consideration, he decided it would be best to check with the sheriff and let him know the guy was here. That way he'd at least have covered his ass. *Let the guys downstairs take the heat for letting him by.*

"Got any ID?" he asked Sam.

Sam dug out the laminated ID card he carried in his wallet. The card bore his photograph, and had his name and position printed beneath the nursing home's seal. He handed the card to Collins, who scrutinized it for a minute, then moved off down the hall without saying anything.

Sam slumped into the chair the deputy had vacated. "What's going on, Jer?"

"Shit! You ain't gonna believe this man! Some fucker got in here and sliced one of the old coots to bits." Peters shuddered. "Found what was left of him 'bout a half hour ago. Man, you shoulda seen that room. Blood was freakin' everywhere!"

Sam had heard enough. "Who was it?" he asked, dreading the answer but needing to ask.

"It was, ahh, what's his name? The guy who's always havin' those weird dreams? You now, the guy with the funny last name. Gabe what's-his-face?"

Before Peters knew what was happening Sam was up off the chair and running down the hall, racing past a group of deputies too surprised by his sudden appearance to stop him. His heart lodged like a bone in his throat.

Flashes of light could be seen coming from Room 310, and a group of deputies were clustered in front of that door, their backs to him.

Barely slowing, Sam shoved through them into the room itself, ignoring the protests and evading their attempts to stop him.

The room was awash in blood. Crimson splatters covered every surface.

On the walls.

On the floor.

On the once-white sheets of the bed.

Unidentifiable lumps covered in blood were scattered all about the floor.

As he glanced around the room in shock, Sam's gaze came to rest on the two men who were working inside the room. Dressed in white lab smocks, one used a camera to photograph each of the strange lumps in the place where it had been found, then waited while his partner used a spatula-like device to scoop those pieces into a small plastic bag. The bag was then deposited onto a small, steel cart that stood behind them.

Sam could see the cart was slowly being filled with bags. Numb with horror, he forced himself to walk over and peer at one of the objects through the clear plastic.

The bags were filled with ragged chunks of human flesh.

Gabriel's flesh.

The veteran deputies watching from the door might have been around long enough to have become hardened to the overpowering stench, but Sam had not. He spun around and stumbled back out the door of the room into the hall, desperately struggling to keep his teeth clenched tightly against the tide that surged up from his stomach.

His distress grew stronger than his willpower, however, and he threw up, splashing the shoes of one of the nearby detectives with a semisolid stream of vomit.

25

THE BATON PASSES

The cold water from the basin felt good on his face and hands. After unceremoniously losing his dinner, Sam had stumbled down to the men's room and suffered another attack of retching that lasted almost fifteen minutes. His throat was raw. His stomach ached. He was all but certain the next attack would leave him exhausted.

Sam reached over and yanked several paper towels from the dispenser hanging on the wall and used them to mop his face dry. One glance in the mirror at the bleak, unhinged look in his eyes was enough. As he bent his head beneath the faucet and tried to rinse the foul taste from his mouth for the fourth time, he made sure he refrained from looking in that direction again.

When he felt he had himself together, he left the men's room and stepped back into the hall.

Two uniformed deputies were waiting for him just outside the door.

Damon was talking with one of the responding officers when Collins came up beside him and signaled for his attention.

"What have we got?" Wilson asked while studying Sam over his fellow officer's shoulder.

"Nothing much, I'm afraid." Collins pointed a thumb back over his shoulder. "Name's Samuel Travers. Claims he works here, stopped by to get a few things from his locker, and ran into the commotion downstairs so he thought he'd check things out. The victim was a friend of his it seems."

Collins handed Damon a small laminated card that had Sam's picture and employee information. Damon glanced at the photo, then suddenly remembered where he had seen him last.

Travers had been at the site where they'd discovered the Halloran corpse. Damon wondered if it was just a co-incidence that Sam had shown up at this murder scene as well. *Come to think of it, Jake Caruso had been at two of the murder scenes as well, the two at the Blake estates.* Damon filed the thought away for later investigation.

The sheriff handed the ID back to Collins. "Check this out for me. Find out who his supervisor is and get him on the phone. I want to know everything he can tell us about this guy. You know the drill."

"Gotcha, Sheriff."

As Collins headed down the hall, Damon walked over to where Sam was standing. "Feeling any better, Mr. Travers?" he asked kindly.

"Uh, yeah, thanks. Sorry about the mess." He waved his hand feebly in the direction of the doorway where he'd lost control of his stomach earlier.

"Don't worry about it," Damon replied. "A sight like that isn't an easy one to take." He shook his head sadly. "Unfortunately, when you're in a position like mine you get used to it after a while."

Sam didn't reply. He was barely listening. He knew that he should be paying attention. He was probably in a whole lot of trouble, but he couldn't bring himself to care. His thoughts were a confused jumble, like a swarm of bees around a hive.

He realized suddenly that the sheriff had asked him another question.

"Uhh, pardon me?"

Wilson eyed him calmly. "I asked if you knew the victim."

Gabriel! a voice cried in the back of Sam's mind. "Yeah. He's . . ." he began, and then corrected himself. "He was a friend of mine. I work here, this is my floor." *Forgive me, Gabriel! How could I have known it was all true?*

"Are you friends with most of the patients entrusted to your care?"

"Some of them," Sam replied.

The heavy stench of death filled his nostrils as the ambulance attendants walked past carrying a stretcher on which sat a number of body bags. Sam's gaze followed them the length of the hall until they disappeared around the corner.

Damon waited until he had Sam's attention again. Then he asked, "Do you know who killed Mr. Armadorian?"

Yes! Sam's mind cried, and for a moment he was afraid he'd be unable to prevent himself from telling the sheriff all he knew, that his mouth would disobey the commands his mind was sending to it and the whole sorry story would be revealed, but some rational part of him was still functioning. He knew that if he told the sheriff what he suspected, he'd only wind up at the county hospital awaiting a psychiatric exam. He managed to squelch his desperate need to unburden himself and answered the question in the negative.

Sam's inner turmoil did not go unnoticed, but Damon gave no indication that he'd seen it.

If Sam might know something that could help the investigation of the murders, then Damon was duty-bound to bring him in for questioning. The mayor and the public were screaming for him to make an arrest and end the killing spree that was rapidly turning their town into a frightened community of hermits, too scared to leave their homes. He couldn't arrest Sam just for being in the wrong place at the wrong time, but bringing him down to the station house for questioning wouldn't violate any of his civil rights. Something stayed his hand, however.

Maybe it didn't make much sense, but in his gut Damon was certain that Sam had no connection to the murders. While there was no evidence yet linking this one to the others aside from its sheer savagery, Damon was certain that they were all connected. They had to be. There was no doubt in his mind that all four murders were committed by the same person. Or animal, if he were to use Strickland's theory. While Sam's appearance tonight might indicate he knew something about the murders, not for a moment did Damon believe that Sam was capable of committing them. It took a certain maliciousness to kill in such a brutal manner, and his gut reaction told him Sam wasn't capable of that.

Which left him back at square one.

Except for whatever it was that Sam knew.

Damon watched as Sam dug a crumpled pack of cigarettes out of his back pocket and stuck one between his lips. His hands trembled as he tried to light it, and after three unsuccessful tries the sheriff took pity on him and lit it for him.

Sam weakly smiled his thanks.

Damon came to a decision. "Look, Mr. Travers. I get the feeling you know a bit more about all this than you're letting on. I'm giving you a chance to come clean right now. Is there anything you wanna tell me?"

Sam merely shook his head. "Is it okay if I go now? I'm not feeling all that great and . . ."

Damon cut him off. "Yeah, all right. I'm sure the whole situation has been a shock. There are a few other questions I want to ask you about Mr. Armadorian, but they can wait until the morning. I'll expect you in my office sometime tomorrow, all right?"

"Yeah. Okay." Sam turned and began walking down the corridor. He'd only gone a few steps when Sheriff Wilson called out to him.

"Mr. Travers?"

Sam turned back around to face him.

"The stairway to the locker room is this way," the sheriff said, indicating the other end of the hall with an outstretched hand.

For a moment Sam was completely confused. The locker room? What the hell did that have to . . . ? Then he remembered the cover story he'd told Deputy Collins. He smiled weakly, doing his best to cover his lapse. "Thanks. In the midst of all this I guess I forgot why I came here." Sam turned and walked back past Wilson and down the hall in the other direction. He knew the sheriff wasn't fooled.

Damon watched him go, then walked down the hall and reentered the room where the old man had died. He stared at the splattered bloodstains while the crime scene technicians went about their business around him.

Jesus H. Christ! he thought. *Who the hell could do something like this?*

The mutilation of the Cummingses had been bad. The memory of the man's head stuffed into the toilet bowl rose in his mind, but he quickly shoved it away again. It was bad enough that he saw it in his dreams; he didn't need to see it while he was awake.

Yet that horror had been something he could understand. It was sick, sure, but normally sick, if that made any kind of twisted sense. Mutilation of a victim's body wasn't all that uncommon in psychotic killings.

But this. . . .

This was beyond anything he'd ever seen.

The poor guy had been torn to shreds, for Christ's sake.

He shook his head. *What kind of animal am I after? How the hell did it get in here without being seen or heard? How intelligent is this thing?*

Sheriff Wilson's right hand unconsciously slipped down to caress the butt of his service revolver.

There was one question he did know the answer to, however.

What do you do with an animal that is running wild in the streets?

Damon smiled grimly.

You hunt it down and kill it.

Sam felt like he'd been caught up in a giant whirlwind that was hurtling his body relentlessly forward without his control. He sat slumped on the floor in the basement locker room, his back resting against the cool metal of the lockers. He was doing his best to stop the palsied trembling of his body, which had started as soon as he'd sought refuge there.

He wasn't having much success.

The events of the last hour had been too much for him.

His mind and his body were numb with shock. It was hard to believe that Gabriel was dead. He knew it was true, yet a part of him resisted the notion.

Sam was overwhelmed with guilt. There was no way he could deny the fact that he had killed his friend. He hadn't harmed him physically, but in his own mind he was as responsible as whoever had actually performed the violence. He had dismissed his friend's fears as the harmless ramblings of an old man rapidly approaching senility, even when there had been no evidence that Gabriel had begun in any way to lose touch with reality, and that had killed him as surely as if Sam himself had wielded the knife.

If he'd listened, he might have been able to save him. He and Gabriel could've faced the old man's enemy together. Gabriel might have survived.

If only he'd listened!

But he hadn't, and Gabriel had paid the final price for Sam's own ignorance.

With his heart aching and filled with guilt, grief finally broke through. His face in his hands, Sam wept long and hard, his shoulders hitching with the force of his sobs.

After a time, grief slowly gave way to anger.

Gabriel's death would not go unavenged, he vowed to the empty air around him.

With the backs of his hands, Sam wiped the tears from his face and rose slowly to his feet. Knowing the police might still be outside, he knew he had to maintain his appearance, particularly in the light of Sheriff Wilson's obvious suspicions. He went to his locker and spun the combination, intending on removing the extra coat he kept there to support the story he'd told the sheriff and Deputy

Collins. When the lock clicked he yanked open the thin metal door and froze, staring at what lay inside.

A thick package wrapped in brown paper rested on the top shelf inside the locker. Sam's name was scrawled across the front in Gabriel's script.

The package hadn't been there the day before yesterday.

It was just a simple package, no bigger than a couple of paperback books.

Yet something about it sent chills racing up and down Sam's spine.

He had the distinct impression that it had been waiting there for him; waiting there in the darkness of his locker, quietly, patiently, like a spider hanging suspended in its web.

He stared at it for several long moments, his heart beating painfully in his chest.

Very slowly he reached in and picked it up. He held it gingerly, half-expecting it to scuttle swiftly out of his hands.

It did not.

It merely sat there, its very presence seeming to mock him, daring him to open it.

A voice in the back of his mind told him to toss it back into his locker. Better yet, straight into the nearest trash can. *It's probably nothing important anyway*, the voice said. *Get rid of it. Forget you ever set eyes on the damn thing. Let it sit there and rot until there's nothing left but a thin film of fuzzy mold growing in its place.*

Ignoring the voice, Sam took a deep breath, ripped the package open, and peered inside.

The black face of a videotape stared back at him.

26

REVELATIONS

Jake awoke.

He lay flat on his back in bed, his eyes straining to see in the darkness. His muscles tensed, and he was surprised when, a second or two after awakening, he realized he was holding his breath.

For several long moments, there was silence.

Just when he'd convinced himself that he was imagining things, the loud pounding that had awoken him resumed.

The front door, Jake realized distantly.

He glanced at the glowing hands of his watch.

Who the hell was banging on his door at midnight?

Finding his jeans where he'd dropped them beside the bed, Jake swung his legs out from under the sheets and pulled the jeans up over them.

The knocking continued.

"Hold your damn horses. I said I was coming!" he called in the direction of the front door.

The pounding had awoken Loki, and the dog added his barking to the din.

"Quiet, boy!" Jake said as he rounded the corner and

snapped on the foyer light. Loki stood in front of the door, barking furiously, but when he saw Jake, he backed off and settled down.

The sudden quiet left in the wake of Loki's silence was interrupted a second later as the pounding resumed for a third time.

Jake lost his patience. He turned the lock, disengaged the bolt, and threw the door open violently.

"Look you stupid son of a . . ."

He got no further.

The flood of words leaving his mouth trickled to a stop the moment Jake realized who it was standing on his front steps.

It was Sam, and his friend was a mess.

The knees of his jeans were stained with mud and grass. His shirt was buttoned improperly and on its front was a long streak of drying vomit.

Sam looked up and Jake knew something terrible had happened.

At last he found his voice. "Sam! What the hell happened?"

Travers smiled sadly. He opened his mouth to answer, but nothing came out.

His chin dropped, his shoulders slumped, and without uttering a sound he collapsed directly into Jake's arms, unconscious. The beer can he'd been holding behind his back clattered to the floor.

"Aw shit, Sam," Caruso muttered as he manhandled his friend into the apartment and out into the living room.

As they passed through the foyer something slipped out of Sam's half-tucked shirt and fell to the floor. Loki scooted in and retrieved it as Jake dumped Sam unceremoniously onto the couch.

Jake struggled with his friend's limp body for a few moments until he'd managed to get the soiled clothes off him. He tossed them into the wash and got a spare blanket out of the hall closet to cover him up. He retrieved the beer can from the floor, then went outside and looked in the window of Sam's car. The other five cans of the six-pack were on the front seat, still in their plastic binding. Satisfied that Sam wasn't going to die of alcohol poisoning in the middle of the night, Jake went back inside.

Loki was lying on the floor, gnawing on his newfound toy, whatever it was. His own hangover forgotten in the excitement, Jake reached in and pried whatever it was from between the dog's jaws, ignoring the low growls that he got in return.

"Shut up, boy," he replied distractedly as he turned the object over in his hands.

It was a videotape. There was no jacket and no writing on the label; nothing to identify what it might contain.

Jake's curiosity meter rose a notch.

He walked into the kitchen, the dog trailing eagerly at his heels. "See what you did, Loki?" Jake said as he held the tape in front of the dog's nose and indicated the saliva hanging from it. "You got slime all over the tape. How am I supposed to watch it now, huh?"

The Akita whined as if in apology.

"Yeah, I know. You just couldn't help it, right?" The banter with his pet helped take his mind off Sam's condition and he relaxed a little as he cleaned the outside of the videotape.

Jake returned to the living room, slipped the tape into his VCR, and switched on the television. Settling comfortably onto the floor with his head against the cushion of the couch behind him, he sat back to watch the show.

The face of an old man filled the screen as the tape began to roll, and without having to be told, Jake knew this was Sam's friend from the nursing home, Gabriel. The man smiled and began speaking.

"Well, Sammy. If you're watching this we both know it's too late to do anything for me." He smiled grimly. "Don't worry, my friend. I've waited a long time for this day. Longer than you could ever know. My time is up, but I'm afraid that yours has just begun."

Jake leaned closer to the television, his interest aroused. The old man was talking as if he'd passed away. *Could that be why Sam was so upset? Because Gabriel had died?*

He glanced over his shoulder. Sam looked half-dead himself. His head was thrown back at a strange angle, his mouth agape. If it weren't for the steady rise and fall of his chest, the illusion would've been perfect.

Shaking his head in sympathy, Jake turned back to the screen as the old man resumed his speech.

"I know you didn't ask for this, and I know if you had your choice that you wouldn't want it either. But there is no choice here. You must do as I ask. You must! You're the only one who might possibly understand, the only one who won't dismiss the entire story as pure nonsense."

Say what?

"You've got to believe what I'm about to tell you. I know it'll be hard. It'll seem strange, even unbelievable at first. But it is true. On that, you've just got to trust me."

The old man paused. He was staring straight at the camera, and from Jake's viewpoint it seemed as if Gabriel was staring straight out of the screen, directly at him. Though it was completely irrational, Jake had the odd feeling that even now Gabriel could in some way actually see him.

It gave him the creeps.

But what Gabriel said next was even more frightening.

"If you don't believe me, more innocent people will die."

Jake straightened up. *Gabriel was talking about the recent murders! Did he have something to do with them?*

Little fingers of unease began caressing the back of his neck.

Jake made no move to turn the tape off, however.

Just a few more minutes, he told himself.

"Remember the story I told you a few weeks ago?" Gabriel was saying. "About the Beginning? About the Nightshades and the world before the coming of man? You've got to believe me Sam when I swear to you that it was all true! Every word of it!

"And now it is up to you to take up the fight.

"I am the last of the Elders, the last of my people. We were a brave and noble race, but when I am gone we will exist no more. We will pass out of this world, and only a faint echo of our glorious times will remain, meager memories that your people believe are nothing more than myths and legends."

Time-out here! Jake thought, frowning. *Nightshades? Elders? What is he talking about?* It sounded as if the old guy didn't think he was human, which was completely absurd. Had the guy gone completely off his rocker?

"As I told you before, millions died in the Great War between our two races. When it was over, only a handful from each side survived. A few of us cried out for peace between our two peoples. They believed the Elders and the Nightshades could exist together, side by side in harmony, working to rebuild a world we'd come close to destroying in our greed. But others among us, myself included, disagreed." The old man's fist clenched, and his voice rang with remembered pain. He shook his hand in the air. "White-hot hatred burned in our hearts, and in our minds there was only rage. We swore we would obtain vengeance for our dead or die ourselves in the attempt."

Despite himself, Jake was moved by the man's impassioned words, even as his mind sought to deny their authenticity. It was clear that Gabriel believed what he was saying to be the truth.

He watched as the old man lowered his fist and stared at it, as if surprised to find it there. Jake could see small red half-moons in his palm where his nails had pressed savagely against the tender flesh of his palm when Gabriel uncurled his fingers.

Gabriel went on, but the passion was gone as swiftly as it had come. His voice was now little better than a whisper and thick with the knowledge of choices made in error.

"We hunted each other through the ages, neither side gaining the upper hand. Hiding from the humans who had grown in number and spread their own civilization across the globe, we continued our war in the shadows. Savage clashes occurred whenever we met. We fought, and fought, and fought some more, until there were too few of us for it to matter any longer. Yet still we continued. We knew nothing else by then; the fight consumed us, body, mind, and soul. In the end, it became our only reason to live.

"It continued that way for centuries, until only two of us remained. Myself, and a Nightshade by the name of Moloch."

Gabriel's eyes burned with fanaticism. "He tried to flee, to escape my wrath, but I was better than he. I tracked him relentlessly, never tiring in my chase. I had the conscience of an entire race on my shoulders, and I swore to myself that I would not fail, that they would not have died in vain. Moloch would pay for his crimes. Victory would be ours at last!

"The chase led me here, to Harrington Falls, which at that time was nothing more than a small, pioneer settlement. Moloch had taken refuge in the home of a human, a man who sought to harness the 'Powers of Darkness,' as he called them, for his own evil ends. I confronted the Nightshade there and the battle was intense. The fighting between us went on for days, and many times it had me on the brink of defeat. Each time I would recall the faces of all those who had fallen before me and my strength would be renewed, until I could turn the situation to my advantage.

"In the end, it was Moloch who was defeated.

"It was then that I made my greatest mistake. As he lay there at my feet, awaiting the final blow that would send him into the darkness forever, I found I couldn't finish what I'd begun. For decades, destroying him had been the sole purpose of my life, the very reason for my continued existence. When I thought of what it would be like to live without that burden, all I could envision was a bleak life, living without the company of my people. Even the world was something I no longer recognized, Man was everywhere; the last, wild sacred places dwindling by the day. In that moment of triumph, I realized the irony of my existence.

"If I destroyed him, I would in fact be destroying myself as well.

"Despite my loneliness, I did not want to die.

"In the end, I compromised. I used the last of my powers to rob him of his physical existence, imprisoning the rest of his being, his soul if you will, inside a void, a sphere of nothingness. That was in turn sealed inside a stone likeness of him that his human ally, Sebastian Blake, had fashioned. I sealed the statue and its precious contents away in a place where I thought it would never be found while the townspeople were sending Blake on to his last reward.

"I was no longer the Hunter. I was the Guardian. Once again, I had a purpose in my life, a reason to continue.

"Decades passed and the beast remained locked in its cell. It had lost its body, but its mind still functioned; it was helpless, trapped with only its thoughts for companions for all eternity. I hoped it would eventually lose its mind, but not before it suffered long and hard for what it and its kind had done.

"Such was the nature of my vengeance." Gabriel's voice rose once more. "I was a fool! The years passed. I roamed the world as one of you, pretending to be an ordinary human, hiding my true identity. Nightly I would let my consciousness return here to check on my captive, to ensure that all was well with Moloch's confinement. In time I grew overconfident. My visits became weekly, then monthly, and before long entire decades would pass before I would return. I was enjoying life as a human, crude though it was in comparison to our world, and sought the kind of pleasures from life that I had missed in my earlier years because of the war.

"My people have much longer life cycles than your own, and so I watched generations pass me by while I remained as I was and always had been, young and strong.

Eventually, time caught up with me and took its toll. Our lives may be longer than yours, but we are every bit as mortal in the end.

"Knowing my death wasn't far in the future, I returned here to live out the last of my days.

"That's when it happened.

"Moloch escaped."

Jake was staring at the screen with his jaw hanging wide, absolutely astounded at what he was hearing. *Everything the old man said was bullshit, but what bullshit it was! The best part of it all was the fact that Gabriel believed it all. Every word. You could see it in his eyes and hear it in his voice.*

Gabriel went on. "I am too old to fight him as I once did. My body is weary, and my power wanes. If you are watching this, then you know I was too weak to defend myself and the war is at last over. But you are young. You have the power of truth and righteousness on your side, as I had so long ago. You can defeat him!

"He has killed several times already and will no doubt kill again and again unless he is stopped. You must find him and destroy him once and for all. You must succeed where I have failed."

The old man's face took on a look of chagrin, as if he were begging for forgiveness. "I wish I had more time to teach you what I know. But I waited too long, hoping against hope that I would be strong enough to finish the deed. How wrong I was! I can tell you this; he has gained new abilities since his release, abilities even I am uncertain of. But he has gained a weakness as well. He requires blood to remain corporeal, or the sorcery he used to release himself will be undone. Do not repeat the mistakes I have made, my young friend. Remember, when he comes, he will come on night's velvet wings. Watch for him. Find him and destroy him. The fate of your world now hangs in the balance."

With that final statement the tape ended.

The screen in front of Jake went blank.

Holy Shit! Jake thought a few moments later, once his mind had managed to digest everything the old man had said. *Nightshades? Civilizations long before the rise of man? And that shit about chasing the Dark One down through the centuries, that's rich. The guy was a certifiable loon, that was for sure, but hell, he had one heck of an imagination, you had to give him that.*

No wonder Sam liked him.

Shaking his head in amazement, Jake flipped off the set and headed back to bed, intending on catching some sleep. He could talk to Sam about things in the morning.

He was in the process of double-checking the lock on the front door when something clicked in the back of his mind.

Jake stiffened and his eyes widened involuntarily. His mouth opened, but no words came out.

Images flashed inside his head, one after another, coming so fast that they seemed to blend together into a hideous collage.

Halloran's corpse.

The statue they'd found inside the crypt.

The news reports about the murders.

The butler's body.

The visions Katelynn had been having.

Gabriel pleading with Sam to stop the thing from killing again.

Good Lord! Jake thought. *Could everything Gabriel had said be true?*

At that moment Jake felt a mental hinge beginning to let go in the back of his mind. With it, his entire foundation of rational thought began sliding down a long dark ramp.

All right, Jake. Don't freak out on me here, he told himself. *Get a grip and just think this whole thing through logically. There's got to be a better explanation for all this. There has to be!*

There wasn't.

A part of him deep down inside knew it.

Calming himself, Jake went into the kitchen and sat down, considering the whole situation step by step.

The killings had begun Tuesday afternoon or evening, only a short time after Kyle Halloran's body had been discovered in Sebastian Blake's crypt. Since then all hell had broken loose. In the space of forty-eight hours, five, possibly six, people had been hideously murdered. Jake knew from the news reports that the bodies had been ravaged as well. In one case, the death of an elderly couple, the victims had been mutilated so badly that the police hadn't been certain how many bodies they were actually dealing with when they first arrived at the scene. Jake had even heard rumors that parts of the bodies had been eaten.

Judging from the frantic pressure the papers were putting on the sheriff's department, Jake suspected that the authorities were no closer to catching the killer than they had been from the very start.

Why?

Because they were looking in the wrong place?

Because the killer wasn't human, as they so naturally assumed?

While the logical side of his mind was telling him to knock off the bullshit and go back to bed, the other half—the one that loved to read horror novels and play Swords and Sorcerers—was saying, *Why the hell not? Weirder things happen all the time, right? Take a look around. How many UFO sightings were there last year? What about the Loch Ness monster? Sure, and the* National Enquirer *is up for the Pulitzer Prize this year.*

Suppose the creature did exist.

That would account for the police having so much trouble finding the killer, wouldn't it? A demon, or whatever you wanted to call it, wouldn't leave the usual sort of evidence that police investigations relied upon. There'd be no motive, no connections between the victims. There wouldn't be any fingerprints, or fiber traces, or paper trails for them to follow. There'd be no murder weapon; no pistol, no knife, no lead pipe or candlestick. Any blood or tissue samples the police recovered wouldn't do them any good. What could they match them to? The same went for teeth marks on the victims.

The creature could leave behind a trail of corpses and still be practically untraceable!

This is crazy, he told himself, but he wasn't quite ready to let it go.

Not yet.

His theory would also go a long way to explaining what it was that Katelynn was seeing in her "visions." Once he made the simple jump in logic that said such a thing might be possible, everything else fell solidly into place.

Okay.

Say it does exist.

How can I prove that?

Jake got up and poured himself some coffee. He had a hunch he was going to need it. He crossed to the junk drawer and dug around until he found a clean sheet of paper and a pen. He took them both back to the table.

After a couple of minutes, he began writing.

27

CONNECTIONS

While Jake was wrestling with the idea that something paranormal was happening around him, Katelynn was pacing her living room, lost in thought.

Blake's Bane, she kept repeating to herself as she moved about the room.

Blake's Bane . . . Blake's Bane . . . Blake's . . .

She tried to sleep, but after lying in bed awake for half an hour she'd given up and gotten to work. The innate curiosity that had led her into a life of research assumed control and pushed her emotions back where they couldn't interfere with her work. There they could simmer until she was ready to deal with them.

For the time being, Jake was forgotten.

Katelynn had bigger fish to fry.

Blake's Bane . . . Blake's Bane . . .

Father Castelli's phrase had rung a bell somewhere in the dark recesses of her mind. Katelynn was positive she had heard it before. It didn't even occur to her to doubt that the phrase was genuine; she was convinced that they had, indeed, been speaking to the deceased priest.

But when had she heard it? And where?

She had a hunch that if she could find the answer to either of those questions, then she'd also discover the answer to what had been happening to her lately.

Back and forth . . .

Back and forth . . .

Blake's Bane . . .

With a sharp cry she dashed across the room to her desk and frantically dug through the stacks of books piled haphazardly on the floor, at last pulling forth a small, leather-bound volume that had seen better days. The book's cover was torn, the corners bent, even the pages had taken on the yellowish brown hue that belied old age.

She seated herself behind the desk unconsciously and, after turning on the light, began slowly scanning page after page of the small work.

I know it's here somewhere, she told herself over and over again. *I know it is.*

Indeed it was.

On page 243, to be exact.

The volume itself was the traveling diary of Edward Beckett. It was a slim volume, one she'd found only after acting on Gabriel's advice during her fourth search of the library's rare books collection. Beckett had been a circuit-riding minister who traveled from settlement to settlement in the country's early years, bringing the word of the Lord to any and all who would listen. Beckett had passed through Harrington Falls several times in the 1760s and she had been using his firsthand observations of the area as a sourcebook for her thesis. Harrington Falls had been well established by then, having swiftly spread into the surrounding countryside as the Blake family's wealth brought more people into the region. Beckett's observations provided a clear and accurate picture of life on the frontier. He apparently rode several hundreds of miles a year, preaching as often as possible.

A meticulous man, he recorded every little detail in the volumes of travel diaries he prepared along the way.

As chance would have it, he arrived in Harrington Falls on a cold evening in October of 1763, the same evening Sebastian Blake was accused of practicing witchcraft and wizardry.

The townsfolk had decided his guilt right then and there and passed judgment on their neighbor.

The sentence: death.

Beckett had watched the trial and the punishment that followed, and, as always, had recorded his observations in his journal.

He had been the one to coin the odd term, "Blake's Bane."

Now, reading the words of a man who had long since turned to dust, Katelynn discovered some of the answers she'd been searching for.

And something else, as well.

She discovered that she was more frightened than she'd ever been in her entire life.

28

FOREST GREEN REVISITED

Having left Sam asleep on the couch, Jake stood beside his Jeep, staring across the street at the entrance to the cemetery, driven by his own logic to see if his theory was true.

Two spotlights lit the concrete arch in a brilliant glare, making the darkness just beyond seem that much darker. It looked to him to be a solid wall of black, and as he strained unsuccessfully to see into it, Jake had the uneasy feeling that something was hidden within its swirling depths, hiding just beyond the range of his vision, crouched there in hungry anticipation of his arrival.

You don't want to go in there, an inner voice warned. *There's nothing on the other side of that arch; no grass, no graves, no cemetery. Just one great, sprawling nothing, and it's waiting for you.*

Waiting to swallow you whole.

"Bullshit!" he said aloud. The echo of his voice in the otherwise empty silence of the night made him jump in surprise. *It's just dark, that's all. That's why you brought the flashlight, remember?* he told himself. Though he knew he was being ridiculous, knew it was just an illusion created by the contrast of the lights and the night's darkness, he still couldn't help but cringe when he passed beneath the arch, expecting in that instant to be sucked away into the void, never to return.

Of course, nothing like that happened, and he emerged on the other side unscathed.

"Nothing to it," he muttered beneath his breath as he wiped the thin sheen of sweat from his brow.

Turning on the flashlight, its beam lighting the way before him for a good twenty feet, Jake set off, knowing if he hesitated, he might lose his nerve and turn back.

The darkness pressed in from all sides.

It was a hungry beast waiting to pounce, and more than once he stopped in his tracks and swung the flashlight in a slow arc around him, assuring himself that he was, indeed, alone. On the last such pass, a sudden realization came to him, and it was one that did nothing to improve the state of his already frayed nerves. Seeing the glistening marble of the headstones that stood in silent rows on either side of the path on which he stood, Jake remembered he wasn't alone.

Not really.

Not by a long shot.

He had the dead for company.

He imagined them in their holes beneath the ground, lying languidly in their coffins, their flesh rotting from their bones, their lips pulled back to reveal grinning teeth, their eyes open and staring. Eyes that were alive with unnatural life. Eyes that could see him despite the wood and earth that separated them. He pictured their grins growing wider at the sight, their arms slowly rising off their chests to reach upward toward him . . .

Jake shook himself violently, trying to dispel the images. He wasn't entirely successful. The hair rose on his arms and the back of his neck. He had to force himself to keep moving. It couldn't be much farther, he figured.

If you go on, you might not be able to turn back, that disturbing little voice whispered in the back of his mind, but he ignored it and continued on.

Five minutes later he turned off the path, his feet seeming to know the way of their own accord. Despite his unease, Jake really couldn't believe he was doing this. Back home, with the night's excitement still rampaging through his system and Gabriel's voice echoing in his ears, the idea that some supernatural being was hunting in Harrington Falls had seemed possible. The strange coincidences that had been occurring around him had added fuel to the fire, seeming to add up to that conclusion as naturally as two and two make four. But here, in the depths of the cemetery in the heart of the night, Jake was no longer so certain.

Jake wrestled with his thoughts for several more minutes, until he realized he had reached his destination.

There, not ten feet away, was the tomb.

Maybe it was the sense of evil that pervaded the place, or the nerve-jabbing feeling that all was not as it should be there, or the perception of wrongness that penetrated to the bone like an ice-cold February rain, but whatever it was, Jake suddenly knew beyond a shadow of a doubt that his conclusions had been right. He could feel it in his heart, in his head, and in his soul. Where five minutes before he had come close to convincing himself that it was all nonsense, now, staring at the crypt, all his suspicions were swept away by a mental tide of profound certainty.

The beast was real.

As if in confirmation of that fact, the open door of the crypt creaked loudly.

Jake felt his breath vanish in a sudden rush. "Oh, God," he said softly.

Shining the light out on the ground before him, his feet suddenly unsteady, Jake cautiously made his way closer to the crypt until he stood only a foot or so in front of the door.

He was sick with dread.

Praying that his mind was right and his instincts wrong, Jake lifted the flashlight until its beam shone directly into the tomb.

He felt his mind tilt crazily at the sight before him, and his knees grew dangerously weak. He knew that if he fell there, that close to the tomb, he might not have the strength to get back up. That was the last thing he wanted just then. If he didn't get away from there, he knew he'd go crazy. As it was, he couldn't bear to look any longer.

Try as he might as he slowly backed away, Jake found he couldn't tear his gaze away from the sight before him.

The beam of light shone directly on the rear wall of the tomb.

The emptiness of the chamber seemed to mock him in return.

As impossible as it was, it was true.

The tomb was empty.

29

DECISION TIME

"Can I come in?"

Jake nodded and stepped back slightly, allowing Katelynn just enough room to get through the door before he quickly closed and locked it thoroughly. He then checked the locks twice before peering out the peephole into the night.

Katelynn watched all this without a word.

Jake didn't look so good. His hair was uncombed and wildly tangled. A five o'clock shadow lay heavy on his face.

Jake turned to face her. He put one finger to his lips and motioned for her to follow with his other hand.

They went through the living room, where Katelynn saw Sam asleep on the sofa, looking even worse than Jake. The large circles under his eyes were exaggerated by the pale, pasty color of his skin. One hand lay atop the blanket that covered his body, and Katelynn could see that it trembled while he slept.

Jake took a seat at the table and, with an unsteady wave of one hand, indicated she should do likewise.

"What happened to Sam?"

Jake shook his head. "He showed up here a few hours

ago but passed out before he could tell me anything. I haven't bothered to try to wake him."

"What's going on, Jake?" she asked in a quiet voice.

For several long moments she thought he wasn't going to answer. He sat there without moving, silently staring at the table, a distant glazed look in his eyes. When at last he did answer, his voice was a low monotone. "Earlier, when I told you that you must have been dreaming, I was wrong. It's real, Katelynn. It's real, and it's out there somewhere. Waiting to kill again." He told her everything that had happened from the time she left him in the Hemingway until he called her to come over.

Katelynn didn't say a word the entire time he spoke, just patiently heard him out.

When he was finished, she got up without a word and started out of the room.

"Where are you going?" he called after her, then reluctantly got to his feet and followed.

He found her in the living room, sliding the video back into the VCR.

Watching it a second time, Jake felt the fear that had been gnawing at his gut for the last few hours come back for a second course. Knowing Gabriel was telling the truth gave his plea for help that much more of a punch. It was no longer the fanciful ravings of a lunatic; it was stark, cold reality. Jake shivered with the implications.

Again, Katelynn didn't say a word; she quietly got up when it was over and returned to the kitchen.

Jake spared a quick glance over at Sam, saw that he was still asleep, and followed her.

She was sitting at the table, waiting for him.

"I'm afraid there's more, Jake," she said.

He looked at her, thinking he was about to get the second half of a one-two punch.

"Does the name Edward Beckett ring a bell?"

He shook his head.

Taking a deep breath, she began her story. "Beckett was a minister, a traveling one, who spent a good deal of time around these parts in the late 1700s. He kept extensive journals of all he did and saw. I've been using some of his works as references on my thesis.

"In October of 1763, Beckett arrived here in Harrington Falls just in time to witness the one and only witchcraft trial this town has ever seen. The man who was accused, and later convicted, of the crime was Sebastian Blake."

"What's that got to do with Gabriel and the thing you keep seeing in your dreams?" Jake asked.

"I'm getting to that. It seems that Blake was practicing what everyone considered to be black magic. Among other things, he supposedly had a demon familiar, a kind of magical companion, that followed him and did his bidding."

Jake nodded that he understood. He was familiar with the concept of familiars from their weekly session of Swords and Sorcerers.

"At the trial, several witnesses came forward and admitted to having seen this familiar. One of them even claimed to have survived an attack by it. The authorities took them at their word and searched Blake's house, but they never found the familiar. They did find a statue of a demonic-looking creature carved from stone, so lifelike in its appearance that they believed Blake had used a living beast as a model. That was all the evidence the authorities needed to convince the jury that the witnesses were telling the truth. For Blake, it was the final nail in his coffin.

"Beckett recorded all this in his journal, including a description of the beast, and went so far as to name it Blake's Bane. I believe the statue you found in Sebastian Blake's tomb is the statue Beckett mentions in his journal."

They sat in silence for a moment, digesting the implications.

"What happened to Blake?" Jake asked.

"They supposedly sealed him alive inside a tomb as a warning to anyone else who might be tempted to fool around with witchcraft," she answered matter-of-factly.

Jake stared at her in surprise. "Are you kidding?"

She shook her head.

"Nice neighbors," said Jake.

Katelynn went on. "It is my belief that statue was not a model of Blake's familiar, it was the familiar itself, somehow transformed into stone. And by breaking into the tomb, Kyle unwittingly provided what the Nightshade needed to secure its release," Katelynn finished.

They sat in silence, lost in their own thoughts.

"What do you think happened to Gabriel?" Katelynn asked.

"Something broke into the nursing home and ripped him to shreds."

Then Jake and Katelynn jumped in surprise. They looked up to find Sam leaning against the doorframe, wrapped in the blanket in which he'd been sleeping. On his face was a blank expression, and his voice was utterly devoid of emotion.

He's in shock, Katelynn thought.

Sam went on, "I went to the nursing home. I managed to sneak past all the cops and got to the third floor in time to see them photographing the scene. What was left of him looked more like raw meat than the remains of a human being."

He shuffled into the room and took a seat opposite Jake, retreating into silence.

Loki chose that moment to come wandering in, eyed them all, and settled on the floor at Katelynn's feet.

She reached down to stroke his fur in an effort to calm her own rapidly fraying nerves. "So it was Gabriel who was trying to warn us through the Ouija board?" she asked.

Sam nodded. "I should have known it was him. Only Gabriel called me Sammy. When that message came up, I was simply too stunned to act, then Dana's seizure delayed us all. By the time I got to the nursing home, it was too late. Gabriel was dead."

"Then what I am seeing in these visions . . ."

"Is this Nightshade Moloch," Jake finished for her.

"What do we do now?" Katelynn wondered.

Jake answered without hesitation. "We've got to stop him."

She looked at him. "What do you mean 'stop him'? How?"

"Kill him, I suppose. What else can we do?"

"We're not talking about some rabid dog that you can just track down and put out of its misery. This is a, uh . . ." She struggled, not quite sure what to call the thing. *A beast? A demon? Just what in the name of God is it?*

Jake watched her confusion, thinking that while he might not know what to call it, he at least knew what it was.

Evil.

With a capital E.

"What do you suggest we do?" he asked Katelynn in reply. "Just let it keep killing people?"

"Of course not! I just think there might be someone else better qualified to do the job. Why don't we tell the cops? They can call in a SWAT team, or the National Guard, or somebody. They're trained for this kind of thing. We aren't."

Jake laughed. "Yeah, right Katelynn. I can see it now." He mimed picking up the telephone and dialing a number. "Yeah, hi. Is this the police? Good. My name is Jake Caruso, and I just wanted to let you know that there's some creature from Hell loose in Harrington Falls and that's what has been killing people. What's that? Oh, of course I have a description. He's red, with cloven hooves and a forked tail, and usually carries a pitchfork."

Katelynn stared at him for a moment, then sighed. "Okay. I get the point. But I still don't think it's a good idea for us to get involved. We don't know anything about stopping this thing. We don't know where it lives, what its weaknesses are, nothing. How are we supposed to kill it? Drive a wooden stake through its heart? Shoot it with silver bullets? Wrap it in iron chains and drop it in running water? What?"

"I don't know. But there's got to be some way to stop it, or else there'd be thousands of them out there. The Elders managed to do it, according to Gabriel. So can we!"

"Come on, Jake! This isn't a game of Swords and Sorcerers, where you can drink a healing potion or receive a resurrection spell and everything will be all right again. Wake up to reality. This thing has been savagely killing people, including two cops. And you can bet your ass they had guns and knew how to use them!"

Jake turned to Sam, who'd been silently watching their exchange. "What do you say, Sam? Are you with me?"

Sam's gaze met his own, and in his eyes Jake could see a rage that smoldered like a white-hot ember. Sam's voice was flat and hard, but this time full of emotion, his anger barely held in check. "I want to kill that motherfucker. I don't care how we do it. I just want it dead."

"All right! That's my man!" Jake said, clapping him on the back. "We're gonna send this mother right back to whatever hell it crawled out of!" He turned back to Kate-lynn. "So? Are you with us or not?"

Katelynn stared at the two of them. They were really going to do it, whether she agreed to go along or not, she could see that. *Have they both gone completely nuts?* She was convinced they had.

"No." she said, then once again more firmly. "No, I'm not going with you. And I won't sit here listening to you anymore. You've got to be out of your mind, Jake. You heard what Sam said. This thing ripped Gabriel into little pieces. If he was one of these Elders with their mystical powers and still got torn to shreds, what do you think it will do to the two of you?"

"I guess we'll just have to take that chance," Jake replied calmly.

Katelynn could see the hurt in his eyes, but she ignored it. If he wanted to be mad at her for trying to save his life, let him. He'd done dumber things before. "Then you'll do it without me."

Katelynn got up and walked out of the kitchen.

A few moments later the two men heard the front door

open and close, then the sound of her car starting in the driveway.

Katelynn wasn't coming back.

Jake looked at Sam, then shrugged. "So be it. We'll just do it on our own." He got up, filled a mug with coffee for each of them, then sat back down and started to plan.

30

RIVERWATCH

Sam awoke to a hand gently shaking his shoulder. In the dim light he could see Jake standing over the bed. "Time to go," his friend said.

Sam nodded to show he understood.

As Jake disappeared back into the living room, Sam swung his legs out of bed and quickly dressed. A passing glance at the clock told him it was 4:00 A.M.

He slipped out of the bedroom and moved down the hall to find Jake waiting silently by the front door. Loki stood beside him, but Jake indicated to the dog that he was to stay, and the Akita complied. Sam nodded that he was ready, and the two of them left the house and climbed into the Jeep.

They had settled on a simple plan. The two of them would climb the Rock, a tall outcropping of stone that overlooked the Quinnepeg River and set up a watch. As the highest place in town, and one that overlooked the Riverwatch mansion, it seemed a logical place to start. All of the attacks had been at night, under the cover of darkness. That had led the two of them to hypothesize that the beast either chose not to be out and about during the daylight or could not. Either way, it would attempt to return to its hiding place before the sun came up. The Rock's height gave them the best possible chance of spotting the Nightshade in the air, and there was always the possibility that it might actually be hiding in Riverwatch, despite the search the police had made of the premises earlier. Jake and Sam intended to be on the Rock before then, so that they would have the opportunity to see it when it returned. That would give them an idea of what they were up against.

After that, they'd figure out the rest of the plan.

For his part, Sam found himself wondering just what the hell they thought they were doing. He didn't doubt for an instant that the beast really existed. He'd seen enough in the last two days to convince him of that. He also knew just what horrible acts of violence the beast was capable of committing, and yet, here he was actively going to seek the thing out, to discover where it lived. His anger had cooled slightly, and this gave him some perspective on the situation. Katelynn had been right. They had to be nuts to try a stunt like this. This thing could kill them without batting an eye. He turned to voice his opinion to Jake, when his friend said, "We're here."

Sam glanced out the window as Jake pulled the Jeep over and parked it on the side of the road. From where Sam sat, the woods seemed to extend for miles out from the road, though he knew that just a few hundred yards away they suddenly dropped off at the edge of the Quinnepeg River. Next to the shoreline loomed the Rock, though they couldn't see it from the street.

"I don't know about this anymore, Jake. It seems kind of crazy to me."

Jake wasn't pleased. "I thought we agreed."

"We did," Sam said. "It's just the rest of the plan that bothers me. Sure, we might actually see this thing, but then what? What happens if it discovers we're up here? Have you thought of that? Gabriel didn't give us information on how to stop the Nightshade. I don't particularly like the idea of trying to fight it off with my bare hands!"

"It's not going to find us," Jake said as he climbed out of the Jeep, looking back in through the open door. "We'll be hidden in the trees, well out of sight. All we've got to do is hang around long enough to see if it's still in the mansion, then we'll get the hell out of here and call in some help."

"Like who?" Sam wanted to know, making no move to get out of the car.

"How the hell should I know?" Jake replied in exasperation, and shut the door in Sam's face.

Sam watched as Jake crossed to the other side of the road, stepped over the old stone wall that lay crumbling at the edge of the trees, and disappeared into the darkness on the other side.

The silence that settled on the Jeep in his passing seemed to weigh heavily on Sam. Fear had come to replace the anger he felt earlier when they'd decided on this course of action and seemed to settle about his shoulders like a wet cloak. Being alone in the dark was not the best idea at the moment. Should he stay there, and hope the Nightshade didn't see him hiding in the car, or join Jake and pray it never looked in their direction? Neither alternative held that much appeal to him. It only took him another second to make up his mind.

Sam opened his door and got out of the Jeep. "Hey, Jake!" he hissed into the darkness. "Wait up!"

Ten minutes later they were settled in on the top of the Rock, doing their best to blend in with the landscape. The stone they sat upon was wet with the evening's condensation, and its coldness quickly sapped the heat from their bones. The wind whistled lightly through the trees around them, rustling the leaves, sounding like voices calling out to them from the darkness. Below, a thick fog lay a few inches above the water, swirling about in the light breeze like ghosts dancing in the night. Nothing in their situation made Sam feel any better about his decision to leave the Jeep.

Sam glanced out over the water. From where they sat, the tall spires of Riverwatch were clearly visible in the light of the moon. It was there that they suspected the Nightshade had been hiding since the most recent killings.

They sat quietly in the darkness, ignoring their discomfort, lost in their own thoughts, until Sam broke the silence about half an hour into their watch.

"I think I have it figured out."

In the dim light Sam could see Jake's head turn toward him. "Have what figured out?"

"Why there's been no evidence of Gabriel's version of history."

"Why's that?"

"Because mankind just hasn't recognized it for what it was when we saw it."

Jake chuffed, a trait he'd probably picked up from Loki. "Run that by me again."

"Think about it. If these things were supposed to have had their own civilization like Gabriel said, there should be some kind of physical record of their existence, right? I mean, if we can find evidence of man's earliest ancestors walking across the plains of Africa, then there should be some clues left behind that these two great races inhabited the world before we did. Hell, Gabriel even bragged about the Elders' great cities. Why isn't there any evidence of them?"

Jake pondered this for a moment. "Beats me."

"Maybe there is evidence. Think about it, Jake. How many unexplained coincidences and unsolved mysteries are there concerning the ancient world? Hundreds, right?" Sam's voice started to rise in excitement.

"So?" replied Jake. He wasn't sure where Sam was going with this. "And lower your voice, will you?" he added irritably.

"I'm talking about hard, substantive evidence that Gabriel's story of the Age of Creation is true. Evidence that's always been right under our noses, we just didn't recognize it."

"Like what?"

"Like who built the statues on Easter Island, for instance. They've stood there for centuries, yet no one knows one iota about the people who built them or why they were built in the first place."

Jake stared at his friend in disbelief, though the darkness prevented Sam from seeing his expression. "That's your evidence? A bunch of lousy statues no one knows who built is your proof that some highly developed civilization ruled the earth before we did? Don't you think that's pushing things?"

"But that's just it, Jake. It's not the only evidence. It is just one example. There are others just like it. Look at the pyramids. Even today, with all of our modern technology, we still couldn't replicate even one of those pyramids and get it as mathematically precise as the Egyptians did, and they used only their hands. And what about the Mayans and the Incas? Two incredibly advanced civilizations with both a spoken and written alphabet long before our ancestors in Europe had learned the value of writing. Both groups also had enough respect for geometry and astronomy to create a calendar that many argue is even more accurate than the one we use today. How else could they have done it, Jake, if not with a little help from someone else, like the Elders?"

Jake was interested now. Sam was actually making some sense. He remembered such theories had been put forth in the past, though they usually revolved around some extraterrestrial intelligence landing in flying saucers for a neighborly visit. Such ideas had always been scoffed at, with valid reason, in Jake's opinion. But Sam's idea struck a little closer to home. A prehistoric, intelligent race of "others," for lack of a better term, was just as good a theory as any for explaining how man had managed to rise from naked, bestial savagery in such a short period of time, if you looked at things on the cosmic scale. It seemed impossible for them to have done it on their own. Jake turned back to stare out into the night, pondering this new twist.

Sam's mind was still going a mile a minute as he sought to collect his thoughts into a coherent sequence. Everything suddenly made sense, and one simple answer could explain hundreds of mysteries.

"But why don't we have any relics, any ruins, from these people? Every other civilization has left something behind, some record of the past, why not this one?" asked Jake.

"There wouldn't necessarily be any ruins left. It's the way they did things back then. Look at Troy, for God's sake. That's a perfect example. By the time Heidelmann actually found the place, he found not one city, but twenty-two cities, each one built on the ruins of the others, the materials of the former scavenged to form the building blocks of the next. Maybe that's why some of the earliest human establishments were built where they were; they were building on the ruins of the civilization they remembered of old."

Jake wasn't buying all that, however. "There'd still be something left, Sam. Some reference, some clue that they'd been there before us."

"But there is, Jake! What's the one constant myth that can be found in hundreds of cultures? The myth of a great and shining civilization destroyed by some tremendous cataclysm in the earliest days of recorded history. Atlantis.

"Can't you see it, Jake? Those last violent days, as the race you've nurtured grows into adolescence while your own dwindles into its final days, your ranks and those of your enemies diminished beyond recovery by centuries of warfare?"

Sam began pacing back and forth across an exposed portion of the Rock, no longer hiding, completely in view should anyone be looking in their direction.

Knowing that in his excitement Sam had forgotten what they were doing there and the need to remain undetected, Jake turned to tell him to shut up and sit down.

The words froze on his lips.

From over Sam's shoulder, Jake could see a long, dark shape diving out of the night, its form darker than the darkness it descended from, silhouetted in the light of the stars it blotted from view.

The sight shocked Jake into immobility.

Down, down it came, traveling dozens of feet in seconds, hurtling toward its target, Sam's unprotected back.

Jake tried to yell, tried to scream, to break the paralysis that gripped him, as raw, undiluted fear squeezed his heart like a vise and threatened to shut down his nervous system. Yet still he couldn't move, couldn't warn his friend of death approaching from the night sky above.

Everything seemed to happen at once.

A sharp, shrill shriek filled the air, as the Nightshade gave voice to the sheer pleasure and anticipation of the kill to come.

Sam spun around and looked up, seeing for the first time that dark shape streaking toward him.

The moon reflected off the claws of the beast's outstretched talons as they prepared to rip and tear into its prey.

Jake's paralysis broke.

He reacted without conscious thought; his body swung sideways without a word, his legs extended out before him in a wild kick with all the weight of his six-foot frame behind it.

His ankles struck Sam's legs at a point just above his knees, knocking his friend's legs out from under him, throwing him into an uncontrolled fall that forced him right over the edge of the Rock toward the water below.

With a sharp cry, Sam disappeared from view.

Knowing he had scant seconds to escape, Jake wasted no time in thinking about his response. He simply let his body continue the arc it had begun, throwing himself sideways and following Sam off the edge.

One moment the solid surface of the Rock was beneath him, the next he was falling through space. The drop seemed to last forever, until with a sudden impact he plunged into the icy waters of the Quinnepeg.

The fall took him deep, and the cold of the water seemed to suck the air straight out of his lungs. He frantically fought to the surface, feeling the weight of his wet clothes trying to drag him under, and he gasped with relief when his head broke clear of the water.

He found Sam coughing up a mouthful of water just a few feet away.

"You okay?" Jake asked him.

"Yeah."

"I guess we found it," Jake said weakly.

Sam chose not to reply.

Jake was about to continue when a whistling sound alerted him to the oncoming danger.

"Down!" he cried, not even bothering to look up, instinctively knowing that what he heard was the sound caused by the rush of air over the surface of the Nightshade's wings as it plunged toward them from above.

Jake dived again, dived deep to evade the deadly claws that plunged into the river in search of his tender flesh. He struck out for shore at the same time, hoping that the Nightshade's eyesight wasn't sharp enough to see him beneath the water in the darkness. He planned to come to the surface a fair distance from where he'd gone under, hoping that would buy him enough time to figure out how to get out of this situation.

Jake stayed down as long as he could, until his lungs were screaming for oxygen and he knew beyond a shadow of a doubt that he couldn't hold out another moment.

He broke the surface of the water some thirty-five yards from where he'd gone under, having covered two-thirds of the distance to the other bank.

A quick, frantic look above told him the sky was empty for the time being.

It was a blessing, though there was no telling how long it would last.

Still, he'd take whatever time it gave him.

Where's Sam? Jake thought, and looked around, doing his best to pierce the layer of fog that floated an inch above the dark water. A subtle motion in the haze and the rhythmic sounds of a swimmer's strokes through the water reached him, and his heart began beating again.

They were both all right, for the time being, it seemed.

Jake knew if they didn't come up with a plan quickly, they were finished. The noise they were making was sure to bring the Nightshade down on top of them, and each successive moment they spent in these freezing waters would quickly leech away their strength, slowing their reaction time. They might not move fast enough to get out of the way of the next attack.

Jake didn't even want to consider what might happen then.

He struck out after Sam, quickly catching up to him as he floundered toward shore.

"You all right?" Jake asked softly, when he had reached him.

"Shoulder's bleeding, but I don't think it's too bad. Not sure if that thing got me or if I hit the rocks on the way down. The cold is helping to numb the pain, though. I think I'll be all right provided we get out of here soon. Any ideas?"

Jake shook his head in reply.

They didn't have much time to debate their choices.

As they spoke, they kept looking up into the sky, struggling to catch a glimpse of their pursuer. Which was why they failed to see it, when, minutes later, it swept out of the fog only an inch or two above the water, suddenly appearing like a wraith in the night, its claws extended and eager for flesh.

"Look out!" Sam cried, spying the beast, shoving himself backward at the last moment in an effort to get away from those deadly talons.

Jake was not as quick. The Nightshade's claw caught him a glancing blow across the face, carving a deep furrow in his left cheek.

As quickly as it had come, the beast disappeared back into the concealing darkness.

The pain was sharp, and Jake could feel the blood flowing freely down his face, but he could tell that the wound wasn't bad. Another inch or two and it might have been a different story.

"Jake! Over here!"

Glancing in the direction of the sound, he saw Sam treading water several yards off, closer to shore.

"Look!" his friend cried, and pointed toward the shoreline.

High above, Moloch caught a rising thermal and drifted with it, watching his prey in the water far below. His eyesight was exceptional, and he had no trouble picking out the heat of their bodies despite the camouflaging coolness of the water around them.

There was no hurry. He would take his time, for he got a perverse sort of pleasure out of playing with his prey.

The humans, as he had learned they now called themselves, had aroused his curiosity. They would never be more than cattle to him. But it was obvious that they had come a long way since he had hunted their kind in the rich, verdant forests they had begun to settle many centuries ago. They had taken to heart many of the lessons the Elders had taught them and had spread in numbers Moloch never would have dreamed possible. That made them more interesting as prey; still no match for one of his kind, but interesting nonetheless.

Especially these two.

It almost seemed as if they had been waiting for him. As if they knew he would be coming.

How is that possible?

The information he gleaned from his first kill told him that humans had long since forgotten the winged predator that once hunted them in flocks. Time had erased their fears, changing memories into myths. Those myths were altered so heavily as to be almost unrecognizable. The Na'Karat had ceased to exist for them.

What are these two doing here?

Moloch was merely curious; the truth mattered little. The end result would be the same. As the thrill of the hunt rose in his breast, he cast aside his ruminations and turned his attention once more to those floundering in the water below.

Jake peered in the direction Sam had indicated. The fog was thick in that area, and while Jake was thankful for its presence since it helped hide them from the vicious presence above, he cursed it for hiding whatever it was Sam was pointing at.

"What?" he called softly. "I don't see . . ." But then he did. Out of the gloom at the edge of the river he could just barely make out the crumbled remains of a small structure. Looking at it, Jake realized that if they could reach it, it might provide enough of a shelter to protect them from the creature's attacks.

"Can you make it?" he asked Sam. Even from where he was he could see the savage gashes the beast's claws had torn in Sam's leather jacket, and he could only imagine the condition of the flesh beneath. The pain had to be severe, and Jake knew that Sam's swimming was probably opening the wounds even farther.

Staying there was not an option, however.

Apparently Sam had come to the same conclusion. "Do I have any other choice?" he replied, smiling weakly.

As Sam headed in the direction of the structure as swiftly as the cold and his injury allowed, Jake hesitated a moment, casting his gaze heavenward, wondering just where in hell the creature was. The fog, earlier an ally, was now their enemy, hiding the beast from sight. He strained his ears, but the thick fog deadened all but the loudest noises. Even the sound of Sam swimming several yards away came back sufficiently muted as to be easily missed.

Let's hope that thing's hearing sucks, Jake thought to himself grimly as he struck out after Sam.

The object of Jake's attention was at that moment soaring high above the river, leisurely preparing for another attack. Moloch was in no hurry; the cattle were trapped below, floundering about in the cold waters of the river. Even from far above he could smell their fear.

He'd missed twice on purpose, playing with them in

the same fashion in which a cat will tease its prey, letting fear and adrenaline push them closer and closer to the edge. He knew he could catch them whenever he wanted; he might as well enjoy the game for a while longer.

He glanced down at the water, his heat-sensitive vision easily picking out the two forms below, thrashing toward shore.

His tongue danced over his teeth, and Moloch grinned to himself, his mouth salivating in anticipation of the hot, living flesh to come. With one final glance downward, he folded his wings and dropped like a stone toward the water below.

They were only ten yards from shore when Moloch struck again. This time, Jake was alert and waiting. He recognized the sudden tension in the back of his mind as an instinctive warning signal and reacted quickly.

"Dive!" he cried, and instantly followed his own command, praying as he did so that Sam could follow suit. Sucking a quick lungful of air, he hurled his body beneath the surface of the water, kicking desperately, clawing with his hands for more depth. A small voice in the back of his mind whispered that Moloch's plunge from above would in turn propel him a long way beneath the surface, and if they weren't deep enough, they stood little chance of surviving.

The water was dark as pitch at midnight, impossible to see in, and after a few seconds Jake stopped trying. The lack of his most commonly used sense disoriented him, so he was surprised when his outstretched arms encountered the slime-covered mud at the bottom of the lake.

Too shallow! his mind screamed at him, irrationally begging him to go deeper.

There was nowhere else for him to go.

Jake stayed down as long as he could, skimming the river's bottom, fearful of resurfacing, uncertain as to what awaited him above. *Did we make it in time? Are razor-sharp claws even now reaching down through the gloom above, ready to rip through my skin, shredding it from my bones? Has Sam gotten away or is his blood staining the water crimson?* There was no way of knowing for sure except by surfacing, something his oxygen-starved lungs were ordering him to do.

Jake gave in to the demand.

Unable to see, the ascent was as harrowing as the descent and seemed to take twice as long. For a moment Jake wondered if he'd gotten turned around somehow, if he was actually swimming laterally instead of vertically. The fear grew as his lungs struggled to inhale; the moment stretching into what seemed like infinity, until he broke the surface with no more warning than when he'd touched the bottom. His mouth sucked in great whooping lungfuls of air, unmindful of the noise he was making in his need to assuage the burning in his tissues.

Amazingly enough, Sam was there as well, no more than a few feet away.

"Thank God!" his friend exclaimed when he saw him, the fear in his eyes easing slightly. Jake knew exactly what he was feeling. Facing this thing together was bad enough, but doing it alone would be infinitely worse.

For his part, Sam was amazed they had survived this long.

They had been lucky.

Sam was acutely aware that luck had a way of running out when it was needed most.

He glanced around, looking for the Nightshade. As far as he could tell, the sky above them was clear. The fog was still around them, but was getting noticeably thinner. A slight gray tinge had begun to seep into the sky, and Sam found himself praying the dawn would come soon.

They had only moments to get out of sight before the Nightshade regained enough altitude to begin another attack, and Sam was certain they'd already used a good portion of that time regaining the surface. *They had to keep moving!*

Despite his exertions, the pain in his shoulder began to abate, no doubt a result of the temperature of the water. The cold had slowed the bleeding as well, for which he was grateful.

Jake could see the structure clearly now. It was the remains of a boathouse. While it looked like it might offer them some protection, it was still several yards away and would require effort to reach.

There was no time to waste. Ignoring what was left of the pain in his arm and the deep cold that was slowly working its way through the rest of his limbs, Sam doggedly resumed swimming, heading for what he hoped was safety.

Two of the four walls remained standing, the others having succumbed to the ravages of time and weather, collapsing inward against the others to form a ragged lean-to. The roof had collapsed down over the walls as the wood beneath decayed. Most of the dock on which it stood had long since collapsed as well, submerging the lower third of the structure beneath the waterline.

Looking at it, Sam felt his heart sink.

What he had hoped would be strong enough to protect

them from the beast's attacks didn't even look strong enough to survive being touched. The dock itself didn't look any better; at any minute what remained might collapse the rest of the way into the lake.

When they reached it, they discovered that there seemed to be room for them to hide beneath it. It appeared they could swim underwater and come back up inside the boathouse, safe from view from above, hiding in the pocket of air trapped beneath what remained of the roof.

They wasted no time debating it. Jake dived beneath the surface with Sam quickly following, determined to occupy their makeshift sanctuary as quickly as possible.

They resurfaced, relieved that their suspicions had been correct. By clinging to what remained of the dock support pillars, they could gain a small measure of rest for their weary limbs, but both knew they couldn't remain in the water for long. If the Nightshade didn't get them, hypothermia would.

The morning around them was quiet. Other than the barely heard sound of the river gently lapping at the remains of the dock, no other noise reached their ears.

Where the hell is that thing? Jake wondered anxiously.

At that moment, Moloch was circling the river, rage burning like an inferno in his breast. Only moments ago he had them trapped. Nowhere to go, no room to run, no means for them to escape. Yet that was exactly what seemed to have happened. They had inexplicably disappeared from sight.

Moloch was furious. Never before had the cattle outsmarted him. He would not let these two be the first.

He swept down low across the water, swiveling his head to and fro as he searched the bank near where he'd made his last attack. He searched for both a trail through the weeds to indicate where they might have gotten out of the water and for the heat residue left behind by their bodies in passing, but he found neither. The frigid temperature of the water and the rising sun to the east worked against him in this endeavor.

It would be dawn soon. Moloch hated the sunlight; too much of it affected his vision, blurring everything with the sudden avalanche of heat, making it difficult for him to see. While he could still rely on his other senses, he did not like to be placed at so clear a disadvantage. With the gray light of dawn slowly beginning to filter into the sky, Moloch knew he did not have much time unless he wished to be seen during the day. Tiring of the low-level passes across the water, Moloch swept toward the remains of a small structure against the shoreline and settled tentatively atop the peak of its roof, relaxing comfortably once he determined that despite the groaning it made it would not collapse beneath his weight. He lowered his wings to his sides so he could listen to the night around him without distraction.

Through the holes in the roof, Sam watched as the Nightshade lowered its frame upon the roof above them. Sam froze, not daring to move, even to breathe, the fear like a grapefruit stuck in his throat. He was terrified that the beast would hear them.

A sound suddenly intruded on the silence, a deep, rhythmic drumming from somewhere close. Sam frantically swung his head around, seeking the source, praying that it wouldn't draw the Nightshade's attention. He was surprised to see that Jake seemed to be ignoring it, his attention on the dangerously sagging structure around them, and it took Sam another moment or two of confusion before he realized that the sound was the drumming of his own heart in his ears.

Jake, too, was worried, but for an entirely different reason. For one long moment he had been certain the rotting structure would give way when the beast had landed above, plunging it down into their midst. The roof had held firm, though, and now they were trapped not an arm's reach from the very creature hunting them.

Now what? he asked himself.

He had no ready answer.

A quick glance in Sam's direction confirmed his worst fears. His friend's face was drawn and pale from the blood he had lost, his lips blue from the cold. If they didn't get out of the water soon, Sam would be finished.

He began carefully examining their surroundings. Maybe there was something that could be used as a weapon, something that could hold the creature off long enough for the two of them to climb out onto the shore.

A few minutes were all it took to dash such hopes. There was nothing but water and rotting wood, slick with many years' accumulation of lake slime.

The boathouse groaned as the beast shifted its weight.

Glancing up in dismay, Jake wondered if the damn thing was just going to hunker down and wait them out.

If it did, the wait wouldn't be a long one.

Luckily for them, that proved not to be the case.

Moloch didn't know that the prey he sought was scant inches away because the high, thick scent of the marshy shore hid the usually strong scent of the humans and the lapping of the river against its banks masked any telltale sounds they might make. The rising sun in the east forced Moloch to abandon the chase. He took one last look around the immediate area and unfurled his great wings. Anger coursed through his veins like quicksilver as the realization struck that the humans had escaped. Never before had such a thing occurred. It was obvious to him that the humans had grown more cunning during the years of his confinement, and he vowed not to let them outwit him again. For the time being, he would return to his haven in the garret across the river to await the setting of the sun.

It didn't really matter that they had escaped; they would not go far. When night once again spread its glorious wings across the world, he would find those two humans.

When he did, he would kill them.

Slowly.

With that satisfying thought in mind, Moloch leapt from the roof, a few quick thrusts from his wings carrying him up into the brightening sky and across the river to the mansion.

Beneath the boathouse, Sam's strength finally gave out. The pain and the cold had taken their toll. With dismay he watched as his fingers lost their grip on the support piling, and his body slipped down beneath the surface.

Frantically, Jake grabbed for him, his fingers snaring the folds of Sam's jacket. He hauled him above the surface and close to his side, keeping Sam's head above the water through sheer adrenaline-driven strength.

The two of them stared fearfully overhead, every nerve

in their bodies tight with anticipation as they waited for the wood above them to splinter beneath the awful force of the creature's blows, waited for the descending claws to savage their unprotected flesh.

No attack came.

Was it waiting for them to make the next move? To dash out from their protective cover, so it could cut them down in the open?

Still, nothing happened.

"Where is it, Jake?" Sam asked, his fear giving back a little of his energy, enough so that he could cling to the pilings unassisted again.

"I don't know," Jake whispered in reply. He hung there in the water, listening intently for some small sign that might detect the presence of the beast.

Nothing came to him.

He glanced up at the roof and noticed something different.

It was easier to see.

Not by much, but certainly better than it had been several moments before. A gray light was seeping through the holes in the roof, allowing him to make out some details of the structure and to see Sam's face more clearly.

Had the rising sun driven the creature off, like some vampire out of legend? Or was it now crouched above them, out of sight, trying to fool them into believing it had taken off? Maybe it had left, yet was only circling high above, ready to plunge down as they emerged from the water and stood exposed on the bank?

As he debated the question, the light coming in through the roof grew discernibly brighter, and in the end it was this fact that Jake used to make his decision. Jake decided that if the beast were still on the roof waiting for them, then the light would in some way be blocked by its bulk. At the very least, it would throw a shadow that they would be able to see. Therefore, the creature must have taken to the air. If that was true, and they moved quickly, they might just be able to get out and onto solid ground before it attacked.

It was only a slim chance, sure, but it was all they had.

Jake hoped they could pull it off.

He explained his idea to Sam, who by know was too weak to protest even if he'd wanted to. Jake slipped his arms under Sam's and around his chest.

"All right," he said to his friend, "a quick breath, then down we go. I'll do all the work, you just hold on. Okay?"

Sam nodded.

"I'll get us to the surface. Once we're there, get yourself another deep breath, just in case that thing is waiting for us and we need to dive again. If we do, I'll get us back here under cover, and we'll think of something else."

Jake paused, looked Sam over, then said, "Are you sure you can do this?"

"Let's do it already."

Behind him, expression hidden from view, Jake smiled. *Maybe they'd get out of this alive after all.*

Breathing a silent prayer that the beast had truly left, Jake said, "Okay. One. Two. Three."

Each took a deep breath, and they dived.

31

REPERCUSSIONS

"We've got to go back."

From his seat at the kitchen table, where Katelynn was disinfecting the wounds on his shoulder and preparing to cover them with a heavy padding of surgical gauze, Sam looked over at his friend.

"What?" he asked, incredulous. *"What?"*

Jake turned to face him. "We have to go back," he said more forcibly this time. The shocked, vacant expression he wore since they escaped the creature was gone from his face, and in its place Sam could see the first shining gleam of determination that he knew from past experience always meant trouble.

Sam wasn't going to be persuaded. As a matter of fact, he'd had just about enough of Jake's bullshit.

"No way, Jake. Not on your fucking life. Time to let somebody else take care of the mess. Gabriel was crazy to think we could handle it!"

Jake shook his head in denial. "We've got to stop this thing. We're the only ones who know about it."

Sam snorted in disgust. "So we tell someone else. Anyone. The cops, the National Guard, I don't really care."

Sam seemed to remember that that had been the original plan. Prove it exists, then get someone else involved. He said so to Jake.

Jake didn't immediately answer, so Sam took his silence for agreement and turned his attention back to examining the cuts on his shoulder. The Nightshade's claws had sliced through his leather jacket and left four deep furrows across his shoulder and three inches down his back.

He winced as Katelynn began applying the bandage, and turned to watch her to take his mind off the fact that he'd come within inches of dying. She kept her mouth shut during the exchange between him and Jake, and upon seeing the look on her face, Sam instantly knew why.

She was pissed. Angrier than he'd ever seen her, in fact. She'd been at Jake's house when they'd returned, pacing the front walk in sharp, hard strides, but on seeing their condition she'd followed them inside and simply begun tending them without a word. Now her wall of calm seemed to be eroding, and Jake's comments just made the stones start falling faster. Sam spared another glance in Jake's direction and discovered to his dismay that his friend had retreated a thousand miles away, if the dazed look on his face was any indication.

A sudden pain flared in his shoulder, and he flinched.

"Hold still!" Katelynn said sharply, gripping his arm tightly in order to reinforce her words.

"That hurts," he replied through teeth clenched against the pain, but he did as he was told. He knew he wasn't about to get any sympathy from her. She said that they were liable to get killed if they went, and they had certainly come awfully close to making her prediction come true. Katelynn didn't like it when her advice was ignored.

Jake broke Sam's thoughts.

"Fine. I'll go alone."

Sam surged to his feet, ready to tell Jake what a thick-headed fool he was, but Katelynn beat him to it.

"Are you out of your fucking mind?" she screamed at him suddenly. She moved closer, still yelling, each word seeming to Sam like a hammerblow directed at Jake's head. They made *him* flinch, and he wasn't even the target of her attack.

"Haven't you figured it out yet? This . . . thing . . . kills people! That's *all* it does. Kills people! It's stronger than you, faster than you, and about four hundred times deadlier than you. You almost got yourself killed. Now you want to go back and try to fight this thing? How? With what? Haven't you had enough already?"

Katelynn was standing directly in front of Jake by the time she finished, her hands clenched into fists at her sides as if to prevent her from physically beating the idea out of him. Sam waited for Jake to blow his cool in return, to lash back at her in self-defense; but, after several long, tense moments, when he finally did answer her, his voice was calm and even.

Hearing that tone, Sam knew they'd lost, even before his friend's words had sunk fully into his mind.

"You're right, Katelynn. This thing, this Nightshade, does kill people. It's killed six in the last few days alone. Six that we know of. Who knows how many others? No one else in this town will believe us if we tell them. That's why it's up to us. We'll get the pistol from my trailer, search Riverwatch until we find where this thing goes to rest during the day, and then put a couple of bullets through its head. End of story."

"No. That's stupid and too dangerous," said Katelynn, doing her best to regain her composure. "Let's take Gabriel's tape to Sheriff Wilson. Sam was supposed to meet with him later this morning anyway. Wilson will believe you. He has to!"

Jake shook his head. "The tape doesn't prove anything, Katelynn. It's just the disjointed ramblings of a sick old man on the brink of death. We don't have time to gather the type of proof we need to convince anyone else, let alone the sheriff. We don't have time. Every minute we delay is another minute someone else might lose their life. I couldn't live with that. Could you?"

Katelynn started to cry halfway through Jake's explanation, and by the time he finished speaking she turned and moved away from him, tears streaming silently down her cheeks. Jake started to reach out to her, apparently thought better of it, and let his hand fall softly back down to his side. He turned to face his other friend.

"Sam?" he asked, and the rest of the unspoken question was clear in his eyes.

He did not want to go alone.

A moment ticked by, neither of them moving, their gazes locked, unspoken words flying between them; memories of all the times they'd stood against whatever was the enemy, imagined or otherwise, memories that only a deep friendship could ever supply.

Then slowly, almost imperceptibly, Sam shook his head. No.

Not this time.

Jake held Sam's gaze a moment, then looked away. Crossing the room to the door, he opened it and, without turning, said, "Give me two hours. It won't suspect that I'd come right back after it. It will still be thinking it scared us off. Now's my chance to catch it off guard. Two hours. If I'm not back by then, well, then I'm probably not coming. Go to the police and tell them everything you can. They won't believe you, but at least we will have done our best to warn them."

Without another backward glance, Jake stepped outside and quietly closed the door after him.

32

ATTACK PLANS

Outside on the steps, Jake hesitated a moment, torn between his desire to go back inside to talk his friends into coming with him and the need to protect them from what he was about to do. Deciding that it just might be best if he went at it alone, he turned away and moved down the drive to where he'd parked the Jeep. Loki came running out of the early-morning light, having followed him out through the doggie door in back. Jake let the dog into the Jeep, then climbed in after him. He took one last look at the closed front door, then started the car up and pulled away.

It took only a few minutes to reach the construction site. He stopped at the end of the drive and headed for his trailer. Jake knew that very soon it would be full daylight. For that he was glad. Knowing that his friends would have continued trying to talk him out of going, Jake had already decided that his best chance of going after the beast was when it returned to its lair. That was the time to strike, when it felt safe, when its defenses were down. Believing itself to be protected from harm by secrecy, it would be totally unprepared for an attack.

So attack he would.

He pulled the key ring off his belt and unlocked the trailer door. He moved quickly, having already decided exactly what he would need on the drive over, a vague plan being slowly formulated as he raced through the quiet city streets, intent on his mission of destruction. Moving inside, he marched over to his desk and slid open the top drawer, withdrawing the 9mm Beretta lying there.

Jake crossed over to the storage closet that dominated one whole end of the trailer and unlocked it. He was more convinced than ever that the Nightshade had taken up refuge in the Riverwatch estate, and that was Jake's destination as well. He was fairly certain the electricity would still be on; it was, after all, the scene of a current police investigation, but the last thing in the world he wanted was to get over there and find himself trapped in the dark with that thing, so he was taking no chances. From the closet's third shelf he took down a large Coleman lantern and an extra bottle of propane fuel. He checked to make certain that both the lantern and the propane bottle were full, then shut and relocked the cabinet.

At least I'll get a good look at the thing, he thought with a touch of black humor, smiling grimly at his own joke.

He turned back to the door, surveying the small, cluttered room around him as he did, wondering if there was anything else lying around that might be useful. *Just what the hell do you take on a monster hunt?* he asked himself sarcastically.

Your will, a voice said in the back of his mind. He quickly left before the voice made him lose his nerve altogether.

Once back in the Jeep, he gunned the engine, swerving around the dirt lot that formed Stonemoor's makeshift parking area and rushed back down the drive, not stopping at the end but turning directly onto the road without slowing, knowing the streets of Harrington Falls would be empty at that hour.

It took him only a few minutes to reach the stone arch that formed the gateway to the Riverwatch estate. He stopped and took a moment to mentally prepare himself.

If you're going do this thing, Jake, do it right, he told himself, and took several deep breaths to slow his breathing and get his heartbeat back under control. *Won't do you any good to go in there half-cocked. That will only get you killed.*

He decided to leave the Jeep there, at the base of the drive. When he was ready, he climbed out. Loki tried to follow him. Jake had allowed Loki to come along because he intended to use the canine's keen instincts to help track down the beast, but now, at the moment of choice, he had a last-minute change of heart. Jake shooed the dog back inside the vehicle, not wanting to endanger his closest companion.

"I'll be right back, Loki," he said soothingly, and turned away from the dog's whining, his heart breaking with the thought that he might not see his friend again. He took some comfort in the fact that Sam or Katelynn would care for the Akita as if he were their own, and that got him focused again on the problem at hand.

The rising sun was reflecting off the waters of the river as Jake started walking up the drive. *Just how intelligent is this thing?* he wondered, a bit uneasily. *Does it already know I'm here? Is it going to be waiting for me inside the mansion?* The answers to those questions could mean the difference between life and death.

Equipment in hand, he began walking up the drive toward the mansion, the road stretching out before him. By the time he reached the wide wooden steps that led onto the veranda, he was grimly resolved to carry out his task or die trying. He didn't believe the beast would give him a second chance, so he determined it was all or nothing. He'd said his good-byes, at least as much of a good-bye as he'd ever give, and he was certain that if he failed to return Sam would go to the cops, the newspapers, and everyone else he could think of in a wild attempt to get someone to listen. If they failed to pay attention, then Sam would be sure to get himself and Katelynn as far out of town as possible. Knowing those he cared about would escape even if he didn't, Jake felt some of the tension leave his frame. He was in no way certain he would succeed, but at least things would be taken care of in his wake.

The steps loomed up before him, and Jake cast aside such thoughts, clearing his mind as much as possible, readying himself for the coming confrontation. At the foot of the steps he stopped and looked up.

The twin elms that lined the drive draped the mansion in their shadows, lending it a dark, brooding presence all its own, as if it were a living, breathing thing that gaped at him; the dark windows like eyes that sought him out where he stood. They seemed to stare disapprovingly in his direction. It was as though the structure was watching him and didn't like what it was seeing. He looked quickly away. His gaze came to rest on the pools of darkness that crept out from beneath the porch. This was no better, as his fear-filled mind began to imagine it saw movement there beneath the wood.

In that moment, Jake thought about turning around, getting the hell out of Harrington Falls altogether, and running for the other side of the country just as fast as he could, but his reasoning of a few moments ago quickly rose up and cast the idea back into the depths from which his mind had dredged it.

I am going in there, I am going to do what has to be done, and that is that.

Do your best, Jake thought in defiance, and stepped onto the first riser of the veranda.

In the silence after Jake's departure, Sam and Katelynn stared at each other, uncertain of what to do next.

Katelynn broke the silence first, "Do something, Sam!"

He just looked at her, saying nothing.

"Come on, Sam! Don't just sit there. You've got to stop him. He's going to get himself killed!"

Sam knew it was useless, that once Jake made up his mind about something, nothing short of a bullet to the back of his head was going to stop him from doing it. The panic-stricken look on Katelynn's face made him realize that he had to at least make an effort.

But he was already too late.

Even as he turned toward the door, the sudden roar of the Jeep's engine could be heard outside. Opening the door, Sam was in time to witness Jake's brake lights disappearing around the corner at the far end of the street.

He felt a hand on his good shoulder and turned to see Katelynn behind him, the anguish plain on her face. They had no idea where Jake was headed, and neither of them could summon the courage to meet him at Riverwatch.

Katelynn spoke softly, "Oh, Sam, what are we going to do?"

He didn't know. Unless they did something, however,

there was a very good chance that Jake was going to become the Nightshade's next victim.

An idea suddenly reared its head.

"Stay here," Sam told her, and disappeared back inside the house. A few minutes later he reappeared, carrying his backpack.

"Let's go," he said.

Sam tossed the backpack onto the rear seat of his car and climbed in behind the wheel. Katelynn quickly followed. When Sam pulled out and headed down the street, she said, "Riverwatch is the other way, Sam. Where are you going?"

"We're not following Jake," he replied. "We've got an appointment with someone else." He handed her a piece of paper.

In the light from a passing streetlamp, Katelynn recognized it as a page torn from the phone book. A name and address about halfway down the page was circled in red ink.

The name was Damon Wilson.

At that moment, Damon was seated in his study, staring at the pages of the reports in front of him without really seeing them. He didn't need to; he'd read through them so many times over the last few weeks that he practically had them memorized, even down to McClowski's spelling errors.

Nothing in them told him what he so desperately needed to know.

What was killing the citizens of Harrington Falls?

After three frustrating days of relentless investigation, he was no closer to the truth than when he'd started. It was wearing on him. By day he was short-tempered and mean, taking out his frustrations on his staff in one fashion or another. By night he was an insomniac, words and phrases from the investigation scrolling through his mind. On the rare occasions he did sleep, he was tormented by nightmarish visions of the victims themselves, torn and mangled. He'd taken to downing several shots of Scotch before heading to bed, hoping the liquor would deaden the memories enough so that he could get some rest.

It was a vicious cycle with no end in sight, and Damon knew that unless he found some answers soon, something, somewhere, was bound to break, and it would probably be him.

Damon turned, glancing out the sliding glass door behind him. Through the glass he could see that it was well past dawn.

He breathed a sigh of relief at the sight.

For days, the dark had been bothering him.

It had gotten to the point that he couldn't look out the window at night without growing uncomfortable. It sat there on the other side of the glass, black and thick, watching, waiting, looking for the smallest opportunity to break into the light and snatch another life out from under his very nose.

Damon turned away from the door, intending to return to the papers in front of him, when the sound of car doors slamming reached his ears.

He glanced at the digital clock on the other side of the room—7:30 A.M.

Who the hell?

Maybe there's a break in the case, he thought suddenly. *Maybe they didn't want the information to go out over the radio for fear of the press catching wind of it.* While he knew it was wishful thinking, Damon's steps grew lighter, a sense of heady anticipation welling inside him.

The bell sounded, and its echoes hadn't even faded before he slipped the lock and opened the door.

"Mind if we come in?" Sam asked the sheriff. "We really need to talk to you."

Without a word Damon stepped back, allowing Sam and Katelynn room to step inside. After Sam introduced Katelynn, Damon indicated the hall that led to the living room and they all headed in that direction.

Katelynn took a seat on the sofa, Sam beside her, and, without thinking, Damon chose the seat across from them, the coffee table like an unconscious dividing line between them. It was only after he sat down that Damon felt the first traces of the adversarial nature of their choice of seating, a feeling that grew as his police instincts recognized he'd been right; Sam and his friends did know something about what was happening in Harrington Falls.

Damon spoke first. "I know I suggested you make an appointment to see me this morning, Mr. Travers, but I didn't expect to see you this early," he said lightly, hoping to dispel some of the tension he could feel slowly enveloping them. "What can I do for you two?"

He watched as they glanced at each other, saw Katelynn nod to Sam, and so wasn't surprised when it was the latter who addressed him in reply. The ball had quite clearly been dropped into Sam's court.

"Sorry it's so early, but we needed to speak to you."

Damon nodded for him to continue.

"I, we, need to tell you a few things, but before we do, we need to get your promise that telling you won't cause us further trouble. If we don't get your word on that, I'm afraid we can't continue."

Puzzled, Damon stared at the two of them for a moment without answering. *Just what have they gotten themselves into?*

Cautiously, Damon said, "As long as whatever it is doesn't break the law and would therefore violate my oath as an officer, I guess I can agree to that."

Sam hesitated, and glanced at Katelynn.

"I think that's the best we're going to get, Sam. Tell him," Katelynn replied, and Damon was surprised to hear the pain and resignation in her tone.

Turning to the sheriff, Sam said bluntly, "We know what has been committing the murders."

So shocked was he at the announcement that Damon didn't pick up on Sam's choice of words. He leaned forward eagerly in his chair. "Who?"

Taking a deep breath, Sam told him.

About the statue.

About Gabriel and his tale of the Age of Creation.

About the Nightshade and the attack at Riverwatch.

He told him everything they knew. When he was through it all, Sam told the sheriff where Jake was headed and what his friend intended to do.

Then he sat back and waited for a response.

For his part. Damon had been running a gauntlet of emotions ever since Sam had started speaking. Now, forty-five minutes later, he didn't know what to think. He'd started with disbelief, moved to sarcasm, then developed a deep-rooted conviction that they had both gone crazy. As Sam had continued speaking, this gradually gave way to a surprising sense of belief.

As crazy as it sounded, God help him, it also made a weird kind of sense.

Provided you believed in monsters.

"What, exactly, is it you want me to do?" Damon asked Sam.

"Go with us to Riverwatch. That's where Jake is headed. If my story is true, you'll get your shot at the killer that's been terrorizing this town. If it's not, I apologize for wasting your time."

Damon thought about it for a few minutes. *What would it hurt to go with them?* he asked himself. It was likely they really had seen something out by the river; Sam had not displayed even the slightest sign of lying, something Damon's trained eyes would have detected instantly. And the fresh wounds on his back and shoulder were certainly proof they'd run into something. It was entirely possible that they had seen the animal Strickland had been talking about after the autopsies, and had simply let their imagination run away with them. *Could he blame then for that, considering the present circumstances?*

Damon didn't think so.

If there was a chance they had actually seen the thing, he was duty-bound to look into it.

Besides, it was the only lead he had.

"Okay. I'll go with you."

He stood up and moved to the gun cabinet on the opposite wall. Taking the key ring from his belt, he unlocked the doors and selected a high-powered rifle from the rack within. He reached inside a second time and filled his pockets with spare ammunition for the weapon. If it turned out that Sam was right, Damon did not want to be caught unprotected.

When he was ready, he turned to face them.

"Let's go have a look at this thing," he said.

33

FIRST STRIKE

Jake stared at the Nightshade with a mixture of awe, fear, and dreadful fascination. It was hanging before him, suspended by its feet upside down from one of the ceiling rafters in the garret, its claws gripping the rough wood securely, its body swaying slightly in the light breeze that entered through the open window. The low light from the lantern glistened off the creature's form, the beast's scaled hide wet with the dew that gathered during the early-morning hours. He could see that it was large, probably over six feet when standing. The multiple folds of its wings meant they would probably be something over ten feet when fully extended. Now they curled gently about the creature's body like some kind of protective screen, making it seem that the beast had wrapped itself in its own awesome embrace. The Nightshade's head was tucked down against its chest, the edges of its wings against its temples, and Jake was suddenly glad that he wasn't going to get a good look at the creature's face.

Jake set the lantern down slowly, gently, taking care to be as silent as possible, not knowing how good the creature's senses actually were. *Does it know I'm here?* he wondered. *Can it sense me? Smell me?*

With his right hand Jake reached behind his back and slowly withdrew the pistol from the waistband of his jeans, never once taking his eyes off the beast. So far it hadn't moved; that was good. *Maybe I was right,* he thought to himself with sudden hope, *maybe the damnable thing goes into hibernation during the day after feeding so much at night. Maybe I'll be able to end this right here, right now, before it even has a chance to defend itself.*

Adrenaline kicked and surged through his system, forcing him to take a more secure grip on the pistol as his hands began to sweat. Slowly, he shifted into the classic shooter's stance; legs slightly bent and shoulder width apart, left hand cupped over the bottom of his right, arms extended before him. His sneaker scuffed the floor as he shifted weight and instantly he froze; but the beast never moved, never even flinched. After a long, fear-filled moment, he released the breath he had been holding and prepared to fire.

He surveyed the beast's form for a moment, settling on the head as his best possible target. He knew he had to make the first shot count, hoping it would be enough to slow the creature down long enough for him to empty the whole magazine into the thing. If nineteen bullets weren't enough to stop it, then there wouldn't be much else that he could do except to say a quick prayer and run like hell for the staircase behind him.

The Nightshade still hadn't moved. *If it was going to wake up, it would have already done so,* he told himself.

Steadying his aim, Jake crouched slightly lower in his stance and locked his arms in their current position. He drew in a deep breath and slowly began letting it out, squeezing the trigger as he did so, the motion one long steady pull just the way he'd been taught at the range, his eyes never leaving the target.

The creature opened its eyes and looked at him in the same instant that the gun fired.

The Nightshade took the shot high in the space between its shoulder and its neck, snapping its head back with an audible crack. As force of the shot slammed its body against the wall, its feet suddenly lost their grasp on the crossbeam overhead, causing it to drop to the floor.

Jake adjusted his stance, sighted, and fired again before the sound of the first shot stopped echoing around the small room, putting the second bullet cleanly into the side of the beast's head. The passing slug tore a hole through the creature, taking a large chunk of skull with it as it tore its way back out, spraying the wall and floor with a grisly mixture of blood and bone.

Silence filled the room as the echo of the two gunshots faded away.

Jake held his ground, waiting for the beast to move.

It's dead, it has to be. Nothing can take that kind of damage and survive, he thought to himself. Even so, he held his ground, his breath frozen in hopeful anticipation, the adrenaline surging through his body like a raging river.

The minutes slipped away.

Neither he nor the beast moved.

Jake waited a full five minutes before lowering his arms, his muscles shaking with the sudden release of tension and the overload of adrenaline in his system. It seemed he suddenly remembered to breathe again, and the air came rushing into his lungs.

Relief flooded his system.

Then the sudden rasp of a claw on stone sent his heart slamming into overdrive.

The Nightshade was moving!

The beast had pushed upward on its arms while at the same time drawing its feet underneath itself for support, forcing its body up into a crouch, its claws scraping the floor as its limbs fought to obey the commands its damaged brain was sending out to them. Yet that wasn't what made Jake stare in dumb amazement; it was something far worse.

The Nightshade's skull was slowly beginning to heal right before his eyes.

The bullet had left an exit wound the size of a grapefruit, as he knew it would. The edges of this cavity were slowly drawing themselves together, new flesh and bone flowing out of the skull like clay, mating themselves to the other sides and knitting them together. In a matter of moments there would be no evidence that the wound had ever existed.

And then the beast again opened its eyes.

In the space of a second, Jake realized two things with cold, hard certainty.

The first was that the creature was laughing at him.

The second was that he was about to die.

It was a testament to his stubborn pride that the first fact unfroze him from his pose of immobility and got him moving again, his right arm swinging back up, his finger tightening on the trigger even before the gun was in line with its target.

Unfortunately, this time the Nightshade was faster.

Jake managed to get off one shot, the slug slamming

into the creature somewhere between its left shoulder and rib cage. Then the beast's clawed hand smashed into Jake's own, leaving bloody furrows down the length of his forearm and knocking the gun from fingers that had suddenly gone numb from shock and pain. Without any hesitation, the same arm that had struck him seconds before came back around in the opposite direction, this time striking the side of his head with the back of its hand, the blow hard enough and strong enough to knock Jake clear off his feet and halfway across the room.

The Nightshade moved closer, and suddenly it did laugh, the sound striking Jake like ice pouring into his veins, causing the hair on the back of his neck to rise in response.

The laugh was low and chilling, and utterly inhuman.

Unless he did something, and did it quickly, Jake knew he was going to die.

He could clearly see that his left leg was bent at an unnatural angle just below his knee. Moving caused white-hot pain to flare in his leg, and he had to clamp down his teeth to keep from screaming aloud.

The creature was halfway across the room by then, no more than ten feet away. Its arms were outstretched, its hands, if you could call them that, clenching and unclenching in what Jake imagined was anticipation at sinking those great claws into his unprotected flesh. As it approached, the Nightshade unfurled its wings like a cobra spreading its hood. Their length cast him in shadow as they blocked out some of the light from the lantern on the other side of the room, the sound of their movement like the rustling of reeds in the gentle spring breeze by the riverside.

The sound was anything but reassuring.

Knowing that he had only seconds before the beast was upon him, Jake gritted his teeth against the pain he was feeling and tried to gather his good leg underneath him, using the wall against his back to support his weight as he pushed himself into a semistanding position.

By the time he managed to accomplish that, the beast stood before him.

Jake stared into the creature's inhuman eyes and fear washed over him in a wave.

But the stubborn side of him, the one that had forced him to try to shoot the beast even after he'd seen it heal itself, that side again rose and coaxed his courage back out of hiding.

If he was going to die, at least he would do it on his feet, facing whatever was to come. His left hand tightened into a fist at his side, a meager defense considering what he was facing, but reassuring in its own, simple way.

All right, you bastard, he thought fiercely, *let's see what you've got.*

As if in answer, Moloch reached out swiftly and grasped both of Jake's shoulders in his iron grip. He dragged Jake closer, a hideous smile splitting his mouth open to reveal the double rows of needle-sharp teeth that lined his jaws.

The pain from the motion of his broken leg was too much for Jake.

Darkness closed in around him.

Out of that darkness came a voice, a voice full of menace and hatred, a voice that scurried up his spine with millions of tiny, ice-cold feet to reverberate against the walls of his skull with enough intensity to cause physical pain. It was a voice that was felt, not heard, directly inside his mind.

"You are cattle," said the beast, with the confidence of a predator trying to explain to dull-witted prey. "You have always been cattle. That is your rightful place. Watch!"

Suddenly the darkness was swept aside, to be replaced by visions of violence and gore, of a land and a time long since forgotten and passed behind. Jake's senses were overwhelmed by the blood and sudden violence, by the smells and sensations that came through the tide of the Nightshade's memory. They were so real, so vivid, a drama of such scope that he was not only an observer but also a participant, locked within the creature's mind.

As he hung there, desperately trying to fathom a way out of his predicament, the beast's voice echoed inside his mind.

"Cattle! If it were not for the meddling of the Elders, things would not have changed; the balance would not have been disrupted. Now you can find no solace amongst them. This time, things will return to the way they were supposed to be." His tone turned to one of grim satisfaction. "Cattle you were, and cattle you shall become again.

"There are none left to oppose me!"

Moloch leaned forward, his mouth opening wide to reveal those rows of gleaming teeth. A forked tongue flicked out to dart here and there about Jake's face, leaving trails of glistening mucous where it came in contact with his flesh.

Moloch's vile laugh filled the tiny room.

Jake stared death in the face, and realized that he no longer had the strength to resist. The pain in his leg was overwhelming, and it had quickly sapped what little strength he had left, so that all he was able to do was hang limply in Moloch's grasp and meekly wait for what he knew was to come.

As the beast's jaws came slowly closer, Jake braced himself for the pain. The mocking scorn in the creature's laugh told him it would be anything but swift and painless.

The teeth descended.

Katelynn was riding in the back of Damon's Bronco, listening only vaguely to the conversation going on between Sam and Damon when it happened. Her left hand held the necklace Gabriel had given her, sliding the stone back and forth on the gold chain as she gazed out the window nervously, praying they would be on time. When the stone first glimmered with the faint flickering of red light from deep within, she didn't immediately notice. It was only several moments later, when the faint glow suddenly flashed into blazing incandescence in the blink of an eye, filling the backseat with its eerie red glow, that she did.

Katelynn felt a faint tickling in the back of her mind, a sensation she barely noticed over her surprise at the light emanating from the stone. When that tickle turned abruptly into pain, like two great icy hands squeezing her mind between them, she realized that she was in trouble. By then it was already too late, for she only had time to gasp softly in pain before the darkness that had begun swimming on the edges of her vision rushed in like the swell of the tide, and she lapsed into unconsciousness without uttering a word.

The first sign that Sam and Damon had that anything was wrong came when they felt something violently strike the back of their seat. Turning to investigate, Sam almost caught Katelynn's next kick full in the face. As it was, he was struck high on his shoulder with enough power to elicit a sharp grunt of pain.

"Holy shit!" was all he managed to utter in surprise.

The rear seat was filled with a deep scarlet glow that sprang from the stone clenched tightly between Katelynn's fingers, a bright, lurid light that made everything it touched seem to be drenched in a thick tide of blood. In the middle of it, Katelynn thrashed back and forth violently, lashing out with her feet, slamming her sweat-drenched head from side to side against the leather of the seat, obviously in the grip of some kind of bizarre convulsion.

For one long moment, Sam could only stare.

The sheriff glanced back over his shoulder and, seeing the weird light and the seizure that held Katelynn securely in its grip, he reacted with the quickness of years of training.

He skidded to a stop on the shoulder of the road abruptly enough to toss Sam against the security of his seat belt. Damon was out of the car and opening the rear door to get to Katelynn before Sam even realized they had stopped.

For her part, Katelynn felt a sudden, sickening swirl of light and color, and the sensation of falling down a long dark well, where she found herself looking through the eyes of the Nightshade.

Directly into Jake's face.

He was there, no more than three inches in front of her, and she could tell by his position that the beast must be holding him in its grasp. Jake's face was covered with a fine sheen of sweat, his brow contorted with pain. The

Nightshade continued to stare directly into his face, so Katelynn was unable to see the rest of Jake's body to determine how badly he was hurt, but at least he was still alive.

The question was, for how long.

The two of them stood that way for what seemed like hours to Katelynn, but what in reality was only a few seconds, before Jake's eyes suddenly popped open and she found herself staring into their depths. Her heart cried in anguish at the intense pain she could see reflected within them; he was suffering, there was no question of that. Along with the pain, Katelynn could see the blaze of his anger and determination; a wave of emotion that caused those usually gentle eyes to go icy blue with resolve. Jake was still fighting, but Katelynn wondered how much longer he could keep it up.

They had to get there in time!

Suddenly, she sensed a third presence in the link, one that emanated from the Nightshade itself. It was aware of her presence in return, might have even pulled her into the link intentionally, for the waves of anger and fury that were directed at her almost swamped her.

A realization came to her; the necklace worked in both directions! As long as she had it, the beast could seek her out in turn, at any moment, anytime it liked, and could pull her into the twisted depths of its mind.

Before she could react to that knowledge, the beast suddenly plunged both her and Jake into the well of its memories.

She came to in the back of the Bronco, with the doors open on either side and Sam and Damon leaning in to help her. When they saw that she was conscious they released her and backed up slowly, the concern on their faces evident.

"Sam!" she cried, grasping his arm tightly. "We've got to keep moving. The Nightshade has Jake!"

Sam didn't have time to answer. Damon was already sliding behind the wheel, and Sam had to hustle to keep from being left behind. In seconds the car was moving, speeding toward Riverwatch.

34

A FIERY END

In the end, it was Loki who saved him.

Jake was unable to move, frozen in place by the pain radiating out from his left leg and the mental weight of knowing that no matter what he did, he wouldn't be able to stop the beast.

As those savage jaws descended, Jake gave himself up for lost and sent a quick prayer skyward that his friends would take his death as a sign to get out of town as quickly as they could.

As he felt the Nightshade's hot, fetid breath on his face and heard the rumble of eager anticipation in his ears, Jake turned his face away, unable to face his own destruction. In doing so, he caught a flicker of motion out of the corner of his eye and watched in spellbound fascination as Loki hurtled through the doorway, aimed for the Nightshade's back.

Loki's form seemed to glide through the air in slow motion, all grace and power, his lips pulled back from his teeth in a vicious snarl of ferocity and rage, 140 pounds of solid muscle aimed at the thing that threatened his master.

As Loki reached the zenith of his leap and arced downward, his paws extended before him to absorb the impending impact, Jake found the energy to wrench free from the creature's grip and fall to the floor.

He was just in time.

The Nightshade's jaws snapped shut with an audible clack in the space where Jake's face had been only seconds before.

The beast whipped its head around, following Jake's motion instinctively, and in the cold gleam of its eyes Jake could see the raw, undiluted hatred as the beast realized that its prey had managed to elude its fate.

Before it had time to act on that knowledge, however, Loki slammed into it from behind, driving its body against the wall with incredible force.

Something snapped with a loud crack, and the beast roared with pain.

Jake moved along the wall, away from the vicious confrontation happening behind him. Pain welled up from his leg, and his feet didn't want to cooperate with what his mind was telling them to do, yet he managed to put several feet between him and the Nightshade. A voice in the back of his mind was wondering just how Loki had managed to get loose from the Jeep; but he ignored it, knowing he was still in incredible danger and needing to concentrate on finding a means of escape.

He had to find some way to stop the beast long enough that he and Loki could get out of the confines of the garret and into the rest of the house, where they might be able to lose the beast and escape with their lives.

Behind him, the beast roared in anger. The answering snarl of fury let Jake know that Loki was still alive and fighting.

He looked around desperately, trying to find something to stop the beast, even if it was for only a short time. His glance showed Loki standing a few feet away snarling, his back to Jake, his legs tensed and his belly slung low to the ground. It didn't appear as if the Nightshade was afraid of the dog in any way, though Loki must have hurt it since the creature stood with its right side forward, favoring its left. From where he stood Jake could see that the beast's left wing hung limply at its side, and he wondered if that was what he had heard snap when the creature had been forced against the wall. Was it really that fragile?

As he watched, Loki dashed in at the beast, keeping low, snapping at its legs the way a wolf will worry the legs of a deer. Every time he would rush in, the creature's claw would lash out in a vicious strike. Jake knew that if the beast managed to connect with even one of those blows, Loki would be in trouble.

Jake had to find a weapon before that happened.

Had to.

But where?

The only objects in view where those few things he had brought with him, along with several rotting beams that had broken away from the room's walls. The gun had proved useless, and the short pocketknife he always carried would be as effective as throwing stones.

A sharp squeal sounded from behind him, and Jake knew he was about run out of time. The beast had scored a blow, and it was just a matter of time before Loki jinked when he should have jagged and ended up a bloody ball of fur on the floor.

Jake's gaze fell on the Coleman lantern, and he knew he'd found what he needed.

°   °   °

Swerving into the drive, Damon slammed on the brakes just in time to avoid smashing into the back of Jake's Jeep. Before the car had even come to a full stop Sam was out the door, running over to his friend's vehicle. Katelynn and Damon joined him there a second later.

A great, gaping hole could be seen in the Jeep's windshield. Shattered glass covered the hood as if something had burst free from the inside.

Some of the shards were edged with drying blood.

Without a word Damon walked back to the Bronco and opened the back, removing the rifle from the rack he kept there. He chambered a round, and the sound was strangely loud in the still morning air.

He smiled grimly.

"Let's go," he said.

The lantern stood on the other side of the room near the doorway through which he'd entered. Jake dragged himself across the room, scooping up the pistol as he went by, ignoring the searing flash of pain that radiated from his injured leg. Gun in hand, he reached the opposite wall and picked up the lantern.

A glance across the room told him he didn't have much time. Loki was still harrying the beast, barking up a storm to confuse it; but his motions were slower, weaker, and with each attack he came that much closer to the beast's claws. It would only be a matter of time before another blow connected. Jake could see a wide wound in Loki's flank where the first blow had struck, and the brilliant red of the dog's blood was shocking against the pure white of his fur. He would need extensive care at the hands of a good vet if they got out of this alive.

When they got out of this alive, Jake corrected himself.

With his right hand he twisted the fuel knob on the lantern, turning the gas up as high as it would go, then yelled to get the Nightshade's attention.

"Hey, asshole! Over here!"

For just an instant, the creature took its eyes off Loki and looked at Jake.

That was all the two of them needed.

With a snarl, Loki dashed in under the reach of the beast's deadly claws and sank his teeth into the soft underside of the creature's knee, severing the muscles there as neatly as if it had been done with a knife, pulling the beast down and off its feet. It crashed to the floor. At the same time, Jake hurled the lantern at its head as hard as he could.

The Coleman smashed into Moloch's shoulder just as his arm came up and around to brace his fall, trapping the flaming lantern between wing and chest.

The Nightshade let out a howl of pain and anger.

Damon, Sam, and Katelynn dashed up the stairs and into the house. From high above, the sounds of the conflict drifted down to greet them, and Damon wasted no time rushing up the stairs in hot pursuit.

"Come on!" Damon called to the others as he reached the final staircase, but there had been no need, for Katelynn and Sam were right on his heels.

At that moment, a shot rang out from above.

Once the beast collapsed onto the lantern, Jake called out to Loki to heel. At once the dog stopped his attack and backed away, snarling all the while, clearly unhappy but obeying his master, as always.

Jake loved him for it.

Moloch used his good wing to push himself partially off the floor, his injured arm and leg hanging limply at his side. As he rose, Jake could see the lantern on the floor beneath him; the beast's weight had smashed the glass but hadn't smothered the flame.

As Moloch roared out his challenge, he called on his power, ordering his tissues to begin healing ravaged bone and muscle.

In that moment of hesitation, Jake saw his chance and took it.

Raising the pistol in his right hand, he took aim at the cylinder of gas that fed the lantern and fired.

The sheriff entered the garret ahead of the others, and what he saw there froze him in his tracks.

A great hulking beast was slowly dragging itself to its feet on the other side of the room, and as Damon stopped in the entryway, it turned its yellow eyes on him and snarled in rage. The intelligence and hatred in those eyes caused the blood to freeze in Damon's veins. It was clear the thing was injured, yet even as he watched, it seemed to be gathering strength, using one of its long, winged arms to push itself up off the floor and into a semierect position.

Off to Damon's right, Jake Caruso lay on the floor with his arm outstretched and pointing a pistol at the beast. Jake was slumped against the wall, one leg twisted at a peculiar angle. Between him and the beast crouched a dog, torn and bloody from the fight, but still in the game.

The sudden sound of Jake's second shot made Damon jump.

Jake stared in dismay as the shot went wide, the recoil pulling the gun to the left so that the bullet slammed into the wood floor with a report barely audible over Moloch's snarls of anger.

The beast was slowly getting up, moving away from the lantern.

Jake couldn't let that happen!

He fired again, peripherally aware of movement on his left but ignoring it, concentrating on getting the shot where he wanted it, praying for it to connect before the beast got too far away. He gripped the butt of the gun as tightly as he could to prevent as much drift as possible; praying, praying, needing the shot to be true, knowing if it wasn't he might not get another chance.

His second shot went wild as well.

Oh, Jesus! he thought, watching in horror as the beast climbed to its feet, the damage Loki had done to its hamstring by then completely healed so it could support itself on both legs, its wing slowly knitting itself back together as well.

Jake realized that in less than a minute it would be completely healed.

Suddenly other shots rang out in the room, and Jake watched in awe as the power of the impact drove the beast right back down to its knees, huge chunks of flesh ripping out of the side of its head and shoulder, the gun obviously in the hands of someone who knew how to use it, the sound of the shots echoing around the walls of the small chamber.

Jake twisted to see the sheriff, Katelynn, and Sam framed in the doorway, the former pointing a very large rifle at the beast while chambering another round.

Their gazes met, and Jake could see the fear and horror in the sheriff's eyes, the disbelief being shoved aside in favor of action; the mind's need for survival waiting until later to rationalize the presence of the deadly thing before them.

Their weapons went off in unison this time.

Damon's shot took the Nightshade high in the side of the head, driving it backward, just as Jake's struck the gas canister of the Coleman lantern with a metallic whine.

The resulting spark ignited the propane inside, setting it aflame with a loud thump and miniexplosion. Burning fluid splashed over the beast's neck and shoulders as it was forced down by the power of Damon's rifle.

Amazingly, within seconds, the Nightshade's whole head was ablaze, covered with the burning fluid.

A loud, piercing scream of pain came from the thing's mouth as it struggled to its feet. Loki was barking furiously now; Sam was at the door screaming, "Kill it! Kill it!" and Damon was readying his rifle for another shot, when suddenly the fire that was consuming the beast leapt to the rafters above. The flames spread quickly on the dry and rotting wood.

Within seconds, that entire side of the room was a raging inferno.

"We've got to get out of here!" Katelynn yelled to them over the hideous cries of the beast, and she rushed over to Jake and grabbed him under his good arm. Supporting his weight, she began dragging him toward the door and out of the room. Sam rushed over to help while Damon let loose with another shot.

Before Jake knew it, the four of them of them were rushing down the narrow staircase, the eerie cries of the beast being drowned out by the roar of the flames as they hungrily consumed the fuel on all sides. Loki dashed past and led the way before them, still barking like crazy.

They reached the second floor as the smoke began to flood the hall before them in great, billowing, black clouds. By the time they descended the stairs and dashed across the living room to the front door, the flames were rushing from the room and consuming the third floor in their fiery grip.

The group raced from the house and took refuge behind the vehicles farther down the drive, turning as one to watch the spectacle unfold behind them.

The entire upper portion of the house was in flames, the fire raging out of control as it burned through the wood. The garret was one mass of flames so bright they were forced to shield their eyes to see it. Damon opened the door of the Bronco and slid inside to put out the fire alarm over the police band. The others lowered Jake to the ground, leaning him against the fender so he could see, Loki crouched at his side, refusing to leave his master.

"Look!" Katelynn cried suddenly, and pointed to the upper level, where the wood surrounding one of the windows had burst free and a blazing form stood for a second framed in the light.

It was the Nightshade, its entire form shrouded in flames.

For just a moment it hung there, those eerie cries of pain and anger still issuing forth from its maw, then, with a massive shove of its powerful legs, it launched itself into space.

The beast spread its wings, and those below could see that they, too, were ablaze as they beat frantically for a minute against the air, trying to raise the beast's form into the sky, yet the beating of its wings did nothing but fan the flames.

With a great cry the thing plunged earthward, a fiery comet on the last leg of its journey, roaring down through the sky, blazing, crashing into the placid waters of the Quinnepeg River.

35

AFTERMATH

"   . . . and I cannot say enough about the bravery and professionalism that these men exhibited in the face of danger. They were a testament to themselves, this town, and this country."

The news clip jumped from Sheriff's Wilson's eulogy to the long procession of fellow officers who had come to pledge their support to the families of Deputies Jones and Bannerman. The line of blue-and-tan uniforms stretched down the street, unquestionably the largest gathering of officers Harrington Falls had ever hosted. The two fallen brothers-in-arms were being recognized as heroes, and the town wanted everyone to know they understood and appreciated the sacrifice that the men had made.

"As you know, these brave officers were slain on duty while trying to apprehend a murder suspect in Harrington Falls, a small town just north of Montpelier. Shortly after their deaths, a confrontation occurred between the alleged killer and Sheriff Damon Wilson, who we just saw delivering the eulogy for these fine men. That confrontation ended in the death of the suspect and the accidental fire that razed the town's oldest estate, Riverwatch, to the ground. Back to you, Steve."

Jake used the remote to turn off the television set. All the networks were carrying the funeral. The news channels had been covering the events that had occurred that morning at Riverwatch. Knowing everything the reporters said was false made it a lot less interesting, Jake realized. He shifted in his hospital bed, trying to find a comfortable position. He had been doing so repeatedly for the last three days, since being admitted. Having his leg in traction made getting comfortable difficult. He was fiddling with the straps around his leg when he saw a figure standing in the doorway.

"It's too bad we just can't tell them what really happened," Damon said, removing his sheriff's hat and entering the room. He closed the door, giving them some privacy.

"They'd never believe us anyway," Jake replied. "I suspect it was hard enough convincing you."

"How's the leg?"

"Okay, I guess. They say I've got months of physical therapy before I can even think about walking; but they did say I'd walk again, so it can't be all that bad."

Damon took a seat in one of the plastic chairs next to the bed. "What you did was crazy, you know."

Jake shrugged. "I felt responsible, in a way. It was a member of my crew that released that thing into the world. If I had the slightest bit of common sense, I'd have sealed that damn tunnel up right after discovering it and would have saved everyone a lot of grief." He met Damon's frank, appraising stare with one of his own. "What would you have done in my place?" he asked.

"Probably the same thing," Damon said with a grin. "I just wanted you to know the official opinion before I gave my personal one."

Jake inclined his head at the television. "Think they'll buy it?"

Damon understood right away that Jake was referring to the press and, by extension, the public. "We've gone through the worst of the scrutiny. The 'suspect' I created is strong enough to hold up. We'll see some problems when they don't find any remains a few weeks from now when they sift through what's left of Riverwatch, but I'll figure something else out by then. We'll get through it."

"Thanks for getting me out of there that night. I wouldn't have made it without you," Jake told the sheriff.

"The thanks really belong to your two friends. They were pretty convincing."

At that moment the door to Jake's room opened and Katelynn came in. She kissed Jake on the forehead, said hello to Damon, and took a seat on the end of the bed.

"You're not wearing your necklace any longer," Damon noted.

"Never will, either." She reached into her pocket and pulled out a small wrapped package. "I'm not quite sure what to do with it, though. It seems wrong to just throw it away."

"I'll take it," said Jake. "It'll make a nice reminder of what we went through."

"What do you think it really is?" Damon asked, referring to the stone's unique properties.

"I don't know. I've been thinking about that for the last few days, ever since Katelynn told me what happened that night in the car. My best guess is that Sebastian Blake created it so that he could communicate with the Nightshade in a closer fashion."

"Speaking of the Blakes, any word on Hudson?" Katelynn asked the sheriff.

"Nothing," replied the sheriff. "Officially, we are listing him as missing, but I think that creature got him at the same time it killed his butler. It seems unlikely that he escaped. We're still looking though."

They talked for a bit, until it was time for Jake's next dose of painkillers. Knowing they put him out like a light, Damon and Katelynn said their good-byes when the nurse came, leaving Jake in her care.

He awoke later that afternoon. His room was empty, but a long white cardboard box rested atop the nightstand, wrapped with a blue ribbon. Reaching over, Jake picked it up and set it on the bed beside him. On the outside there was no card; no indication of who sent it or what it contained. Untying the ribbon, he opened the box.

Inside was a cane, carved from mahogany and with a silver handle in the shape of a wizard's head. A note lay in the bottom of the box, tucked beneath the gift.

"Jake," it read. "Thought you might need this in the weeks ahead. Sorry I wasn't there sooner." It was signed, Sam.

The note was short but explained a lot. Jake hadn't seen Sam, except for one quick visit, the entire time he had been in the hospital. It was obvious from the note that Sam was feeling guilty about not accompanying him back to Riverwatch.

While Jake hated the thought that he was going to need a cane, he knew that he would have to get used to the idea if he intended to walk anytime soon. "Thanks, Sam," he said aloud to the empty room, wishing his friend were there.

Downstream from Riverwatch in a small canyon formed by the twists and turns of the river as it flowed down the mountain, something crawled from the depths of the river. It dragged itself into the darkness of the dense undergrowth and slowly began to heal.

36

THE BEGINNING OF THE END

It was a gorgeous night. The air had that crisp, clean quality that comes with the fall. The stars overhead shone brilliantly. It was a good night for a walk, and since Jake's physical therapy required several of these a day, he had chosen to take advantage of the evening.

From the corner on which he stood, he could see Columbus Park.

His street met the park on the opposite side, and he always ended his exercise by cutting through it.

He passed through the gate and entered the park. In the distance he could just barely make out the dark, squat shapes of the merry-go-round and the jungle gym. The baseball diamond was directly in front of him. A slide and a set of swings were there somewhere as well, he knew, but what little illumination extended from the streetlamps behind him did not reach that far.

From center field to the exit on the far side, the park lay nestled in a darkness broken only by the faint light of the stars above.

A sudden unease about crossing that distance struck

him then, and for a moment he considered going back and taking the longer route home.

Get on with it.

Settling the grip of his cane comfortably in the palm of his hand, he started across the park. A wide stretch of grass marked the area between center field and the playground. As he headed across this no-man's-land, Jake was struck by the sudden stillness of the night around him.

The park was silent.

Utterly, eerily silent.

Not a breeze blew, not a bird chirped. The swings hung still and motionless. Even the street behind him was empty and therefore silent.

Jake's nerves began jangling like high-tension wires.

This is weird.

Jake stood there and tried to gather his thoughts.

So it's quiet, he informed himself. *Of course it's quiet. It's close to 11 P.M. on a weeknight in the middle of October.*

But why does it feel so empty? he wondered.

He glanced behind him.

The darkness seemed thicker behind him, denser, blackness with blackness, each level somehow more sinister than the last.

No, he wouldn't be returning in that direction.

"So, it's the other side or bust. So be it."

Despite his bravado, Jake wished he'd taken the long way around. Looking ahead of him, it dawned on him that once he reached the playground, he'd be in the dead center of the park.

In the center of the darkness.

His feet started moving almost of their own accord, and

this time his pace matched the accelerated beat of his heart.

The darkness and the silence pressed in on him, as if they had gained sentience through the admission of his fear.

By the time he crossed into the gravel of the playground, he'd worked himself into quite a state. His cane had trouble finding a purchase on the rock-strewn ground, and when combined with his nervous excitement, he almost pitched forward on his face. His teeth were chattering from the cold, the sound only serving to remind him of empty rooms full of skeletons, their bones clicking away in the dank darkness that . . .

"Hold on there Jake!" he told himself, suddenly angry. *This is absolutely ridiculous. There is nothing to be afraid of.* He knew his imagination had run away with him, and he wasn't happy about his loss of control. Ever since his encounter with the Nightshade he'd been seeing ghosts in every shadow, demons behind every doorstep. *He'd proven the damn thing had been flesh and blood, hadn't he? Proven it could be killed? It hadn't been some unholy, supernatural being that couldn't be stopped. He, Jake Caruso, had stopped it!*

Replaced by his anger, the fear slipped away into the back of his mind.

Jake moved on, confident he had gotten himself under control. Off in the distance, he could see the glow of streetlamps from the parking lot on the far side of the park, and it was toward those that he headed.

After only a couple of steps he found his pace quickening.

"Here you go again," he told himself aloud, his words hanging in the night air.

He didn't slow down, however. The unease that had been poking away at the rational wall inside his mind suddenly blossomed into a heavy sense of dread. It was gathering momentum inside him with every step he took. He had only one objective in mind, and that was to reach the lights ahead of him. In the lights he'd be safe.

He broke into a shambling sort of run, leaning more heavily on his cane and dragging his bad leg behind him, his eyes trained on the lights before him.

He left behind the slide, the seesaws, then the swings, and was coming up on the jungle gym.

One minute he was running in his lumbering gait, the next, he found himself lying facedown in the gravel, dazed and disoriented.

The pain in his shoulder made itself known just about the same time the first warm trickle of blood oozed around the side of his neck.

Jake pulled himself into a sitting position. Supporting himself with his left arm, he used his right carefully to reach under the edge of his jacket.

Pain tore through him as his hand made contact with his ravaged flesh.

When he pulled his hand back, it was covered with blood.

Carefully, Jake moved the shoulder of his jacket around to where he could see it and stared at the three long gashes that extended completely through the thick material and into his flesh beneath.

He realized then that he had been struck viciously from behind and that it had been the force of the blow that had propelled him face first into the gravel beneath him.

But there was no one behind him.

Maybe it came from above.

He froze at the thought, afraid of the implications.

But it's dead! one side of his mind cried out. *You killed it! You saw its final, blazing plunge into the river three months ago!*

But the other side, the logical, calculating side that threw away the emotion and faced the facts as he found them, knew that he was right. Somehow the Nightshade had survived, managed to stay hidden throughout its recovery, and had come back to finish what it had begun back in the garret of Riverwatch.

It had come back to kill him.

The voice of a dead man echoed in his mind.

"When it comes for you, it will come on night's velvet wings."

He looked upward, despite the pain, twisting his body around to see behind him, straining his eyes to see into the darkness.

He knew the beast was out there, yet the sky was empty as far as he could see. *Why had it not circled around for another attack? Was it out there? Watching? Waiting?*

Seeing nothing but blackness around him, he decided he'd stayed in one place for far too long. He located his cane, climbed to his feet, and headed for the lights ahead as quickly as his legs and fear could carry him.

High above, Moloch wheeled about in the sky, watching the human as it climbed haltingly to its feet, making its way across the park.

His bloodlust was high, but there was time.

The human would die.

And then, Moloch would feast.

Folding his wings tightly against his body, he plummeted toward the earth.

Jake was moving toward the edge of the park when the Nightshade suddenly swept into view immediately in front of him, so quickly and unexpectedly that Jake actually took another step before his brain registered the danger.

The beast hung in the air a foot or so off the ground, the steady beat of its great, leathery wings blowing the cold night air into his face, air filled with the peculiar odor he'd noticed the last time he'd faced the beast, the smell of damp wool and wet fur.

For one long moment they stared at each other.

Predator and prey.

It seemed to Jake the moment would stretch forever, leaving them locked in that timeless space between the world and time itself, until with a sudden flash of emotion in those pupils, the beast lashed out with one clawed hand and struck Jake full in the face.

The blow sent Jake to the ground, his head spinning, his mind still trying to come to grips with the fact that he'd been struck. The blow came so fast that he had only seen it when it connected with his face.

The beast had struck with calculated force; Jake knew it could have taken his head clear off his shoulders had it wanted to.

Jake looked up to find the creature standing a few feet away, grinning at him, its razor-sharp teeth glinting in the moonlight.

And then the Nightshade crossed the few feet that separated them and struck again.

And again.

And again. Each time pulling his blows just enough so that his prey was damaged but not incapacitated.

Jake hauled himself up off the ground. His head was spinning, his vision was blurry, and blood was flowing freely across the side of his face in a thick caress.

The Nightshade stood a few feet away again.

Watching.

Summoning what was left of his strength, Jake turned to face the Nightshade, his silver-handled walking stick gripped tightly in his hand as a weapon.

37

REQUIEM

Sam stared down at the body of his friend, rage and despair washing over him.

Jake was dead.

His friend had fought, fought like a demon himself, that much was clearly evident from the tableau laid out before him. Jake's body lay crumpled where he'd last fallen; one arm lay trapped beneath him, the other flung over his head across the metal rail of the merry-go-round, his outstretched fingers firmly frozen into claws to ward off the evil that had flung him there like a used-up rag doll, discarded like so much waste.

His hands were covered with small plastic bags tied off at the wrists, the crime scene techs having worked quickly to preserve any and all evidence of the struggle, determined to drag from the ruins something to work with, some clue with which to trap the killer. Through the plastic Sam could see the splashes of violet that had dried beneath Jake's nails, blood left behind from whatever injury Jake had managed to inflict on his attacker.

A technician pushed by, jostling him as he went past, causing him to look over at the expression on Jake's face.

Raw determination and defiance were etched there for all to see, as if his last act had been to spit in the thing's face. His lips were pulled away from his teeth, frozen in a vicious rictus of a smile. A smile that even the pain of his death had been unable to erase.

When Sam first arrived, after receiving the call, Damon hesitantly filled him in, letting him know what they had managed to reconstruct of Jake's last movements and the tragedy that followed.

Apparently he'd been out for a walk, and, as was his habit, he'd chosen to cut through the park instead of taking the long way around. Some hundred yards away from the road, he'd been struck and had fallen; the technicians had marked and measured the spot already, the marks of a scuffle clearly evident in the soft dirt of the ball field. The long ragged track left behind indicated that he'd reinjured his bad leg, dragging it behind him into the grass of the outfield as he tried to reach the safety of the lights in the playground. Halfway there he'd been attacked again, his blood staining the ground where he collapsed the second time. He must have turned to fight at that point, because bright blotches of the Nightshade's own violet blood colored the grass along with his own. Somehow, and Sam couldn't understand how, Jake had managed to pull free of the beast one more time, driving his fingers into the soft loam and pulling himself forward, ripping chunks of it free as he dragged himself, vainly believing the light might save him.

It hadn't.

Moloch had caught him and dashed his body down on the hard, unforgiving surface of the merry-go-round. From the angle of Jake's body it was clear that he had struck the metal bars from a height, the shock of the landing snapping his spine like a dry twig. From there, the end had come quickly.

They hoped.

The officers were all around Sam now, trying to do their work, so he backed away, his eyes never leaving his friend's face.

I'll find it for you, Jake, he breathed silently. *I swear to you, I will find it.* He turned away then, unable to look any longer, as the medical examiner's team began loading Jake's body into the dark plastic of a body bag. Tears welled in Sam's eyes, spilling down his cheeks. He looked around, into the gray light of the near dawn, wondering where the Nightshade had gone once it had finished with Jake. It was out there somewhere, hiding, waiting for the darkness.

He would find it, wherever it was, even if it took the rest of his life.

Then he would kill it.

He turned and walked away from the gathering group, and found Damon waiting for him by the Bronco.

The two men stood in silence for a minute, then Damon spoke what they both knew to be true.

"It's back, isn't it?"

Sam could only nod.

Damon thought about it for several long, silent moments, then said, "Whatever you're planning, I'm in. I want to stop this thing once and for all."

For once, Sam had the distinct feeling they understood each other perfectly.

"Where do we start?" Damon wanted to know. "How do we find this thing?"

Sam wasn't sure. He did, however, have an idea. He just hoped Katelynn was strong enough to go through with it. Jake's death had driven her into hysterics.

He turned to face the sheriff. "I have an idea of how to find this thing, but I'll need Katelynn's help in order to do it. Can you get someone to take me to her home?"

Damon nodded and called to one of his deputies. Turning back to Sam, he said, "When you're ready, call me at the station. If I don't happen to be there, have them patch you through to me on the radio, understand?"

"Yeah," Sam replied, his thoughts already far away as he considered what they were about to do. In less than twelve hours it would be dark again.

They didn't have much time.

38

HUNTING ONCE MORE

"You've got to use the necklace, Katelynn. It's our only hope of tracking the Nightshade down."

Katelynn stared at him, hearing his words but not understanding their meaning, as if he were speaking in a foreign language.

After the sheriff's deputies had dropped him off, Sam stayed with Katelynn throughout the morning and into the afternoon. The sedative Sam had made her take had forced her into a deep sleep, but it hadn't kept the nightmares at bay. They'd been ghastly images of blood and teeth and claws, a kaleidoscope of pain and horror that threatened to smother her with its loathsome weight, until she came kicking and screaming back out of sleep. The room echoed with her cries. She found herself being held tightly by Sam when she regained her senses, his soothing voice helping to banish the demons.

Sam.

She realized he was speaking to her then, and she focused her attention on him just in time to catch the tail end of what he was saying.

". . . and that's why you've got to use it."

"Use what?" she asked.

"The necklace!" he replied, exasperated. "Haven't you been listening to what I've been saying?"

She looked at him quizzically, then she suddenly understood.

She went pale at the notion, and her body began to shake.

"No way," she said, her voice a dull monotone. She moved shakily across the room and squatted next to Loki. Damon had dropped the dog off at her place while she'd slept; Loki somehow seemed to sense that Jake was not coming back. Damon had assumed the two might be good company for each other, and he'd been right.

Sam wouldn't give up that easily, however. "It's the only way, Katelynn. You've got to!"

"No," she said again, more firmly this time. *Doesn't he understand what he is asking? Doesn't he realize that whenever I wear it, I am sucked into whatever horrible acts the beast is presently committing? That I can smell the blood, taste the fear, and feel the flesh between my claws?*

Does he have any idea just how horrible it all is?

She didn't think so.

Otherwise, he wouldn't be asking.

Besides, she thought, *we don't even have the stone.* She had given it to Jake when he was recovering in the hospital, and they hadn't talked about it since. For all she knew he had thrown it away.

She certainly hoped so.

She said so to Sam.

"Fuck!" he cried, suddenly furious. Knowing Jake, the stone could, quite literally, be anywhere.

"We're just going to have to find it then," Sam said.

Katelynn couldn't believe what she was hearing. She turned to face him. "No way, Sam."

"What do you mean 'no way'? We have to."

"I said no. Even if you do find it, I won't agree to go through with using the stone. I am not touching that thing again. Leave it alone!"

Sensing her agitation, Loki climbed to his feet and licked her face. She rubbed at his fur and watched as he eyed Sam warily. It was almost as if the dog knew what he was saying, and disagreed with the notion, too.

"I can't leave it alone, Katelynn! The thing that killed Jake is out there somewhere, and I am going to put an end to it!" He turned and kicked out in anger, smashing his foot into the easy chair next to him.

Loki instantly began to bark, and Katelynn had to hold tight to prevent him from lunging at Sam.

"I think you'd better go, Sam," Katelynn said, while the dog continued to bark.

Without answering, Sam turned and headed for the door.

Out on the stoop, Sam sat down for a moment in Katelynn's porch swing to try and calm himself down. He knew that his anger was not directed at her, but at the helplessness he was feeling. Jake had been his friend, and in more ways than one he couldn't stop blaming himself for Jake's death.

The situation couldn't have been worse. Even if Sam managed to locate the stone, he didn't have a clue how he intended to stop the beast. He'd seen that bullets seemed to have little effect, so trying to corner it and blow it away with a handgun seemed to be nothing more than a fancy form of suicide. He didn't have access to anything like a flame-thrower or shoulder-launched missile and doubted Damon did either. Sam supposed he could use a hand weapon, like a fire ax; maybe cutting it into smaller pieces would prevent it from harnessing its regenerative powers. *But what if it didn't? If he managed to chop off a limb, what would prevent the thing from growing a new one right then and there? Hadn't it pushed the bullets right out of its body in front of Jake? Even worse, what if it grew a new limb, and the old limb decided to grow a new body?*

Sam quailed at the thought.

No, an ax was out of the question.

Which left only fire, something Sam knew could harm the beast. It was obvious that it had survived its previous immolation, but that didn't mean it would again if they could somehow trap it in the flames and allow the fire time to consume it completely. They had mistakenly assumed it was dead when it had made its plunge into the river three months ago.

Sam was determined not to make the same mistake twice.

Before he could do that, he had to find the beast.

He knew that tracking it could take forever. Jake had guessed correctly that the thing had taken up residence at Riverwatch, but Sam did not expect to have the same good fortune. That was why he needed the Bloodstone. He didn't know of any other method of contacting the beast.

He'd have to start with searching Jake's apartment. If he didn't find it there, he'd try the trailer. And then the Jeep. And then . . .

An idea drifted out of the back of his mind and he clung to it the way a drowning man clings to a life preserver. He remembered something Gabriel had once said, in that first meeting with Katelynn, about Sebastian Blake's obsession with the dark forces. He'd read the newspaper accounts of the disappearance of Sebastian's descendant, Hudson Blake, and wondered for the first time if there had been a modern connection to the beast as well as an ancient one.

Hudson Blake had disappeared in the midst of some sort of occult ritual, his butler an obvious victim of the Nightshade. Could Blake have been trying to control the beast? If he had been, how had he planned to accomplish it?

Sam glanced around, his thoughts churning. The day was growing late.

Sam was running out of time.

He jumped up and walked over to his car. Climbing inside, he started it up, backed out of Katelynn's driveway, and headed across town.

There was one person who could tell him fully what they'd found at Riverwatch.

That person might also unwittingly hold the answer to their problem of finding the beast before it killed again.

39

MYSTICAL METHODS

Fifteen minutes later Sam was seated outside Damon's office, waiting for him to return. The desk sergeant had a radio on low, and Sam listened to the news reports as they came in; the reporter's information on Jake's death was sketchy and full of speculation. Of immediate concern was whether or not the serial killer police had believed dead in July had returned to Harrington Falls. Since Jake's earlier involvement had been kept from the media, no one made the connection between the two, believing him to be just another random victim.

Sam knew better.

Come talk to me, he thought silently. *I'll tell you the truth. I'll give you a story the likes of which you wouldn't believe.* He knew he never could, though. Jake's death would forever be shrouded in mystery, the file permanently open, the crime unsolved.

Damon came through the door then, followed by a pair of deputies. He saw Sam and nodded in his direction, letting him know he'd be right with him.

From across the room Sam could see the fatigue on Damon's face, the worry lines cut like canyons in his brow. His eyes were hollowed pits in his skull, and for a moment Sam thought the man was ready to collapse; but when he turned and invited Sam into his office, his voice was firm and steady.

The strength Sam was counting on was still there.

Damon ushered him into his office and closed the door. He crossed the room and slumped wearily into his chair, indicating with a wave of his hand that Sam should take one of the two vacant chairs in front of the desk. When Sam had done so, Damon tossed a thick manila envelope onto the desk.

"I shouldn't be doing this, but those are the crime scene photos from your friend's death. They match all the others. It's the same thing."

Sam didn't move to take them. There was no need for a second look. The memory of his friend lying dead would never leave him.

Damon's respect for Sam rose another notch. He continued, "The damn thing is back. The lab confirms it; same teeth and claw marks, same MO. But we don't have any idea where it might be now."

"That's why I'm here," Sam replied. He filled the sheriff in on the evening's events, outlining the use he had intended to make of the Bloodstone, Katelynn's refusal to have anything to do with the idea, and the fact that he had no idea where the stone might be found.

"What can we do then?" Damon asked.

"We use the other one."

Damon looked blankly at Sam for a moment. "What?" he asked.

"I said: We use the other one. Do you have an inventory of the items you recovered at Riverwatch on the night Hudson Blake disappeared?"

"Sure." The sheriff dug around in the stacks of files on his desk until he found the right one. He removed a thick sheaf of paper bound by a paper clip, then selected several pages and handed them across to Sam. "This is a list of everything we took out of the house."

Sam scanned the list, praying that he was right.

He finally found it about three-quarters of the way down the third page. *One small polished red stone on a gold necklace; type unknown.* He pointed it out to the sheriff.

"Do you have all of these items here at the station?" he asked, handing the list back.

"Probably. The bigger pieces would have been left in place or are in storage in the courthouse basement, but everything in the specific room where they found the body was photographed, tagged as evidence, and packed up to be brought over to the lab for examination. Most of it is probably downstairs in the evidence locker by now. Why?"

"I think that Blake not only knew about the Nightshade, but that he was trying to contact it. I'm betting that the stone you found is an exact duplicate of the one Katelynn had, a matched pair. If I'm right, we can still use it to trace where the Nightshade has gone."

Agreeing that it might work, Damon got the keys, and the two of them descended to the basement. Damon walked over to a door marked EVIDENCE. Removing a key from his belt, he unlocked the door and disappeared inside. He returned a moment later carrying a large cardboard box.

"I think it might be in this one," he said.

He carried the box over to a bench and set it down lightly. Inside were several rows of sealed plastic bags and a sheet of paper. Checking the list in his hand against the one in the box, Damon assured himself he had the right container, then he rifled through it until he had found the bag he needed. He pulled it forth, glanced at it, and handed it to Sam.

Sam stared at what he held for a long moment. A slow, grim smile crossed his face.

Inside the bag was a red stone identical in shape and coloration to the one Katelynn had once worn. This one hung on a long chain of gold.

"Is that it?" the sheriff asked.

Sam nodded.

Damon ushered Sam down the hall and into a small room marked INTERROGATION. He took a moment to make certain the observation room next door was empty, then closed and locked the door behind him. It wouldn't do to have anyone see them trying this when the rest of his deputies were out searching for the killer. He might know it was necessary, but there was no way he would be able to explain that to anyone else.

He and Sam took seats opposite each other, the stone resting on the table between them.

"How do we do this?" Damon asked, feeling slightly ridiculous but willing to go on despite it.

Sam shrugged. "Damned if I know. Katelynn said that she has never tried to achieve the link consciously. The first couple of times it happened while she was asleep. The next, while she was busy studying in the library. The last was in the car that night."

He reached out and picked up the stone, letting it hang from his hand. It spun on its chain, casting streaks of crimson light the color of freshly spilled blood.

"Maybe if you just concentrate on it, sort of project your thoughts in its direction?" Damon suggested.

"Worth a try." Sam cupped the stone between his hands and gathered his thoughts about him like a cloak. He cleared his mind, striving to reach a state of calmness. He breathed slowly; in through his nose and out through his mouth, a deep, slow rhythm. Once he felt ready, he began to form an image of the beast as he remembered it from that fateful night at Riverwatch. He projected as much detail into the image as he could, relying on his recollection of the statue to flesh out the parts he was missing. Then he began to assault the image with questions, variations of "Where are you?" hoping the Stone would form the link they needed to locate the beast.

Nothing happened.

Sam kept it up for several more minutes, while Damon sat quietly on the other side of the table, but nothing happened.

"Here, let me try."

Sam passed the stone over to the sheriff, who attempted the same thing.

Again, no luck.

For the next half hour they tried everything they could think of to get the stone to unlock its secrets. They projected their thoughts at it. They set it in the center of the table and spoke to it. They held hands and chanted at it.

Nothing worked.

"Dammit!" Sam got up from the table and began pacing, venting his frustration through physical action.

Damon glanced at his watch. "We don't have time for this, Sam."

"I know, I know. Okay, maybe it takes a certain type of

person to use the stone. Or maybe it needs to be attuned to a particular individual beforehand and we don't know how to do that. Either way, we're screwed. Unless this one will work for Katelynn."

"I can always order her to use the stone," Damon said.

Sam stopped pacing and looked at him incredulously. "Oh, right. And when she refuses, what are you going to do? Force her to do it at gunpoint?"

For just a moment Sam thought that Damon was going to say yes. There was anger in the man's eyes, and a level of frustration that Sam could easily identify with. Common sense must have reasserted itself, however. Damon stared at him a moment, then turned away, shaking his head in answer to Sam's question.

"We're going to have to convince her that it's the only way of locating this thing."

Sam agreed. He didn't know how they were going to manage it, but it was the only option they had left.

Katelynn had to help.

Surely she'd understand that.

She met them at the door with a wary look, but let them in nonetheless. They moved into the living room, with Damon and Sam choosing seats on one side of the coffee table and Katelynn and Loki seated on the couch on the other.

Damon let Sam do the talking, explaining how they had acquired the stone and what they wanted her to do with it.

She listened to their story, a false veneer of calm plastered across her face.

Then, just as calmly, she told them no.

"Can't you see we don't have any other option, Katelynn? You're the only one who can do this!" Sam said in exasperation.

For the first time emotion flared in Katelynn. "Bullshit! You don't know that! You don't know anything; you're just guessing." She wrapped her arms around Loki's neck, a sign of her unease. The dog whined in reply.

Damon nodded, to show his agreement with her statement. "You're right, Katelynn. We are guessing. It won't work for Sam or me. It might not even work for you." He kept his tone calm, reasonable, to help defuse the frustration and anger that was rapidly filling the room. "But what would you suggest we do? We know the stone has worked for you in the past. We don't have the original, but we are hoping this one will work the same way. We need you to try."

Sam looked like he was about to speak, but Damon silenced him with a swift glance.

"I don't want to do it," she answered stubbornly.

Damon could see she that was starting to break. He let the silence stretch for a moment, then played his trump card.

"If you don't, someone else will lose someone they love."

It wasn't fair to play on her emotions like that, but Damon was getting desperate. He agreed with Sam; they needed to find the Nightshade as swiftly as possible, and Katelynn was the quickest and easiest means.

Katelynn stared at him. He watched the emotions flash across her eyes: anger, fear, pain, worry. For just a moment he felt the power of that emotion jump the distance between them. Then Katelynn turned away, and the link was broken.

No one said anything.

The silence stretched.

Loki whined again and licked Katelynn's face.

She turned and looked into the dog's eyes. What she saw there Damon didn't know, but when she turned back to face him, he knew before she had said a word that she would do it.

"Okay. Give me the stone."

Sam suppressed a grin and dug the object out of his pocket. He tried to hand it across the table to her, but she refused to take it. He left it lying in the center of the table in front of her.

"It will be okay, Katelynn," Damon said. "The other times you've done this you weren't prepared for it. You had no one to help you out of the trance if you got into trouble. This time both Sam and I will be here. At the slightest sign that you're in danger, we will pull you out of it."

Katelynn ignored him, knowing that while his intentions were good, they would be of no use to her if she did get into trouble. She knew how powerful the Nightshade actually was. She had done her best to free herself of its loathsome grip in the car that night; in the end, she had failed.

Now she was being forced to put herself in danger again, and she wasn't happy about it. Who knew what kind of power the beast could send back through that link with the stone? And yet, the sheriff was right. She didn't have much of a choice. To let the thing roam free and continue its slaughter was unthinkable.

She would have to use the stone.

Pure evil seemed to emanate from it, and Katelynn had to force herself to pick it up.

She lay down on the sofa, the stone clasped between both hands. Loki sat on the floor next to her. Sam took a seat on the table itself, while Damon stood behind it.

"If I look like I'm struggling, or in pain, do everything you can to wake me up. Taking the stone out of my hands should do it. Shake me, slap me, do whatever it takes," Katelynn told them insistently.

They agreed.

With that said, Katelynn went to work.

Much as Sam had done earlier that night, Katelynn set out to clear her mind of all thought, letting a dark, empty void fill her. Instead of concentrating on the stone, however, she cast her thoughts outward, seeking the beast. She pictured it as she'd seen it in her dreams, its long wings stretched out on either side as it soared through the air. She listened for its heartbeat, the three-chambered rhythm she'd heard before. She imagined the caress of the wind across her flanks, and the flicker of her tongue across her teeth . . .

Abruptly, she made contact.

The Nightshade was crouched atop a high structure, staring out into the night. Through its eyes she could see the university grounds and knew immediately the spot it had chosen for its vantage point.

Keating Hall.

A high stone tower projected up from the building's roof, and it was there that the beast was perched. Instantly, Katelynn knew that this was the creature's new lair. The clock tower had been unused for years, and the beast would be free to come and go at will, provided it avoided drawing attention to itself.

Having achieved her objective, Katelynn attempted to abandon the trance.

Her gaze never strayed from the campus grounds.

She struggled harder, willing herself to awaken.

Nothing happened. She remained linked to the beast, trapped within its consciousness.

A strange lethargy began to seep through her. Darkness loomed, then overwhelmed.

Just as quickly, her vision began to return, but she was no longer seeing the dark campus grounds. Instead, she found herself looking into Loki's face, inches from her own.

The dog growled, deep and low in its throat.

"It's okay, Loki," Katelynn tried to say.

No sound issued forth from her throat.

Katelynn began to panic.

The two men watched as Katelynn quickly slipped into her trance. One minute she was with them; the next, lost in whatever realm her consciousness had fled to. Her body visibly relaxed. Her breathing deepened and slowed. Her eyes flickered beneath their closed lids.

Her hands remained securely locked around the stone.

They waited.

Five minutes passed. Ten.

Katelynn remained locked in her trance.

Suddenly Loki jumped to his feet and moved closer to Katelynn. He sniffed at her face, then pulled back to watch her.

Damon and Sam watched as Katelynn's eyes slowly opened.

Looking at her, the dog growled long and low.

"Did you find it?" Sam asked. "Did it work?"

Katelynn didn't answer.

She turned her head, slowly looking at Sam, then at Damon.

Loki scampered back, growling again.

"What's wrong with him?" Sam asked, still not realizing that Katelynn was reacting strangely.

Damon had noticed, however. He'd noticed Loki's response to Katelynn as well. He didn't like either one. Something had gone horribly wrong.

The fear rose like a spectre in the night and threatened to overwhelm her. The Nightshade had used the power of the link against her, reversing the connection. The beast had taken control, using its mental powers to assume control of her form.

While the sheriff and Sam were waiting for her to divulge the beast's location, the beast was using her to spy on them!

It only lasted a moment, but that was long enough.

Just as Damon stepped toward her, just as Sam was reaching out to her, just as Loki was about to attack, the Nightshade released its hold and the connection between them was broken.

Darkness descended in Katelynn's mind for a second time that night.

Katelynn came to in Sam's arms, a cold cloth pressed against her forehead. Loki was standing next to the sofa, trying desperately to lick her face while being held back by Damon, who stood with a hand wrapped around the dog's collar and his gun pointed in her direction.

"Are you all right?" Sam asked, concern etched on his face.

Katelynn didn't trust herself to speak, so she nodded instead.

Damon still looked suspicious, but lowered his gun nonetheless. "What happened?" he asked.

Katelynn took several deep breaths, doing what she could to get her heart back under control. She was bathed in sweat, her long hair hanging in limp strands about her face. Her hands were shaking when she answered him.

"I found it," she said. "At the university. It's using the old clock tower as an aerie."

"Yes!" Sam cried exuberantly.

Damon had not yet taken his eyes off Katelynn. "And?"

Katelynn continued to meet his gaze. "The link worked both ways this time. There wasn't anything I could do to stop it. Before I could get free, it took control of my senses and got a good long look at the two of you. We discovered where it is hiding, yes, but it knows now that we're coming after it. We don't have much time."

Grimly, Damon nodded.

He had suspected as much when the dog had gone crazy, ready to rip Katelynn's throat out when she opened her eyes the first time.

"What do we do?" Sam asked, his excitement stifled in lieu of what he'd just learned.

Damon turned to face him. "Do?" he asked. "Same thing we had planned to do. We find it and kill it."

"But it knows we're coming. We won't stand a chance," Sam said flatly.

Damon gave him a steely look. "Do we have any choice?"

40

PREPARATIONS

They moved quickly. While it might prefer to travel at night, that didn't mean the Nightshade wouldn't travel by day and simply take to the air, disappearing again, only to find another resting place elsewhere. Who knew if they'd be able to track it down again? The next time they might not be so lucky. They didn't know the range of Katelynn's talent. It was also obvious that Katelynn had survived the encounter because she'd already been trying to break contact when the beast had become aware of her presence. What would happen if it threw the full weight of its mental powers at her the very instant she sought contact? Would she then have the power to free herself? They didn't know and couldn't take the chance. If they could reach the campus before too much time passed, they might be able to stop the beast from leaving, or at the very least, follow it when and if it did.

"Okay," Damon said, a look of weary resignation on his face. "We know where it is, but what good does that do us? We still don't have a clue as to how to stop it."

When Damon looked up, however, the gleam in Sam's eyes made it obvious that that might not be the case.

Sam had a plan. Taking a deep breath, he let them in on it.

As Damon sat and listened, something totally unexpected and all but forgotten bloomed in his chest. For the first time since the killings had begun, Damon felt a surge of hope.

When Sam was finished, Katelynn expected the sheriff to object. What Sam was proposing was as crazy as Jake's original plan of facing the Nightshade on his own. They simply were not equipped to handle such a task. They should be calling in the National Guard, not trying to assault the beast's latest lair on their own. She waited for Damon to echo her thoughts aloud.

Katelynn was in for a surprise. With a vengeful light in his eye that matched the one in Sam's, Damon simply said, "Let's do it." Using his radio, he called one of his deputies and ordered the man to meet them at the sheriff's station with the items they needed. Leaving Katelynn's, the three of them drove to the station, making a brief stop at a gas station along the way.

A short time later, Katelynn and Sam were pouring old-fashioned soap flakes into mason jars and passing them on to Damon, who filled them the rest of the way with gasoline and screwed on spill-proof lids. While Sam and Katelynn packed them carefully into two black knapsacks, Damon moved over to the gun cabinet behind his desk and selected a rifle. Loading up on ammunition for the weapon, he asked them, "Either of you know how to handle a firearm?"

"A little," said Sam. Katelynn shook her head.

Damon sighed. Weapon in hand, he turned to face them, a grim expression on his face.

"Let's end this," he said.

The three of them left without a word to the rest of Damon's staff; they simply had no time to explain.

Like a flashback to that evening three months before, the three of them climbed into Damon's Bronco and headed across town as a light rain began to fall.

When they arrived at the university campus, Damon made a quick stop at the security office to obtain the keys to the campus buildings. About once a month he personally patrolled the grounds, seeing and being seen, so the guard on duty found nothing strange in his request.

Once Damon returned to the vehicle, he drove them over to Keating Hall.

The building loomed above them, and the very sight of it sent chills up Katelynn's spine. She knew what was hiding inside its cold stone walls. *It will be a miracle if we make it out alive,* she thought.

Sam, on the other hand, stared at the structure with fierce expectation. He, too, knew what awaited them there, but he welcomed the challenge. That thing had killed his best friend, threatened a woman he cared deeply for, and terrorized the town he called home. It was due for a reckoning, and Sam intended to be the one to deliver it.

It was ironic that the Nightshade had chosen this place for the final showdown. Keating Hall had been built in the late 1800s and was constructed in a Renaissance style. It looked like a medieval castle, the clock tower rising over the roof like a keep rising over a castle's battlements. He had written it into many a short story, the building's very nature firing his imagination.

Now, fiction would become reality.

Sam was determined to write the ending his way.

Once out of the car, Katelynn and Sam huddled out of the rain on the steps in front of the entrance while Damon retrieved his rifle from the trunk. Damon knew the weapon wouldn't stop the beast; the night they rescued Jake had proven that. It would slow it down, however, and that's what the plan called for. Damon was to use the weapon to render the beast momentarily incapacitated, just long enough for Katelynn and Sam to do the rest.

It was a military axiom that no plan survives contact with the enemy, and Damon prayed that just this once, that would prove false.

Damon unlocked Keating's front door, and the others followed him inside.

The three of them turned on the flashlights they'd brought with them and set off down the hall.

Katelynn's vision had shown the Nightshade to be inside the clock tower that rose above the main building, so they quickly climbed to the top floor.

Damon held up his hand for quiet and listened to any sound in the silence as the echoes of their footsteps in the empty building died away.

He heard nothing besides their own breathing.

The corridor stretched directly ahead of them. In order to gain entry to the tower, they had to traverse the corridor, exit through the door at the other end, climb the stairs just beyond, cross the roof to the tower itself, go through another door, and climb another set of steps to the chamber at the top. It was there that they expected to find the Nightshade.

They'd be exposed to attack from the front and behind the entire time.

Not a very comforting thought, Damon thought to himself.

A sudden crash of thunder from the storm outside was accompanied seconds later by a flash of lightning. For a moment the corridor before them was fully illuminated. Damon was relieved to see that it was empty.

"Looks okay," he said to the others. "Let's go." He started down the hall.

About time, Sam thought as he set out after Damon, Katelynn between them. He knew Damon was correct in being cautious, but the rage he felt was growing. It was like a living thing inside him, and he fought to control it, for he knew that it could work against him, blinding his perceptions and clouding his judgment.

When they reached the other end of the hall, Damon slowly pushed open the door, looked around, and signaled them forward. Passing through the doorway, they emerged onto the roof.

From where they stood, the tower was directly ahead of them, some fifty feet away. The roof between them was shrouded in darkness, but the tower itself was brilliantly lit by the large spotlights erected along the roof's edge and shining on the face of the tower itself. The rain dashed down upon the trio and in just a few steps they were soaked through to the skin.

Maybe she caught a flash of movement out of the corner of one eye, or heard the sudden sound of an extra set of footfalls striking the wet stone of the rooftop; Katelynn wasn't ever certain what made her turn and glance back the way they had come. Whatever the reason, she was in time to discover that there was someone on the rooftop with them.

Whoever it was was running directly toward them.

Her mind registered all this in the space of a heartbeat. She reacted without thought.

"Behind us!" she cried.

The figure was almost upon them when Katelynn dived to her right.

She acted not a moment too soon. As she fell, she heard the whistle of something slice through the air less than an inch above her head and knew in that instant that she had come perilously close to dying.

The sound of metal striking metal reached her ears and Katelynn looked frantically toward the sound. Sam stood nearby, frozen in indecision.

Damon stood several feet away, facing them but backpedaling furiously as a figure in a hooded robe closed in on him. Damon's hands were empty; the rifle he'd been holding only moments before now missing.

Katelynn rose to her feet and tried desperately to figure out what to do in order to help Damon.

It was obvious the man was playing with Damon. The newcomer was dressed in the tattered remnants of what once had been a rather luxurious robe, the front of which was discolored with a dark stain. In the man's hands was a bejeweled sword, something that would have looked more in place in the Smithsonian than on a rain-slick roof in the hands of a madman. The sword came closer with each slash and jab. The sheriff frantically skipped backward, away from its razor-sharp edge.

As the two maneuvered, Katelynn was able to get a good look at the man's face. It was twisted into an expression of utter fury, his flesh so gaunt it appeared to have been stretched across the frame of his bones. Within this mask eyes gleamed with fanatical hatred.

Despite the man's appearance, Katelynn had no trouble recognizing him.

Hudson Blake.

Katelynn watched as Blake swung his weapon, and this time Damon proved to be too slow in getting out of the way. A cry of pain filled the air and blood flowed as the sword opened a long, shallow cut on Damon's ribs as he leapt to the side in an effort to avoid the blow.

Damon's frantic attempts to avoid the blade by twisting and turning away from it were preventing him from drawing his revolver, leaving him all but defenseless against the attack.

Katelynn knew she and Sam had to do something quickly to help.

She glanced around frantically, looking for a weapon, and spotted Damon's rifle lying against the roof's parapet.

She went after it, knowing she had only seconds before Blake tired of the game and skewered Damon.

Sam watched as Blake suddenly switched tactics and thrust his weapon point first at Damon. A cry of pain quickly followed and Sam watched in horror as Damon collapsed onto the rooftop.

The blade of Blake's sword glistened.

Katelynn swung the rifle in Blake's direction, her hands unfamiliar on the stock.

The old man was faster than either she or Sam could have ever expected.

He was there in front of her in what seemed like the blink of an eye, his own weapon swinging through the air and colliding with the barrel of the gun just as she got it pointed in his direction.

The force of the blow carried the rifle up and out of

Katelynn's hands. From several feet away Sam watched in dismay as the rifle went over her shoulder, disappearing into the darkness on the other side of the parapet, no doubt headed swiftly for the ground far below.

A wide smile crossed Blake's face then, and he raised his sword for another strike at Katelynn.

"No!" Sam screamed, suddenly entering the fray by hurling himself directly into Blake.

Sam struck Blake just below his upraised arms, knocking him off-balance. Somewhere in the back of Sam's mind he registered the clang as the madman's sword struck the stone beneath their feet instead of Katelynn's tender flesh.

With Blake locked in his embrace, Sam slammed him against the rooftop.

He landed badly, striking his head against the stone. Dazed, he could not summon the strength to prevent Blake from rolling them over, trapping Sam on the bottom.

Somehow Blake had retained his grip on his sword throughout the struggle and Sam looked up as Blake raised the weapon over his head, the pommel gripped securely in both of the old man's hands, the sword ready for a sharp downward thrust to finish Sam off.

Oh, fuck, Sam thought, too tired and dazed to offer any resistance.

Two shots rang out and something hot and sticky splashed across Sam's face, blinding him momentarily.

Seconds later Blake collapsed onto Sam, the sword falling from his grasp to clatter on the stone beside him.

Katelynn was suddenly at Sam's side, wiping the blood out of his eyes so that he could see. He turned his head and saw Damon crouched a few yards away, one hand holding tight to the bleeding wound Blake's sword had caused in his side, the other still holding the pistol with which he had just shot Blake. The pistol's muzzle was held rock steady, not wavering from the old man's body as Damon waited a moment to be certain he was out of the fight.

When it definitely looked like Blake was not going to get up again, Damon rose from his crouch and walked over to them.

Katelynn helped Sam get out from under the body, glad the man's head was partially hidden by his arms so that she wouldn't have to look at what must be a gaping wound in the middle of his face where Damon had shot him. They stood up just as Damon reached them.

"You two okay?" the sheriff asked.

Katelynn nodded, as did Sam. He was still a bit surprised to find himself alive and didn't trust himself to speak.

"How badly are you hurt?" Katelynn asked Damon.

He grimaced with pain as he moved, but said simply, "I'll make it," and changed the subject. "We'd better check on the status of our weapons."

Katelynn's warning had allowed Damon an extra second to set his knapsack down on the rooftop before Blake's charge had reached them, so the bottles of home-made napalm inside were still secure. Those inside Sam's pack had been less fortunate; he'd been wearing the pack strapped across his back when he crashed into Blake, and the resulting fall had broken them all.

"Why don't you take this, Sam?" Damon said, holding out the pack to him. "That way my hands will be free."

Realizing Damon's pistol was their only means of defense now that the rifle was gone, Sam didn't disagree. He slung Damon's pack loosely over one shoulder and they headed across the rooftop.

Damon moved slower than the others and was therefore a step or two behind them when they reached the door to the tower and stepped inside.

Damon called out to tell them to wait, but the heavy iron door suddenly swung shut in his face seemingly of its own accord, cutting him off from the others.

No sooner had it done so than a loud cry of surprise and fear reached his ears from the other side of the door.

The sound galvanized Damon.

He yanked open the door and moved quickly inside the room, his pistol held out before him, the pain in his side momentarily forgotten.

On the opposite side of the room, the Nightshade stood waiting.

41

ILLUSIONS

Katelynn and Sam were nowhere in sight.

The room was empty, except for the Nightshade.

Damon stared at it, taking in the details. It seemed larger than before, but that could have been a result of his fear.

The beast caught his gaze and stared back.

Damon could see the cold gleam of intelligence and hatred shining forth from its yellow eyes.

The room spun for a moment, and Damon swayed dizzily in response, his grip instinctively tightening on his weapon lest he lose it. He briskly shook his head, trying to shake off the feeling, then looked across the room to assure himself of the beast's position.

To his horror, two other Nightshades had joined the first.

As he watched, the beasts began to spread out around him, moving swiftly in an attempt to cut off his retreat.

Damon glanced swiftly around, trying to keep all of them in sight at the same time, aware that if they rushed him, he wouldn't be able to defend himself. He couldn't cover all sides, and when he turned to deal with one, another would try to close in on him from behind.

Where the hell are Sam and Katelynn? he thought. They'd come in only seconds before him, and he hadn't hesitated when he'd heard Katelynn's cry. *Could the beasts have taken them so swiftly?*

Yet, there were no bodies, no blood. Except for Katelynn's cry, there hadn't even been sounds of a struggle.

So where in hell were they?

One of the beasts took a step forward, forcing Damon to turn toward it to cover the threat, and behind him he heard an answering scrape of claws on stone as another of the creatures took that opportunity to advance a little closer to his back.

Damon swiftly turned to face the new threat, his heart hammering wildly. Other than the door through which he'd entered, now guarded by one of the beasts, the only other way out was directly opposite him on the other side of the room.

Unfortunately, he'd have to go through three of the beasts to reach it.

A thought struck him. *Could Sam and Katelynn have already gone through the other door?*

Damon estimated the distance from where he stood to the door to be about thirty feet. Maybe they had already passed through the other door before the Nightshades had decided to show themselves, and Katelynn's cry had not been cut off by an attack but rather by the slamming of the heavy wooden door as it swung shut behind them.

Movement to his left forced him to spin in that direction, and he was forced to put the others out of his mind.

As he twisted around, doing what he could to keep them all in sight, Damon considered rushing the beast behind him and getting back out onto the rooftop, then just as quickly dismissed the idea. He would be leaving the others completely at the mercy of these beasts, and he wasn't about to abandon them if there was even a chance that they were still alive.

His decision meant he must not only hold the creatures at bay but also destroy them somehow in the process.

He just wished he knew how.

Katelynn didn't understand what was happening.

When she and Sam had entered the room and found the Nightshade waiting for them, she'd let out a not altogether involuntary cry of surprise, which had served to bring Damon rushing into the room behind them.

From there, everything stopped making sense.

Damon had stepped into the room, gotten maybe ten feet past the door, and had frozen in place, staring at the beast in what appeared to be dread fascination. Expecting him to start shooting, she and Sam had moved off to Damon's right, out of the line of fire.

Damon had done nothing.

He'd simply stood there, staring, his mouth open in astonishment.

That had gone on for a moment or two when Katelynn decided she had to do something.

So far, the Nightshade had ignored the two of them, its attention transfixed on Damon. Katelynn thought it had recognized the pistol in Damon's hands as a weapon, and had decided that he was the obvious, immediate threat. While Sam was armed, nothing he carried could be immediately identified as such, and Katelynn's hands were empty.

It seemed the beast had written them off for the time being.

She called out to Damon, trying to get his attention off the beast, which obviously had some sort of hold over him.

Damon either did not hear her or chose not to acknowledge that he had.

Sam added his voice to hers, and although the creature flicked its ears in their direction, it did not move or shift its gaze from Damon's form.

Katelynn broke from Sam's side and headed into the center of the room, not yet knowing exactly what she intended to do but knowing she had to do something.

Damon must have caught the movement out of the corner of his eye. He turned in her direction.

And pointed his pistol directly at her.

One of the smaller Nightshades that had up until then kept against the wall was coming toward him. He didn't want any of the things anywhere within striking distance. Despite this one's small size, there was still no question that its claws were as razor-sharp as the others.

Damon took a step or two backward to widen the distance between them, keeping his target squarely in his sights.

Katelynn stopped in midstride, one foot still raised in the air, as she saw Damon raise his pistol and point it in her direction. This close, the barrel of the gun seemed impossibly wide, and she could almost believe she could look down its length to see the bullet inside.

From the glazed look in Damon's eyes, Katelynn knew he was not seeing her. His lack of response to her earlier cries suddenly made sense as she realized he was seeing something else, some phantom in his mind that the Nightshade must have conjured forth. That Damon perceived her as a threat was not in doubt; the hand holding the pistol on her didn't waver an inch. Katelynn slowly put her foot down, and tried to decide what to do.

She looked up, tearing her gaze away from the gun, and searched Damon's face for any sign of recognition.

There wasn't any.

She saw only hatred and fear.

In that moment, things went from bad to worse.

From where she stood, Katelynn watched in horror as the doorway behind Damon suddenly filled with a human form. One side of the man's face was a devastated ruin, the left eye mangled beyond recognition from the bullet that had torn through that side of his face. Blood flowed freely from the wound, mixing with the steady flow that poured out of a similar wound in the man's upper chest. Despite the injuries, his stance was firm, his smile grim, and in his hands he held the sword.

In the next instant, Hudson Blake extended the sword directly before him and charged at Damon!

Damon saw the beast's gaze flick past his shoulder and knew in that instant that he'd been trapped. Determined at least to cause some damage before dying, Damon ignored the motion behind him for a second, just long enough to squeeze off a shot at the creature in front of him.

A sharp, cold numbness pierced his back as he pulled the trigger. He watched as the beast before him was thrown backward by the force of the shot, but knew instinctively that he hadn't hit it in any particularly vital area, the attack from behind having spoiled his aim.

Then a nova-hot blaze of pain surged up from his stomach and caused him to glance down in shock, only to discover half a foot of cold steel protruding from an area just left of his navel. Blood pumped from the wound in a surging, crimson tide and Damon knew his time had just run out.

So be it.

At least he'd take some of them with him.

His gaze fell on the form on the floor in front of him, and he blinked his eyes in shocked disbelief. That wave of chestnut hair, that long-limbed form was unmistakable, and in a corner of his pain-filled mind Damon found himself wondering how he could ever have mistaken Katelynn for a Nightshade. Whoever was wielding the sword chose that moment to yank it violently from his body. He dimly heard the clatter of his gun striking the floor in front of him, and Damon felt the world around him spin as he slipped into a darkness deeper than night.

Katelynn found herself lying on her stomach, gazing at the floor in dazed bewilderment. She was aware of a sharp pain radiating up from her leg, reminding her of what had just occurred. Blake's attack had spoiled Damon's aim, so she had taken the bullet in the leg instead of the chest. The force of the blow had knocked her off her feet.

She lifted her head and looked around, discovering that Damon's gun lay just inches from her. Damon himself lay crumpled on the floor a few feet away, a brilliant crimson stain spreading across the floor around him.

Blake was raising his weapon for another strike, looking more than anything as if he intended to cleave Damon's head from his body with that one, simple stroke.

It only took an instant for all of this to register in Katelynn's mind.

Then she reacted.

As Blake advanced the last few steps and raised his sword high over his head, Katelynn lunged out and grasped Damon's pistol.

Blake started the downstroke of his sword.

As if in slow motion, Katelynn watched the sword cutting through the air, watched as her own arm raised the weapon and pointed it in Blake's direction.

She had just a fleeting instant to pray, then she pulled the trigger.

The shot took Blake high in the chest for the second time that night, throwing him backward several feet. The sword spun through the air, off to one side.

Katelynn barely noticed.

She was too busy pulling the barrel down in line with Blake and firing again.

And again.

The second shot opened a red wound in his stomach.

The third flung him violently backward off his feet to lie unmoving on the floor.

She inched forward, keeping the gun on him, until she was close enough to see that he was no longer breathing.

Satisfied the son of a bitch wasn't going to get up again, she turned her attention to the wound in her leg. It was bleeding freely, but not heavily, and she clamped her hand tightly to it while using the other to strip off her belt. She wrapped the belt around her leg just above the wound and cinched it tight. The pain was intense, but she was relieved to see that the wound wasn't spraying blood the way it would have been had the bullet struck a major artery.

She glanced around for Sam, but didn't see him or the Nightshade any longer. She then turned her attention to Damon alone.

He hadn't moved since he'd fallen.

When she dragged herself over to him, she discovered he was alive but unconscious. From the amount of blood staining the floor, however, he might not stay that way for long.

Katelynn stripped off her sodden sweatshirt and was wadding it up to use as a compress when Damon opened his eyes.

"Katelynn," he gurgled, blood trickling out of the corner of his mouth.

That wasn't a good sign, she knew.

"Easy, Sheriff. It's okay." She rolled him onto his side and pressed the sweatshirt against the wound in his back, where it quickly became saturated with blood.

She rolled him faceup, his weight causing the sweatshirt to become a makeshift compress on the wound.

Her actions had sent pain flaring up her leg, and she was forced to stop a moment in an effort to fight off the gray haze that was threatening to overwhelm her.

Once she had her equilibrium back, she tore the bottom half of her shirt free and pressed it against the wound on Damon's stomach. It, too, was instantly soaked with blood, but it would have to do. She had nothing else to stop the bleeding. The sheriff's hand moved to hold the bandage in place, causing Katelynn to look up at his face. His eyes were open but free of pain; he was obviously in shock. He maintained enough control, however, to nod toward the door behind her.

"Sam went on alone," he choked out.

Fear seized Katelynn's heart in its stony grip.

Damon indicated the radio on his belt with a feeble motion. "Call for backup. Then follow Sam." He appeared to want to say more, but choked on his own blood and had to turn away to cough it free. That motion alone exhausted him. He slumped back down, barely conscious.

Katelynn didn't think he would make it until help arrived.

She took the radio from his belt and pressed the switch. "Hello? Hello? This is Katelynn Riley. The sheriff has been stabbed and needs medical help. We're at the university, in Keating Hall."

Questioning voices came back over the air, but Katelynn ignored them. She didn't have time to answer any of their questions; Sam could be dying as well. She had to try to help him. Taking up Damon's gun, she left him lying there on the floor and started making her way toward the door.

Inch by painful inch, she closed in on her destination.

Sam had been as confused by Damon's actions as Katelynn; but he'd kept his eyes firmly on the Nightshade and was in a position to see the beast back toward the door on the far side of the room at the moment of Hudson Blake's arrival. It was as if the two were working in tandem, and the beast had just left the unpleasant duty to his subordinate.

After all they'd been through, the Nightshade's dismissal only served to send Sam's anger past the boiling point.

He knew Katelynn and Damon were in trouble, knew that if he didn't do something to help them, they probably wouldn't survive; but he also knew he could not let the beast escape. He chose to act.

He shoved one hand into the pack he was carrying. One part of his mind flashed on the utter insanity involved in attacking a beast of such bloodthirsty savagery with nothing more powerful than glass jars filled with a mixture of gasoline and powdered soap flakes, while the other cocked his arm and hurled the jar at Moloch's rapidly retreating form.

Sam's aim was true.

The jar struck Moloch on the wide expanse of his right wing as he was turning away through the door on the other side of the room. The glass broke under the impact, spraying the beast with the gelatinous mixture within.

Sam already had another jar in hand when the beast stopped and turned its attention back in his direction.

Sam immediately threw the second jar, then watched in dismay, as it smashed harmlessly against the stone arch of the doorway, and the beast disappeared from sight.

Without taking time to think, Sam took off after the Nightshade. He'd crossed the room and was reaching for the door when his ears were filled with the explosive echoes of a gunshot. A sharp cry of pain followed immediately thereafter.

Sam knew the source of that cry.

Katelynn.

For just a moment, he almost stopped. Almost looked back to see what had happened, to discern what had caused his friend to cry out in pain. But Moloch had disappeared through the door ahead of him, and Sam knew that if he didn't catch up with him they very well might lose him.

He couldn't allow that to happen.

"God forgive me," he whispered in anguish as he pushed his way through the door without stopping, never once looking back.

Stepping through the door, Sam found himself in the room that formed the base of the clock tower. The walls rose high into the darkness, where somewhere up above the clock and bellworks had once hung. They were long gone, he knew, victims of the ravages of time and lack of money. The stone walls had been designed with great archways to provide access to the roof proper and to let the sound of the bells free of the chamber. From where he stood Sam could see through several of the arches.

Moloch was nowhere in sight.

The room itself was fairly large. The Nighshade could not have crossed it that quickly.

Which meant it had to have gone upward.

As the thought occurred to him a warm breeze danced across his skin, and Sam's response was near instantaneous.

With reflexes boosted high with fear-induced adrenaline, Sam threw himself diagonally forward, slamming his body violently into the stone flooring underfoot, his right arm outstretched in an effort to protect the mason jar clutched in that hand. Seconds later the Nightshade's deadly talons raked the air where he'd been standing milliseconds before.

Giving forth a loud, piercing cry, the beast disappeared into the darkness.

Sam scrambled to his feet, using his other hand to pull the roadside flare from his pocket.

The Nightshade will try again, he thought, *and this time I'll be ready.*

The attack came only seconds later.

This time Sam knew what was coming, and heard the shrill whistle in the air as the Nightshade's body dropped from high above.

Sam waited, his body tense with anticipation.

Now he could see the dark form above, growing larger with each passing second as the distance between them lessened.

Still, he waited.

Sam could imagine those claws, stretched out, ready to sink into his skin. Instead of running, he simply raised his arms closer to one another and triggered the flare he held in his left hand.

Then he thrust its burning end into the open mouth of the mason jar he held in his hand.

The mixture inside ignited lightning-quick, and flames shot up out of the jar's mouth.

Cocking his arm, knowing death was only scant feet away, Sam heaved the bottle with all his might directly at the beast.

The bottle struck the Nightshade in the middle of its chest, shattering the glass and spreading the burning mixture across its flesh.

Screaming in surprise and pain, the beast was diverted from its attack, crashing clumsily into the stone floor.

Sam yanked the last jar from his pack.

The creature was less than six feet away. Its hide was awash in flame, the mixture sticking to its skin and igniting what was left from Sam's first attack. It screamed again in rage and pain, then slowly began to climb to its feet.

"Die, damn you! Die!" Sam screamed.

Again using the flare as an igniter, he threw the last bottle.

His luck held, the bottle struck the beast across the side of the head, and it collapsed, its body covered with a raging fire.

Sam heard a cry behind him and turned to see Katelynn crawling through the doorway. He rushed to her side but before he could ask her what had happened to her and Damon, Katelynn pointed over his shoulder, and gasped, "Look!"

42

INFERNO

Somehow, the beast had climbed to its feet.

Katelynn and Sam watched in fascinated horror as the Nightshade took one step toward the roof's edge, then another.

And another.

The flames were burning fiercely, the homemade napalm smeared across most of the creature's torso. The frantic beating of its wings simply fanned the flames, adding to its own destruction.

But they could see that it wasn't burning quickly enough.

While the heat was intense, the fire had not spread to the rest of the creature's body, burning only where the gasoline mixture had soaked into the skin. With its supernatural healing, Moloch would survive the burns if he found some way of putting out the flames before they consumed him.

The beast took a fourth step.

A fifth.

Each step brought it closer to freedom.

Crouched against the far wall, using his body to shield

Katelynn from the heat, Sam realized what the creature was going to do. Once it reached the edge of the roof, it would launch itself into the open air. While the wind of its flight might fan the flames, it would also allow the beast to reach the river on the other side of campus. Once there, it could plunge beneath the river's surface, extinguishing the flames and finding a place to hide. There it would have the safety to gather its strength and slowly heal itself.

Sam knew he could not allow that to happen; they'd gotten two chances at the beast. They would not get a third.

He had to act now.

The creature's agonized shrieks of pain echoed off the room's stone walls, nearly deafening in their intensity. Sam pulled Katelynn's head closer to his own and put his lips next to her ear so she could hear him over the noise.

"Take care of Damon."

Before she could react, he sprinted across the room at full speed directly at the tall burning figure that was just reaching the edge of the roof.

Halfway in shock from the pain of her wounded leg, it took a moment for Katelynn to realize what Sam was doing.

When she did, she screamed in horror. "Sam! Noooo!"

It was too late to stop him, and deep inside she knew it.

At the edge of the roof, the Nightshade spread its wings wide, preparing to cast itself off the rooftop and escape.

Sam was only a step or two behind it, and with one, great wordless scream of rage and despair, he launched himself at the beast.

In that moment, just before his body collided with the burning form of the beast, Sam realized something.

It was okay to be afraid.

Fear is what makes us all human. It is fear that allows us to rise above ourselves, to reach that much further and that much higher, to strive to achieve just that little bit more. If we had succumbed to our fears, man would never have made it past the ice age. There is too much to be afraid of in our lives; fear of ourselves, fear of others, fear of our emotions and our lack thereof, fear of every action we might take every day of our lives. We rise above that and we move forward, facing our fears with a sense of courage that lives within us all, waiting for the chance to be let out.

As Sam's body closed the distance that separated him from the beast's burning form, he was very, very afraid.

But that was okay.

I guess I'm not as much a coward as I thought, he mused to himself, as his body crashed into Moloch's, the momentum taking them both over the edge of the roof. The intense heat of the flames against his flesh only caused him to lock his arms that much tighter around the body of his enemy, effectively pinning the creature's wings against its sides.

As they dropped over the edge and the ground rushed up to meet them, over the shriek of the creature and his own wordless cries of rage, Sam thought he heard Katelynn call his name.

In the second before he and the Nightshade crashed to the ground, Sam whispered a single word.

"Good-bye."

EPILOGUE

Two weeks later.

Glendale Hospital Intensive Care Unit.

Damon was resting in bed watching television when Katelynn knocked on the open door to his room.

"Come on in," he said, a genuine smile crossing his face, the first in days.

Katelynn crossed the room on her crutches and settled into the chair next to the bed. She was tired; the last two weeks had been a blur of activity as the police and several different agencies worked to understand just what had happened over the last several months. With Sam dead and Damon in ICU, she had been their primary source of information.

"I heard they upgraded your condition enough to let you have visitors, so I wanted to come by and see how you were doing," she said to the sheriff.

"I'll make it. They tell me if it hadn't been for you, I wouldn't have made it off that rooftop. Thanks."

Katelynn shrugged, uncomfortable with the gratitude.

In a softer voice Damon added, "I'm sorry about Sam."

She nodded, not trusting herself to speak on that topic yet.

As it turned out, Sam's action had been a smart one; with the creature's wings pinned to its body, it had been unable to arrest its fall. The added fuel from Sam's clothing had helped spread the fire, so by the time the two of them crashed to the ground below in a tangled heap, the Nightshade had become a pyre. The added injury from the fall had been too much for the beast's regenerative powers. It simply could not recover in time to defeat the flames. The beast perished in a raging conflagration on the ground, which burned for nearly twenty minutes until firefighters arrived on the scene. Since the beast's remains were so badly entwined with Sam's, the whole bundle had been transported down to the morgue, where it was still being studied.

The investigation remained inconclusive; awaiting the results of the forensic studies and scientific evaluations. Katelynn told the entire story, as she knew it, from beginning to end, without leaving anything out. She received a number of strange looks from the investigators the DA's Office sent in until the photos of the scene came back from the lab.

It was hard to argue with black-and-white photographs showing the charred remains of a wing jutting from the back of one of the corpses they pulled from the ground.

"I hear you're leaving the force," she said, by way of reply instead.

"It's true. Even if I could pass the physical again, I don't want to. After what we just went through, there is no way I could return to a life of parking tickets and speeding fines. What about you?"

"If they let me leave town, I think I'm going to go visit my aunt in California. It's too cold for me here now."

Damon knew without asking that she was referring to more than the winter weather.

Neither of them really knew what to say. They had

been through something extraordinary, and the wounds were still too fresh, too painful. Maybe in time they would find the ability to talk about it between them, but for the moment idle chitchat was all they could manage.

It saddened Damon's heart to realize it.

They talked of inconsequential things for a short while, then Katelynn announced that she had to get going.

"Stay in touch, okay?" Damon asked her.

"Sure," Katelynn replied, and they both wondered if she would.

She clambered to her feet with the help of her crutches and bent to give Damon a kiss on the forehead.

"Get well," she said, and turned away before he could see the tear in her eye.

As she hobbled toward the door, Damon called out once more.

"Katelynn?"

She looked back toward him.

"Would you mind?" he said, pointing toward the window.

Through the open drapes, Katelynn could see that it was late; very soon the sun would set, and darkness would be upon them.

She nodded wordlessly, and moved to pull the curtain shut, blocking out the sight.

They'd both grown uncomfortable with what the darkness of the night sky might hold.

She suspected it would remain that way for a long time.

Visit
❖ Pocket Books ❖
online at

www.SimonSays.com

Keep up on the latest new
releases from your favorite
authors, as well as author
appearances, news, chats,
special offers and more.

SIMON & SCHUSTER
A VIACOM COMPANY
www.SimonSays.com

Pocket
Books